Gillian was i

some stranger who called himself an earl and acted like an adventurer found her with tears in her eyes as she faced the uncertain future.

"What is all this now?" he said soothingly, and the fingers he held under her chin moved up slowly to brush back a tendril of chestnut hair from her cheek.

In the flickering firelight he looked very much the rogue. There was a glint of mischief in his eyes, and his unruly dark hair straggled over his forehead. A day's growth of beard shadowed his jaw line and upper lip. But his smile was infectious, and Gillian managed to produce a very small one of her own in response.

"Better, much better. You needn't be afraid, you know," he said, and his fingers trailed down from her hair to trace the smile on her lips.

That, though, was just the trouble. His touch sent fire racing through her veins, and her breath caught in her throat. The ache of uncertainty in her heart was melting and giving way to a very different sort of ache. She was not at all afraid of what might happen—and she had every reason to be. . . .

A Perilous Journey

by

Gail Eastwood

A SIGNET BOOK

To my family, for all their love,
and to Pat, Blanche, Karen, and JoAnn,
with heartfelt thanks!

SIGNET
Published by the Penguin Group
Penguin Books USA Inc., 375 Hudson Street,
New York, New York 10014, U.S.A.
Penguin Books Ltd, 27 Wrights Lane,
London W8 5TZ, England
Penguin Books Australia Ltd, Ringwood,
Victoria, Australia
Penguin Books Canada Ltd, 10 Alcorn Avenue,
Toronto, Ontario, Canada M4V 3B2
Penguin Books (N.Z.) Ltd, 182–190 Wairau Road,
Auckland 10, New Zealand

Penguin Books Ltd, Registered Offices:
Harmondsworth, Middlesex, England

First published by Signet, an imprint of Dutton Signet,
a division of Penguin Books USA Inc.

First Printing, July, 1994
10 9 8 7 6 5 4 3 2 1

 REGISTERED TRADEMARK—MARCA REGISTRADA

Printed in the United States of America

Chapter One

"Devil take it, Rafferty! The woman's blind, or we've suddenly become invisible," the Honorable Archibald Spelling grumbled to his companion. The two young Corinthians sat in the taproom of the Ram's Head Inn with empty tankards on the stained cloth in front of them.

Julian Rafferty de Raymond, the Earl of Brinton, glanced up from the newly dealt cards in his hand with a sigh. "You can't expect normal service under these conditions, Archie. I rather imagine that what we have here is a barmaid's idea of hell."

In the hours since the two friends' arrival, the venerable Ram's Head had become a madhouse. In the taproom every conceivable excuse for a seat had been called into use; people perched on trunks and baskets and even packing crates dragged from the storerooms. They leaned against the wainscoted walls and stood in the spaces between tables. The heat and the noise were nearly unbearable, and the stench of spilled ale overwhelmed all other smells. Through the smoky haze that filled the room, Brinton spied the barmaid struggling through the crowd, mugs aloft, looking remarkably like a foundering frigate in a storm.

Spelling had already tossed down his cards. "I confess I have a prodigious thirst, and I'm hungry enough to eat the elephant in the Tower menagerie."

"How fortunate we are not in London, then," Rafferty teased, setting his own cards aside in a deliberately tidy stack. Only intense concentration on their card play had allowed him to ignore his own discomfort. "The odds on food or drink reaching our table appear to be slight," he added, his words trailing off as his voice suddenly tightened.

He pressed his fist against his chest as a deep, painful cough racked him. He waited for the spasm to pass before attempting to speak again, shrugging off Archie's sharp look of concern. "I think I shall test my invisibility by trying to get into the kitchen," he finished finally.

"Perhaps I should—" Spelling began, but the earl cut him off with a shake of his head. Foraging for food might not be a normal occupation for a peer, but social standing at the Ram's Head had deteriorated to an animalistic survival of the fittest. Brinton was taller, leaner, harder, and tougher than his friend, despite his bad lung. His aristocratic features and confident bearing could communicate a cold air of authority that was seldom challenged. He preferred to take matters into his own capable hands. Grateful for the chance to stretch his legs, he rose from his seat and began to make his way through the crowd.

The state of affairs at the Ram's Head was not immediately discernable from the outside. Porters, ostlers, and patrons alike had been driven under cover by the heavy spring rain, and the sound of water splattering from roof corners and gable ends echoed through an empty courtyard.

In truth the Ram's Head was bursting at the seams like every other inn in Taunton. The first of the early season horse races had been planned to coincide with the usual Saturday market, and a profitable amount of crowding had been expected. The avaricious gleam in the innkeepers' eyes had dimmed in dismay, however, when the morning's drizzle had thickened into a driving downpour. As the turnpikes became quagmires, the steady stream of coach travel through Taunton had stalled there. The inns had quickly filled beyond capacity and beyond any innkeeper's ability to cope.

The earl and Spelling had claimed their space at the Ram's Head early enough in the day to obtain sleeping quarters, although no private parlor had been available. They were a striking pair, the earl's dark coloring and angular features contrasting with Spelling's round face and sandy red hair. Immaculately attired in tight-fitting buckskin and superbly tailored superfine, they exuded wealth and the careless confidence of the aristocracy. They had passed the hours playing piquet, watching and speculating about the steady accumulation of other guests.

Now as Brinton shouldered his way into the front entry hall of the inn, he could see that it was every bit as crowded as the taproom. The place reeked of wet wool and warm bodies. He could not catch his breath in the close, thick air, so he hurriedly pushed on toward the back of the passage.

As he did so, a sudden gust of wind set the candle flames dancing, and cool, fresh air steadied him. The thundering of a new downpour on the cobbles outside became momentarily louder, announcing the arrival of more pathetic souls to join the crush. Curious, he glanced toward the front door, wondering what sort of person would still be journeying on such a dismal night.

He glimpsed a tall, fair-haired youth, who turned to an even younger lad, Brinton guessed, judging by the shorter height and the cap that were all he could see of the second traveler. No servant or older person appeared to be with them.

Poor devils! he thought. They seemed so young to be traveling alone, and to be confronted with such a situation! As he turned again toward the kitchen, he wondered how they would manage. The unpredictable challenges of traveling could be difficult to bear, even for someone as seasoned as himself.

In the kitchen the earl easily rescued a haunch of mutton from the fire while the cook was busy berating a luckless stable boy who had been ordered to help her. Not one of the servants collected in the kitchen paid Brinton any notice. He hacked off a sizable chunk of the meat with a nearby kitchen knife and, skewering it neatly on the blade, carried it off, amused by his success even though he had not managed to find any beverage.

Brinton had never expected to be foraging his own fare now that he was home from the war against Boney. Service in the military, following his family's tradition, had hardened him to inconvenience and discomfort, but his friend Spelling had not shared in those experiences. Archie was probably suffering much more from the present difficulties than he was, the earl reflected as he retraced his steps. The sound of raised voices in the entry passage brought him to an abrupt halt.

"I've got no place left to put you," the formidable innkeeper was booming at the new arrivals. Although the blond youth was taller, the man's girth could have encompassed the lad three times at least. Brinton was impressed that the lad stood his ground. As he positioned himself for a better view, he realized with surprise that the boy was nearly his own height.

The innkeeper waved a pudgy hand helplessly and continued in his rumbling tone, "I've got people everywhere—in the stable, in the cellar, even under the stairs. I've got fifteen people in each part of the attic if I've got five, and that's packing 'em in like pickled herring."

"We won't be turned away," the tall youth replied in a firm and obviously educated voice. "We have been to three other inns already and have traveled a great distance today."

Brinton heard courageous desperation in that voice. He watched in fascination as the young man locked his eyes on the innkeeper and ignored the rude, unsympathetic noises coming from the crowd close by.

"Well, I don't know what you expect me to do," the innkeeper responded uncomfortably. "I'm no magician."

Hoots of derisive laughter met this observation. A large, pasty-faced woman pushed up close to the young travelers. "There's no room here—get on wi' ye and let this man tend to the rest of us, wot's got 'ere first!" She coughed, adding the vile smell of blue ruin to the foul air already around them.

The smaller lad sagged noticeably, and the taller youth slipped an arm around his companion for support. They were so wet the water from their clothing was draining into a puddle at their feet. The tall one, clad in a stylish greatcoat of brown wool broadcloth, held his head high and glared defiantly at the innkeeper. The short one could hardly be seen, muffled up in a voluminous green wool traveling cloak that must have been a crushing weight now that it was thoroughly soaked. A dripping lock of reddish brown hair hung over his forehead.

The earl remembered how it felt to be that wet. He and

Archie might be hungry, he thought, but at least they were warm and dry. He was aware of the calculating looks directed toward the meat he was carrying, and he consciously tightened his grip, torn between the drama unfolding in the hall and his duty to his famished friend in the next room.

More ugly noises came from the crowd. He had no desire to be caught in the middle if the scene he was witnessing turned nasty, yet somehow the pair of young lads had engaged his sympathy. As Brinton continued to watch, the tall youth leaned close to the innkeeper.

"We will pay you double—triple—your usual rates," he said in a low voice that nonetheless could be heard clearly by everyone. Then his proud posture crumpled as his companion very deliberately stuck a sharp elbow into his side.

The smaller lad looked away as he did so, by chance casting his glance in Brinton's direction. The shock of meeting those eyes rattled the earl considerably. They were the most remarkable blue-green color he had ever seen, and they seemed to reflect the most profound distress. They widened slightly as awareness of his own gaze registered, and then the small face abruptly turned away again.

Brinton made a decision at that moment. He knew he was intrigued beyond resisting, and he wanted to do something to help. He forced his way back through the crowd into the taproom where Spelling still waited.

Brinton placed the chunk of mutton on the table with a flourish. "Here, Archie, dinner!" He grinned and, after carefully extracting the knife, cut a few pieces off the meat. He and Archie began to eat them with their fingers.

"Raff, you are admirably resourceful. How did you get this? Seduce the cook?" Archie said with his mouth full. "On second thought, don't tell me. You have more deuced luck than anyone I know. But you have my eternal gratitude."

The earl half listened as he considered how to introduce his new idea to his friend. "Eternal, eh? I hope so," he managed to say between bites, "because what I'm going to propose we do next may not suit you so nicely, and I already consider myself in your debt for providing this escape from my visit to my uncle."

"O-ho, that's rich, considering the chaos we've found

here. Must have been bad in Devonshire. And here I've been feeling blue-deviled for bringing you into this. I'm sure I'm game for anything you might suggest, Raff."

Brinton had been summoned to his elderly uncle's Devonshire estate to hear the old man announce plans to remarry. As the heir-apparent, he knew he was supposed to be shocked and chagrined, but he had refused to give the old fool such satisfaction, bestowing his blessing instead. If the union by some miracle produced a new heir, he would toast the child's health. He had no need of his uncle's estates and titles, and no interest in becoming leg-shackled himself any time soon.

He grinned at Archie and watched his friend's face betray belated second thoughts. The two had shared a number of scrapes and misadventures in their schooldays and later in London.

Archie sighed. "You wouldn't propose we give up the race tomorrow, would you?"

"Never fear, my friend. I truly do wish to view these so-called prime goers, assuming the mud after this monsoon doesn't prevent it. My stables need new blood." Rafferty gazed thoughtfully toward the hall. "No, what I have in mind is more immediate—quite pressing in fact if we want to prevent a riot. I want to offer to share our room."

Spelling choked on the mutton he was chewing, and the earl had to get up from his chair to pound him on the back. While his friend was recovering, Brinton continued. "I recognize the imposition, Archie, especially when we've already been denied the privacy of a separate parlor. But we are among the very fortunate few who actually have a room to ourselves. What harm could it do?"

The ridiculously innocent expression on the earl's face nearly sent Spelling into another spasm. "Harm? Why no harm at all, unless you count robbery, murder, and mayhem. To whom do you wish to make this offer, and why should we help them?"

The earl sighed. Archie always did have a talent for cutting right to the bone of a matter. "There is a pair of half-drowned pups who have found themselves in difficulties—two youngsters as green as they come. I take them for gentry at the very least—the older one speaks well, and they are dressed in quality that shows despite how wet they are."

"And?"

"I doubt we would be at any risk from them—they offered the innkeeper triple his price, if you can credit it, in full hearing of all that mob."

Spelling whistled.

"I admit they are a puzzle. They shouldn't be traveling alone. There is something definitely amiss; that is part of what intrigues me, Arch." He did not mention an elfin face with huge blue-green eyes that refused to quit his mind.

"Think they're runaways?"

Brinton lowered his voice. "If you really want to know, I would wager they are on their way to Gretna Green."

Archie's mouth dropped open as he digested this unexpected twist. Then he slapped his thigh and roared. "A female? Eloping? If that don't beat all!" He stopped to look sharply at Brinton. "How much would you wager?"

"Now, now. I didn't mean it literally. I didn't get a very good look at the smaller one. Whether I am right or not, they would still be better off with us than where they are now or back out in the street."

"Where's your gaming spirit?" Archie persisted. "Stake you a hundred pounds!"

"No, Arch. Save your money for tomorrow. There's a pair of 'legs' over there that will be happy to take it from you then."

In the end the earl prevailed. "Bring that, if you would," he said offhandedly, pointing back to the remains of the mutton and the kitchen knife as he and Spelling quit their table. Archie dutifully scooped them up, ignoring pleas from the new occupants of their seats. He followed Brinton toward the hall, where ominous rumblings could be heard among the crowd.

They found the young travelers still in a stalemate. The innkeeper had given up arguing, dismissing them with a cold challenge to curl up in any vacant corner they could find. The inn's entryway was so jammed, the two had not even been able to move away from their place at the booking desk. They stood there looking thoroughly miserable, with a large portmanteau and a leather satchel between them.

The earl used his voice and presence to clear a path just wide enough to squeeze through, leaving Archie to follow in his wake. "I believe we might be of some service," he said, inclining his head as he approached the pair.

They turned to him, the tall one's face eager with hope and surprise, the short one's frowning with suspicion. Brinton thought they were as mismatched a couple as he had ever seen.

"I realize we are not known to one another, but my friend and I have decided we should place our room at your disposal."

"Your room?" responded the blond youth in some confusion. "You are very kind, indeed, sir! But will you not be needing it? Surely you are not thinking to venture out in this maelstrom!"

The earl chuckled. "I am not sure whether the maelstrom outside is any worse than the one in here, but I can assure you we are not going out. I meant that, as gentlemen, we could manage to share our quarters!"

Brinton couldn't help the slight emphasis on the word "gentlemen" any more than he could resist stealing a quick look at the smaller traveler to see if there was any reaction. Those blue-green eyes were fastened on him for a moment, and he thought he saw the cheeks pale before the face turned away.

The tall youth stretched out his hand with enthusiastic gratitude. "Would you really do that, sir? That's uncommonly kind!" He was interrupted by a sudden jerk on his arm that pulled his hand down. His small companion was attempting to become a barrier between him and the generous gentlemen, shaking his head vehemently.

"What's the matter?"

"We cannot do this, Gilbey." The voice was low and soft.

"Yes, we can," the blond traveler hissed back.

The two stared at each other for a moment, locked in their dispute and unmindful of their audience.

"Why on earth not?" insisted the tall youth. He was attempting to whisper. "Do you want to spend the night in this hallway or back out on the street? It is our only other choice."

The one called Gilbey turned back to the earl and Spelling with an apologetic look. His heightened color betrayed his embarrassment. "My brother doesn't like to accept charity," he said quickly, dropping his eyes. He fidgeted with a button on his coat. "He didn't realize that of course I mean to pay for our share of your hospitality— oww!" He cringed and cast an agonized look toward his companion, who had quite deliberately kicked his shin.

The earl hid his amusement. These two were a far cry from the usual besotted lovebirds who sought marriage over the border.

"Why don't we remove ourselves from this rather public situation," he suggested, inclining his head toward the stairs. "I am sure we can come to an agreement over the details."

Without waiting for an answer, Brinton began to move off in the direction he had indicated.

In two hundred years of service the Ram's Head had acquired a weary but comfortable crookedness that permeated everything from the window frames to the wall timbers. Spelling led the way down a dimly lit passage as narrow and twisted as the stairs.

"Aha! At least we have a fire," he exclaimed as he unlocked and flung wide the door to their room. "Perhaps you'll believe me after all when I tell you this inn is usually top notch."

The little procession filed into the room with Brinton in the rear. Depositing their burdens, they regrouped around the welcoming warmth of the hearth.

The room was small, with a low ceiling, a large fireplace, and one small diamond-paned window. Candle braces on the mantel supplemented the flickering light from the fire. Most of the space was taken up by a huge, heavily ornamented canopy bed swathed in blue damask. Not very generously endowed with quilts or pillows, it was at least neatly made. A small table and two chairs stood in one corner. The room smelled mostly of candle wax and stale pipe tobacco, but from somewhere there was also a scent of lavender.

"They always scent the beds here," Archie disclosed proudly. "It's one of their trademark touches."

"Beats changing the linens," Brinton commented under his breath. Addressing their guests he said, "This may be a bit cramped, but it is definitely a more suitable setting to make one another's acquaintance. However, I think our first order of business should be to see you out of those wet things and warm by the fire."

The smaller traveler had turned toward the hearth and seemed to be soaking in the heat, hardly aware of anyone else. The fire threw its rosy glow on a delicately pointed chin and cheeks that were like flawless ivory.

Brinton was certain now that his guest was female. Coming up the stairs he had positioned himself behind her in order to better observe her. Although the heavy traveling cloak concealed its wearer admirably, it could not disguise her posture or the way she moved, which seemed decidedly feminine.

Shivering and wearing gloves far too large for her, she had also had trouble carrying the meat and the kitchen knife Spelling had handed to her when he had picked up her leather satchel. Now she had removed her wet gloves and was rubbing hands as small and white as Rafferty had suspected. At his words she clutched at her cloak and pulled it closer around her.

The one called Gilbey seemed relieved that introductions were not going to be the first order. He, too, was warming his hands and shed his coat gratefully. As if sensing his partner's reluctance to follow suit, he turned to assist her.

Brinton studied the two carefully. *His hands don't linger the way a lover's should—the way mine would*, he caught himself thinking. As soon as the thought crossed his mind he chastised himself for it. But the young man's tender concern seemed to meet hostility that was almost as tangible as if the girl had slapped him. She glared and pulled away from his touch.

The earl couldn't help smiling, although he wasn't sure why that amused him. As the girl's cloak slipped from her shoulders, he exchanged a telling look with Archie. Wet, her ill-fitting male clothing only emphasized her unmistakably female shape.

As if he could cover her by conversation, her partner turned to Brinton. "With all due respect, sir," he ventured, "couldn't our first order of business be to have a bit of that mutton?"

Rafferty opened his mouth to reply and promptly closed it. Damned if the boy's eyes weren't an exact match for the girl's! He hadn't noticed it before, but now he looked closely to be sure it wasn't a trick of the poor light. "Of course, forgive me!" he said, covering his thoughts. "I thought you would be hungry—that's why we brought it along." Yes, the eyes were that same aquamarine. The lad's blond and alabaster coloring differed from the girl's as dramatically as their opposite statures, but on close inspection his face showed a finely sculptured nose and chin very much like hers.

Ha! Not lovers at all, the earl thought happily. *They are some sort of relations.* But he could not reflect then on why this discovery put him in such good humor. "Sit, eat," he said, gesturing toward the table where Archie had placed the meat.

The tall youth took the shivering girl by the hand to lead her to the table, but she snatched her hand away. As they sat down, he glanced back at the earl with a wry grin. "You must forgive my brother. He's not prone to indulge in small talk."

Brinton replied to the boy with an impishly raised eyebrow and a sidelong glance that included Spelling as co-conspirator. "We are not offended, are we, Archie? We have noticed your brother has his own less subtle way of communicating with you, and I think I may say we are glad to be spared!"

Both Spelling and the young man laughed. The girl, who had already tackled the mutton hungrily, stiffened her spine and turned her back to all three men.

"Allow me to make the introductions, since we have no one else to do it for us," Brinton said more seriously. "I am Julian de Raymond, Lord Brinton." Only his closest friends knew him as Rafferty. He bowed, an impeccably correct and graceful movement. "This is my associate, Mr. Spelling. We are at your service."

The young man called Gilbey paused before answering. "Lord Brinton, Mr. Spelling," he repeated. "It is an honor indeed, my lord, and I'm quite sure it is we who should be at your service as we are most certainly in your debt." He did not, however, offer his own name or that of his companion.

Brinton decided not to push. He thought the tension in the room fairly crackled. He stopped Spelling from speaking with a very readable eyebrow movement and said instead, "Some cheese and port would be an admirable accompaniment to that mutton. Mr. Spelling and I were just thinking we would go in search of some. It shouldn't take us long."

With a slight bow he turned to the door, ushering Spelling ahead of him almost forcibly. They gained the hallway before Archie could utter a syllable. "Forgive me for hastening your steps," Brinton whispered. "I could feel the heat rising, and I quite believe we were sitting on a powder keg!"

Chapter Two

The door had barely closed behind the two gentlemen before Gillian Kentwell rounded on her twin brother.

"Thank God they have gone! I thought I should explode with trying to stay silent! What are we doing here, Gilbey Kentwell?"

The girl was furious, trembling as much from her anger as from hunger and cold. She snatched the wet cap off her head and shook it in her brother's face. "Do you want Uncle William to catch us? You deliberately ignored all my protests, Gilbey! We are in a fine coil, now, thanks to you!"

Gilbey took the cap from his sister's hand and set it on the table. "You can become amazingly irrational when you are hungry," he said cheerfully. He cut off another piece of meat and held it out to her. "Better eat some more, Gillie."

Gillian's eyes flashed deep turquiose and two spots of color stained her cheekbones. "I am not irrational, thank you. I am thinking more clearly than you! Whatever possessed you to take up this offer? The last thing we needed was attention from strangers! I doubt their intentions are honorable! And how long did you suppose I could continue this charade in such close company?" She accepted the meat and bit into it. "We cannot stay here, Gilbey!"

"Did you know of better accomodations elsewhere? You really should have said so." Gilbey signaled his intention to stay by calmly inserting another piece of mutton into his own mouth.

Gillian jumped up and paced angrily away from the table. Her toes squished against the wet spare stockings stuffed into Gilbey's old boots along with her small, cold feet. Men! Sometimes her brother was as bad as the rest of them! Men had created this problem, men were complicating the problem, and if she herself could have been a man, none of it would ever have come up in the first place.

"Fine! Sit there chewing." She made a face at her twin from the unthreatening distance of the fireplace. "You are lucky I don't grab that carving knife and run you through with it, I'm that angry! A fine protector you turned out to be!"

Gilbey was stung into replying. "All I have done is get us a warm, dry place to spend the night against impossible odds. If you prefer to sleep in the gutter, next time perhaps I should let you!"

Gillian crossed back to her brother, bracing her hands on the table and peering intently into his face. "I would rather be hungry and wet and cold than be hauled back to Devonshire," she pronounced with dramatic emphasis. "At least in that hallway, or even in the street, no one would have noticed us—especially if you had not raised such a fuss."

Instead, she thought, she was sharing a room with a strange man whose attention seemed never to leave her. She had felt Brinton watching her from the moment they had started up the stairs. Every time she risked a glance at him, she met his deep-set eyes. They were a warm, distinct hazel.

She thought she detected a hint of amusement in them that was not revealed in his other carefully controlled features. Had his inspection penetrated her disguise? If so, what was he planning to do? She found his ceaseless scrutiny unnerving. She was almost equally discomposed by her own compulsion to look at him.

"We ought to leave now, Gilbey, while they're not here."

Her brother stopped sawing on the mutton to wave the knife toward their belongings by the door. "What we ought to do is change into dry clothes. The last thing either of us needs is to take a chill. And there's no sense in making an awkward situation worse."

"Awkward! Of all the rattle-brained schemes! This is a worse scrape than anything I ever got us into at home." Gillian went grudgingly to the portmanteau and began rummaging in it. The muslin she had bound around her breasts so tightly that morning now felt like a cold, soggy bandage that was loosening with every breath. Her head ached and her limbs were still shaking, but she knew the food and dry clothes would help.

"If I were you, I wouldn't start a debate over who got us into this coil," Gilbey said with an edge of irritation in his voice. "Whose idea was it to run off to Scotland?"

"I didn't invite you to come along," Gillian replied. She had prepared to leave without even confiding in her twin. Gilbey had argued with her when he had discovered her intentions, deciding to go with her when he could not dissuade her.

"I hate to think where you might be already if I hadn't. How had you planned to manage? Did you really think you could pass for a male all the way to Scotland—alone?"

Gillian pulled out a shirt that was obviously too large for her and, scrunching it into a ball, threw it at her brother. Breeches and stockings followed. Finally, she gathered up the smaller-size castoffs that made up her current wardrobe and moved to the fire.

"I wouldn't be sharing a room with two strangers who I don't doubt have designs on our purse, if not our persons! Those two have probably gone to summon their accomplices and will pretend to be robbed along with us when they come back, figuring that we are no match for their men." She pulled off one boot and held it up, letting a stream of water pour out onto the floor.

"Why are you so convinced they want to rob us?" Gilbey's voice was muffled as he pulled his wet shirt off over his head.

"I don't know another reason for them to get involved with two waifs as wretched as we must appear," Gillian said. She and Gilbey had turned their backs to allow each other some privacy. "Did you not wonder why this so-called 'Lord Brinton' stepped in so quickly to take charge of us?" She raised her voice a fraction. "He was standing right there when you advertised our fat purse to the innkeeper and half the population of Taunton."

She had not forgotten that strangely charged moment when she had first looked up, straight into Brinton's eyes in the middle of the crowd. As she had stared, suddenly spellbound, she had seen the odd expression that slipped across his face. When she tried to analyze his unorthodox behavior and the peculiar way she kept reacting to him, that moment took on great significance in fueling her distrust. Why didn't Gilbey see?

For a moment the heartache she was trying so desperately to ignore threatened to break through her overlaying anger. Didn't they have enough trouble already without borrowing more? Despite her pose as the Great Adventuress, she would not have left home if there had been any other way to escape her uncle's plotting. She and Gilbey had tried everything else they could think of to scuttle the ill-begotten betrothal their Uncle William had arranged. She was homesick already, yet she and Gilbey had not even been gone a full day!

Where was the excitement she had felt in the morning when they had first set off? *Washed away in the cold rain*, she thought miserably. At this moment doubt and fear weighed on her in place of that eager anticipation. Could she and Gilbey elude their guardian long enough to reach Scotland? She was no longer sure they had wits enough to make it to their second day.

Gillian got herself in hand with a little shake. She would not give way to the megrims any more than she had given in to her uncle's bleak plan for her future. She looked at the heap of wet things by the fire and sighed, wishing they could stay long enough to dry them. She hated the thought of putting her feet back into the heavy, wet leather boots. But the thought of Brinton and his cohort prodded her. She and Gilbey must not let anyone stop them from getting to Scotland. She padded back over to the portmanteau.

"Are you finished?" asked Gilbey, still with his back politely turned. Gillian wasn't sure if he meant her toilette or their halted conversation.

"Near enough," she replied. She searched the bag for her stockings and the short stable jacket she knew must still be in it. She felt comforted when her fingers came in contact with the soft silk of her Spitalfields shawl, wrapped around the square shapes of her mother's Scottish songbooks. She wondered if Gilbey suspected why the portmanteau was so heavy.

She found the stockings and jacket just as her brother

moved to the hearth and began spreading out his clothes to dry.

"Gilbey, you don't truly expect to stay the night!"

"Of course I do. Honestly, Gillie, don't you trust my judgment at all?"

Gillian frowned. She avoided his gaze by concentrating on buttoning her jacket. "Don't you think those two have guessed that I'm a woman?"

Gilbey returned to the table and reclaimed his chair. " 'Those two', as you keep calling them, happen to be gentlemen. They can't openly dispute my word when I say you're my brother. They'll go along with it." He began to work on the mutton again, cutting the meat into small pieces.

Gillian gave a most unladylike snort. Brinton's incessant staring could hardly be considered gentlemanly behavior. It was rude at best and would have been shockingly forward if she was supposed to be female. But Gilbey obviously had not noticed.

"I expect they think we are easier marks than ever if they have already guessed. I say we pack up our things this moment and be on our way."

Gilbey said nothing. The expression on his face was mulish.

"If you will not do this, Gilbey, at least tell them we have a pistol. Perhaps if they think we are armed, they will not be so quick to chalk us."

Brinton and Spelling had headed straight for the kitchen upon leaving the twins.

"I thought service to my country had hardened me, Archie," the earl said as they made their way down the narrow stairs. "Now I find it is not so."

"You weren't thinking of giving them the bed?" Archie responded in mock alarm.

Brinton laughed. "Would I do that? I was not referring to creature comforts, actually. I meant my heart—either it or my head is still soft after all."

"Better those than a certain other part of your anatomy," Archie teased. "You were always the man for a lady in distress, Raff! But I can't see where your interest will get you if she's already headed for Gretna Green!"

"I no longer think that is the case," the earl answered.

"What?"

"I doubt they are lovers, Archie. More likely relations. Did you not notice the resemblance between them? And I think they are quarreling up there even as we speak."

"Relations don't signify," Archie argued. "Cousins marry all the time! As for quarrels, what better proof of love could you ask for?" He laughed. "I think you've developed a case of wishful thinking! I'll wager my matched grays they're headed for Gretna Green. But I'll not settle for anything less than your Tristan against my famous grays."

Brinton hesitated. He seldom gambled without a good sense of the odds, although his luck was almost legendary. He took pride in the reliability of his instincts, yet what did he know? Nothing for certain. Could Archie be right about wishful thinking? Were emotions clouding his judgment?

He wondered again when he felt the pleasure sparked by the mere sight of the girl as he and Spelling returned to their room, laden with bounty salvaged from the kitchen.

"We were successful beyond our wildest dreams," Spelling announced cheerfully, brandishing a decanter of ruby port and a tray with glasses and a large wedge of cheese.

The girl had been standing bareheaded near the fire, her luxuriant curls fully exposed. At their entrance she clapped a hand to her head and sent an agonized look to her companion, who promptly tossed over the cap she had left on the table.

The exchange amused the earl. He noted with satisfaction the wet clothes spread before the hearth and the drier ensembles that now clothed his guests. The tension in the room seemed at least reduced.

"I'm pleased to see you have both found something dry to put on," he said, nodding in approval. "A further bit of refreshment and you will feel much more the thing."

He moved close behind the girl and, stopping there, gen-

tly removed her soggy cap and tossed it onto the hearth.
"There is no need to be uncomfortable," he said softly.

Her hair was a magnificent color, touched with red
where it gleamed in the candlelight, but dark where a wet
tendril lay against her ear. He could smell the rain-washed
freshness of it. The urge to touch it was so strong, he could
not allow himself to move at all for a moment.

"Your brother here needs to know that he is quite safe
with us," he said, addressing his remark to Gilbey.

The lad nodded, but the girl stood absolutely rigid in
front of Brinton. She was so small! She came no higher
than his shoulder. He could tell she was holding her breath,
and he felt a little twinge of satisfaction to know that he
could affect her.

"You may have difficulty convincing my brother of
that," Gilbey confessed, nervously clearing his throat. "It
shames me to tell you, after all your generosity, but it
seems he is convinced the two of you have designs on our
purse." Gilbey's face was nearly scarlet. "He felt it only
fair to warn you that we are armed with a pistol, and are in
such desperate need of our blunt we would be quite prepared to defend it. . . ."

Brinton and Spelling exchanged amused looks, then the
earl threw back his head and laughed loudly. It was not
quite the cool behavior expected of a fashionable gentleman.

"And now that you have so gallantly warned us," said
Brinton, restoring some of his polite control, "would that
stop us from robbing you if, indeed, that was our intent?"

Gilbey flushed even deeper and looked down at the table.
His silent partner stared stonily into the fire as if she hadn't
heard at all.

"If I might offer some friendly advice," Brinton went on,
"don't let anyone know you have a weapon." A smile was
playing at the corners of his mouth. "That is almost as foolish as letting them know you have a heavy purse! Preserve
the advantage of surprise."

Brinton put his hands on Gillian's shoulders and turned
her toward the table. "Come, sit down and eat and drink.
I'm sure you need to be warmed on the inside as much as
the outside."

Gillian in fact felt as if she was on fire from his touch. If he hadn't wanted her to feel uncomfortable, why had he stood so unbearably close? His proximity had created a warm tingling in her bones that numbed her mind. She had not dared to breathe. Now she felt foolish and confused as well. She stumbled toward the chair and sat down opposite her brother, accepting a glass of port with trembling fingers.

"A toast," proposed Brinton, once Spelling had filled glasses for all of them. "To a journey safe from scoundrels and cutpurses. May your rest be easy this night."

The twins would not hear of using the bed. They gratefully accepted their hosts' dry cloaks for bedding, but were astonished to see the earl take up the big kitchen knife and attack the bed hangings.

"Imagine mistaking good coverlets for curtains," he said wryly, neatly slitting the loops at the top. He offered Gillian his coat to use as her pillow, and raised an eyebrow at Spelling, clearly expecting his friend to do the same for her brother.

"No, please!" protested Gilbey. "The very thought of ruining such fine tailoring would keep me awake!" He went to the portmanteau and opened it, searching for something else he could use. He discovered Gillian's shawl and, pulling on it, dislodged the leather-bound volumes she had wrapped in it.

"Gillian, what the—?" he exclaimed in astonishment, quite forgetting for a moment where they were.

He held up one slim volume, then another. "Songbooks." He looked accusingly at his sister. "I thought you said you would leave them behind."

"I couldn't do it." Gillian shook her head, making her voice gruff and hoping no one had noticed Gilbey's use of her name. She struggled for composure as she felt tears starting. Gilbey was her twin. Why couldn't he understand? She had left so much else behind. The books were her most prized possessions—her legacy from their beautiful Scottish mother who had died when they were eight. The small collection of books had served Gillian as solace and inspiration, comfort and hope. Not trusting her voice and suddenly mindful of the two strangers watching them, Gillian stared at Gilbey, willing him to read her mind.

"I can't believe I have been lugging those all day," he complained, but he laid the two volumes carefully back in with their companions. He left the shawl covering them.

Brinton and Spelling tactfully said nothing during this exchange. When Gilbey came up empty-handed, Spelling reluctantly handed over his coat. The earl and his friend went to bed in their clothes, stripped down only to their shirtsleeves and pantaloons.

Gillian could not sleep, despite her exhaustion. Every time she closed her eyes, she could feel again the swaying, bumping motion of the coach roof where she and Gilbey had spent hours in the rain. The sound of Gilbey's soft snoring was punctuated periodically by loud snorts from Lord Brinton's friend. From Brinton himself she could make out no sound except an occasional cough or rustle of bedclothes. She wondered if he, too, lay awake in the darkness.

He truly was a striking man. His broad shoulders and slim hips had shown to advantage as he had shed his waistcoat and neckcloth, preparing for bed. She felt again the burning of her shoulders where he had touched her so briefly. Was that what it was like between women and men—fire? From her parents somehow she had imagined something gentler.

She shifted, trying to position herself more comfortably. Her muscles ached from tension and fatigue. Despite the layers under her, the floor was hard.

She began to drift off, her mind replaying scenes at random from an intensely emotional day. She worried about her uncle's anger and how he might deal with their household staff. How long would the servants have put him off before revealing the twins' disappearance? How soon had he started the search for them? A seemingly endless array of delays and obstacles aside from the weather flashed through her memory—slow market wagons, mud, and vast flocks of sheep, not to mention slow ostlers and missed coach connections. Was their attempt all in vain? The thought of what she would have to endure if they were caught brought a little cry from her throat.

Gillian turned her face into Brinton's coat, fighting the tears that threatened again. The fabric held a musky masculine smell and a pleasant hint of lime. She buried her nose in it and inhaled deeply, focusing her thoughts on Brinton again.

She didn't know what to think of him now. He had made it clear that he saw through her ruse, yet had said nothing. He had laughed at her notion he was after their purse, but he still had never quite denied it. Could she possibly have misjudged him? She tried to imagine meeting him in London, attending the theater, dancing at a ball. She shook her head. If only fate had been kinder! She would likely never see London.

As Gillian suspected, Brinton, too, lay awake, uncomfortably aware of her restless turnings. He had forgotten Archie's unfortunate tendency to snort in his sleep, but he knew that was not the cause of his wakefulness. It was the confounded girl.

The embers of the dying fire cast just enough of a glow by the hearth for him to make out her shape under the bed curtains. The moments he had stood behind her, fighting his urge to touch, came flooding back with a vivid image of her hair. How he had longed to sink his fingers into those satiny, chestnut curls! As he listened to her stirring in the semidarkness, his imagination was delivering quite unexpected, uninvited images and sensations he struggled valiantly to subdue.

He was out of control, clearly. How could he be attracted to a little chit hardly out of the schoolroom? Was she such an innocent she had no idea how revealing her boy's clothing had been? What was the matter with him that his usual cool resistance had disintegrated so easily?

Rafferty was not a notorious rake. What dalliances he allowed himself were pursued with the utmost discretion and selectivity, to the disappointment of the gossip-mongers and a string of London beauties who would have been willing partners. At least half of England knew the Earl of Brinton was not looking for any entanglements. Between the cadres of ambitious mothers and daughters on the matrimonial prowl and his own mother and five sisters, Brinton quite believed his own half of the species to be endangered.

He wondered what made him so certain this girl was the gently bred innocent he took her for. What sort of breeding led a girl to go haring about the countryside dressed as a boy? *I should never have gotten myself involved with her and her young man*, he thought. Yet he had to admire her courage and spirit. None of the females in his acquaintance could have brazened out the awkward situation in the room with him and Archie, not even his sisters. Who was she? Who or what in her life was so terrible that she had been forced to run away? Who was the young man with her?

His desire to know went beyond all reasoning, but then he seemed to have lost what little sense he'd ever had. How could he have wagered Tristan—his favorite mount, his glorious black stallion—against Archie's grays? How the devil was he to prove that he was right? He had not the slightest inkling of how to postpone parting with his guests in the morning, or of how to learn what he needed to know. *I would never have made a good spy*, he thought ruefully.

Finally, he must have slept, for some unknown disturbance awakened him later. As his eyes adjusted in the gloom, he saw that his guests were gone.

Chapter Three

The darkness in the room had lessened only slightly when Gillian roused her twin. Stealthily they had gathered their belongings and slipped out, closing the door softly behind them.

"This is the best way," Gillian whispered in the hallway. "They will never know who we were, so no one's reputation will be in question."

"I can hardly credit that the champion hoyden of all Devonshire is suddenly worried about reputations!" Gilbey teased her. "I would more likely believe you are just relieved they cannot go to the constable."

As he struggled with the portmanteau on the stairs, Gillian touched his shoulder. "I apologize for being in such high dudgeon last night," she said. "I think perhaps you were right . . . about everything."

It was a sweeping admission, but Gilbey decided he would let it go, at least until later. It was enough to know she trusted him and admitted her error. He answered with a grin he wasn't certain she could even see in the darkness of the stairwell.

The ripe smell of the unwashed multitude still snoring in the passageway downstairs hit the twins like a slap in the face. They stood for a moment, unsure how to proceed. Spaces vacated by some early risers offered a winding path through the semidarkness to the door, and the pair followed it, stepping carefully. They were not prepared for the thick wall of fog that greeted them when they opened the door. All recognizable traces of Taunton had disappeared in the eerie grayness.

"How in blazes are we to find The George in this?" Gilbey asked, more to himself than in expectation of an answer. To his and Gillian's surprise, the innkeeper materialized behind them.

"Eager to quit us, eh?" the man inquired with an ironic twist to his voice. "Accomodations not to your liking?" His blustery tones had been reduced to a whisper, and lines of fatigue showed in his face.

Gilbey bit back the smart retort on his tongue. He pitied the man. After all, the circumstances of the previous night were not of his making. "We need to get to The George," he stated instead. "We are booked on an early coach."

The hosteller snorted. "You'll not find them running in this. T'ain't fit for ducks, nor man nor beast." He shrugged, and told them the way.

Navigating by feel, sound, and instinct rather than sight, the twins set off, baggage bumping at their knees. With a care for their footing on the treacherous wet cobbles, they slowly progressed up the narrow street, using the walls to guide them.

At the first cross-street they experienced the disorienting sensation of being adrift, with no point of reference except their feet on the ground. The looming outline of a street-lamp, still flickering faintly with the remains of the night's oil, marked a corner for them, and they proceeded, thankfully anchored once more against ancient solid walls. They were cautiously negotiating the open space of the second cross-street when someone crashed into Gilbey from behind.

"Ho, there!" Gilbey cried, dropping the portmanteau. He was preparing to excuse himself when he realized that there were hands on his arms and inside his coat, and there were more than one pair. He struggled against a strong grip, trying to extricate himself from one set of fingers as he tried to grab at the others. "What the devil?" he cried in confusion.

Strong arms attached to a hulking shape also grasped Gillian. Incensed beyond caution, she fought back. "You bullying blackguard! Unhand me! Vile, base-born, brandy-faced guttersnipe!"

Her language befit a stable boy, but unfortunately she forgot to disguise her voice. Her assailant turned her roughly for a closer inspection. "B'God, it's a little vixen!"

When Gilbey heard Gillian cry out behind him, he be-

came desperate to free himself. He used his shoulders, elbows, and anything he could against his attackers. Finally,
he threw all his weight away from the arms locked around
him. Unfortunately, whoever was holding him chose that
moment to let go. Gilbey pitched headlong onto the wet
cobblestones.

"Clear out!" called one ruffian to the others. As the man
holding Gillian turned to join them, she managed a sharp
kick to his shins and watched him hobble in obvious pain
for an instant, before the fog swallowed them. Then she
rushed to Gilbey's side.

"Are you hurt?"

"Are you?" Sitting on the pavement, he brushed gravel
from his coat and inspected his sleeves.

She shook her head mutely. "I asked you first."

Gilbey appeared dazed and shaken, but amazement filled
his voice as he responded. " 'Base-born, brandy-faced guttersnipe'? My word, Gillie, where on earth did you pick up
such language?"

At the Ram's Head, Brinton lay motionless in bed for a
moment, straining to recapture whatever sound it was that
had awakened him. All was silent in the dim grayness,
however. He wasn't even sure it was morning. He could not
tell if his guests had been gone for hours, or if the closing
of the door behind them had startled him awake.

They could already be miles away, he thought. He made
a little grimace of self-derision. So much for all his ponder-
ings and lost sleep. He had never anticipated this turn of
events. The depth and bitterness of his disappointment surprised him.

He eased himself from the bed carefully, not wishing to
wake Archie. He almost immediately stumbled over his
boots. Cursing softly, he looked back at his friend. Except
for the barely perceptible rise and fall of the covers, Archie
gave every appearance of being dead.

It seemed extraordinarily dark, and Rafferty moved to
the window as he made a fumbling attempt to arrange his
cravat. At least the darkness prevented him from seeing
how dismally rumpled he must be after sleeping in his

clothes! He had been wise to leave Tyler, his valet, behind for this trip.

He pushed the window open, only to discover the fog hanging like a curtain on the wrong side. No wonder it was so dark! There was not a breath of air, nor even the usual dawn chorus of birds, as if the fog had effectively muffled all other signs of life as well as the light.

The earl searched about the room for his coat, finally discovering it neatly folded on the chair with a small purse of coins and his hat beside it. The foolish pair had left payment for their night's shelter. He swore under his breath, snatching up the hat and purse and shrugging into the tight-fitting garment as he hurried out the door.

At the bottom of the stairs he was confronted by the same scene and stench as had greeted the twins. A few more people were stirring groggily, and he threaded his way between them. It was still dark enough to require candles, and he noticed fresh ones had been lit. He could make out the scent of coffee and followed its trail to the taproom. The innkeeper was supervising some attempt at breakfast for such guests as were awake.

"Any likelihood you saw those two lads this morning?" Brinton asked him with studied casualness.

"Steal your purse, did they, my lord?"

Brinton's face darkened. "More like they left one behind," he said in cold, clipped tones that made the man regret his impudence. "Did you see them?"

"Aye, milord, I did. They wanted The George and asked me the way. 'Tis no fit morning to be out, but they were insisting."

"I can imagine. How long ago was that?"

"Not long at all—not above ten minutes, I'd guess."

The earl clapped his beaver onto his head and showed every sign of going out. The innkeeper looked at a loss.

"Coffee, my lord?"

"Later, my good man." Brinton's humor had improved immensely. "Just tell me the direction of The George."

Gillian blushed at Gilbey's reference to her language. She knew a proper young lady should never even have heard such words. "I suppose I have been spending too much time in the stables. But, really, Gilbey! Didn't you think it was perhaps appropriate to the subject?"

"Dash it!"

She had not expected an oath in reply to her intended humor. She looked at her twin with renewed concern as he attempted to rise, unsuccessfully.

"You *are* hurt!" she cried.

Gilbey subsided with a grimace. Pushing the wet folds of his greatcoat aside, he uncovered a large rent in his pantaloons and an angry, raw knee showing through. With Gillian's help, he again tried to get up, but when he put weight on his knee he was rewarded with a sharp protest of pain. The weight he put on Gillian was more than she could bear, and they both sank back onto the pavement.

"Now we are in it, aren't we," Gillian said gloomily. Gilbey just looked at her and blinked.

Gillian needed to know the full extent of the disaster, although she suspected she was beyond solutions. "Did they get everything?" she asked gently.

Gilbey groaned in reply, feeling his pockets as if somehow it was all a mistake. "Purse, tickets, the lot."

Gillian looked at her noble brother, sitting indecorously in the middle of the wet street, and suppressed a bubble of hysterical laughter. How had she ever supposed things could get no worse? Gilbey could not walk, and she could not even get him up. They had no money and no coach tickets—no way to leave this abysmal city she hoped never to set eyes on again. She regretted the coins she had left in the room at the Ram's Head now. She considered trying to retrieve them, but Lord Brinton might be awake, and how could she leave Gilbey here alone?

"What time do you suppose it is?" she asked, wondering if they were still in danger and trying to think what to do. When Gilbey did not answer, she followed his glance down to the torn and empty pocket of his waistcoat. "Father's watch," she realized numbly. They stared at each other in mournful silence.

Almost as if summoned by her thoughts, Brinton's tall figure suddenly loomed out of the fog, nearly tripping over the twins.

"What the devil has happened here?" he exclaimed, so surprised he gave no thought to his language.

Gillian felt indignant at his tone. *It would have to be him,* she thought irritably. *Why couldn't it have been anyone else?* But a little voice reminded her that she would have been far more distressed to see her uncle.

"We've been robbed," she said in a flat voice, making no attempt to disguise her natural tones. "We don't normally indulge in street-sitting, especially at such an early hour."

He ignored her sarcasm. "Are either of you hurt?"

"Yes, my lord," Gilbey answered, showing a spark of life at last. "I am. Could you give us a hand?"

"Where is the problem?"

"My knee."

Brinton looked carefully at Gilbey's injury. "Will it not stand your weight? Sprained, then, most likely, in addition to being scraped and bruised."

"You sound like a surgeon who has seen a hundred such knees," Gillian couldn't resist commenting. Was the man really such a know-it-all, or did he just always take charge of everyone and everything?

The earl did not reply at first. He held out a hand to Gillian and helped her up from the stones, motioning her to one side of her brother. "I have seen enough of these to know," he said finally. Something in his stern tone forbade further remarks.

He moved the twins' baggage into the recess of a dooryard, promising to send someone back for it. Then he took up a position on Gilbey's other side and helped him to his feet.

Gilbey groaned.

"You have hurt more than your knee, haven't you?" Gillian said in alarm.

"What you need is a warm bath," Brinton declared.

The earl and Gillian provided very unbalanced support for Gilbey as they hobbled back along the road. The difference in their heights made it difficult for Gilbey to help them and Gillian needed to stop and rest every few steps.

She found she was quite distracted by the feel of Brinton's muscled arm, linked with hers to brace her brother. What kind of lord had such muscles, she caught herself wondering. Her hand could not span the hard forearm she gripped. Warmth radiated along her own arm from the spot where his hand grasped it. She tried to catch a glimpse of Brinton's face to see if he was suffering any similarly odd sensations, but he stared straight ahead into the fog.

They had stopped twice for her to catch her breath when Brinton suddenly stopped again, his face ashen. He deposited Gilbey on a conveniently placed mounting block and turned away, seized by a spasm of coughing.

"My lord, are you ill?" Gillian realized that Brinton had been trying to ease her load by supporting most of Gilbey's weight himself. She took a step toward him, uncertain as to which helpless man needed her more.

Brinton shook his head. He stood quite still, slightly stooped with one hand braced against the shop wall beside them. After another moment he straightened and turned back to the twins.

"Forgive me," he said, returning to Gilbey's side. "It is just an occasional inconvenience," he added when Gillian looked at him hesitantly. "Let us proceed."

They took Gilbey back to the Ram's Head.

"You two again!" the innkeeper exclaimed as a group of curious onlookers made way for the trio. "What has happened, my lord?" He waved them into the coffee room.

Depositing Gilbey into one chair, Brinton and Gillian sank gratefully into two others.

"A cloth and some water," the earl commanded. "The lad's been hurt. And coffee now, if you would be so kind."

Amid the hubbub and questions of the surrounding crowd, Gillian was impressed to see how quickly his orders were carried out. Nervously aware of this new attention focused on them by their mishap, she let others minister to Gilbey's injury, lest she appear too sisterly. She slouched a little in her chair, pulling at the collar of her cloak and adjusting her hastily retrieved cap to cover more of her hair.

"Attacked by cutpurses!" Gilbey moaned. "I feel so foolish!"

Gillian risked a glance at Brinton. He appeared less than perfect this morning, and she found it disturbingly appealing. He had not shaved and a dark morning shadow ran along his jaw and upper lip. His hair looked hastily arranged and his neckcloth was tied in a simple style that was slightly askew. He looked vulnerable, she thought, quite in contrast to his autocratic behavior. He showed no sign of being ill. In his rumpled disarray he looked more like a charming rogue than anything else, and she felt herself softening toward him.

He really had been very helpful. She didn't know how she would have managed this morning if he had not come along. Already he had dispatched two stable hands to retrieve their baggage; he had dealt with the inevitable questions of their welcoming committee and had seen that Gilbey's needs were tended. But in the midst of her newfound appreciation, something was nagging her. How was it that Brinton just happened to be the first one to come along after the robbery?

Lost in this thought, Gillian hardly noticed that most of the crowd in the room had left until she suddenly became aware of Brinton's hazel gaze upon her. For a moment she could not look away, staring back fully into the myriad smoky colors she found there. Her pulse quickened, and flustered, she finally pulled her eyes to her lap where they belonged.

What must he think of her? *Brazen and forward must surely head the list by now, not to mention vulgar.* She felt a warm flush creep up her cheeks. Had he been near enough in the street to have heard her shocking language? She had always enjoyed being something of a hoyden, but suddenly her pride in not being "missish" was curiously dampened.

"It is fortunate that neither of you was hurt more seriously," Brinton said, frowning. "I cannot fathom what you thought you would do out there in the murk at this early hour!" He shot a reproachful glance at Gillian.

She bristled in response, quite forgetting the fluttering butterflies she had been feeling moments before. "We thought we would catch our coach, if it is any business of yours!"

"I suppose it never occurred to you that any team venturing out so early in this would break their necks before it got light enough to find the road?"

He was scolding her like a father, and she resented it. What right had he? Yet what could she say? That she was eager to get away from him? That they were fearful of pursuit and dis-

trustful of his assistance? That her reactions to him puzzled
and frightened her? "We have urgent business," she said de-
fensively. "We need to be on our way as soon as possible."

To her relief, he did not press the subject further.

"I have ordered some breakfast brought to you," he said
simply.

She felt his eyes still on her, although she knew he was
addressing her brother as well.

"I trust you will excuse me while I repair to our former
quarters. Mr. Spelling may have awakened by now, and besides, I really must attempt to make a more presentable appearance."

Gillian still did not trust him, but the prying eyes of the
other inn patrons who might return at any moment seemed
an even greater threat than he was.

Perhaps her face betrayed her misgivings, for he smiled
and added, "I will make arrangements that you are not to be
disturbed." With a bow he picked up his hat and left them.

A maid brought them a large Staffordshire basin and
pitcher, soap, and towels. Not long after, the innkeeper delivered breakfast to the twins himself. No one else attempted to join them in the coffee room.

As the man set the dishes before them, he gave Gillian a
calculating look. "Your friend the earl seems very ready to
put himself out for you," he commented. "There's not
many as would go so far."

Gillian and Gilbey exchanged startled glances. An earl?
Brinton had never said he was an earl. Then again, they had
never asked about his title, no more than they had volunteered their own identities. Gillian flushed to her ear tips
when she thought of the suspicions she had harbored. Yet a
little voice in the back of her mind said ungraciously that
even an earl could fall from the right path.

"You're lucky his lordship went after you," the man continued. "There's no one abroad in this soup so early that's
up to any good." His expression made it clear that he included them in this unwholesome group.

Gillian thought she might scream if she heard one more
reference to their foolhardiness in venturing out. She glared at
the innkeeper while Gilbey thanked him curtly in dismissal.

"Well! We have certainly made a fine impression on

him," Gilbey commented. "He thinks we are no better than the footpads who accosted us!"

Gillian had fallen ravenously upon the proffered breakfast and was in the act of passing a plate of thickly buttered toast to Gilbey. She set the plate down abruptly.

"We have managed to make an impression of some sort on nearly everyone we have met," she said sharply. "I had so hoped we could just pass along our way, unnoticed and untraceable." Anxiety made her voice husky as she asked, "Do you think Uncle William could track us to Taunton?"

Gilbey sighed. "Nothing would please me better than to set your mind at ease, Gillie, but in truth I have no more idea than you. We did our best not to leave a clear trail. Perhaps he isn't even trying to come after us."

"You know how set he was that I should marry Lord Grassington. We appealed to both of them, and what good did that do? Uncle William flew even higher into the boughs, and the earl wouldn't even receive you. If only we could have learned the reason! Oh, I've no doubt that Uncle will be after us."

She eyed her brother doubtfully. She had no wish to add to his discomfort, but her impatience with their delayed departure was difficult to conceal. "Does your knee still pain you? Is there any chance that you could walk on it today?" Before he could protest, she explained, "I just thought if we could take to the footpaths, no one at all would know where we had gone!"

Gilbey bit his lip. "Perhaps if I can just rest it a little while longer. But what about Lord Brinton?"

Gillian's earlier charity with the aggravating earl had quite disappeared. "He returned the purse we left for him, did he not?"

"Yes. He did not want us to pay for his hospitality."

"Well, then. We are quits with him. As far as I am concerned, the sooner we are far away from him, the better."

Upstairs, Brinton squinted into the small shaving mirror and stroked the razor carefully under his chin. "It goes without saying there's not a conveyance left to be hired anywhere in this town today," he said to Archie, swishing the blade in the basin and wiping it on the cloth provided.

Spelling was tucking his shirt into his tight-fitting pantaloons and did not reply. A tray of partially eaten breakfast perched on the bed beside him. The smell of the thick ham slices mingled with the scent of shaving soap.

"They could probably still catch their coach at The George," the earl continued, thinking aloud. "They must be listed on the waybill, and the agent might remember them. But they will still be short of funds for tips and meals if they are going any distance." It occurred to him that he might at least learn the young pair's destination if he offered to loan them the money.

"Might I make a suggestion?" Archie interrupted. "You have your own vehicle here, and you have horses bespoken for today. Why not offer to convey them yourself?" He aimed an uncharacteristically wicked grin at his friend.

Rafferty paused before answering. "Assisting runaways is a pretty serious business," he began, but even as he spoke he knew he liked Archie's idea. What better way could there be to prove his bet? Beyond all else, the very adventure of it appealed to him.

On the other hand, he knew he should do nothing more to encourage the connection. He had felt the spark of desire the girl triggered in him as he had watched her sip her coffee. When she had looked up into his eyes, he had barely managed to stop himself from going to her. Instead, he had spoken to her like an insensitive dolt, just because he was angry at the thieves and dismayed by what could have happened to her.

"What about you, Arch? What about the race?" He felt like a sinking swimmer grasping at sticks.

"Oh, pish," said Archie. "Don't leave till after the race! As for me, I'll just go home after. S'posed to head up to London in a few days, anyway. I'll see you there."

"My curricle seats only two," Rafferty protested weakly.

Archie laughed. "You know you want to do it. Indulge yourself. I know you want to spend more time with her. Maybe they'll let you be best man at the wedding!"

Brinton gave up the struggle. "All right, I will do it. I shall prove to you yet this is not about marriage. You'll not get your hands on my Tristan so easily! Perhaps the lad can ride on the tiger's perch."

Chapter Four

The trio in the curricle had passed nothing in the fog for quite a few minutes. After miles broken by occasional lights and other signs of habitation, the emptiness of the barely visible landscape was eerie.

"We have not mistaken the way, have we?" asked Gillian with more than a trace of anxiety in her voice.

Brinton sighed and handed the ribbons over to her. He had discovered soon after setting out that she had not the slightest fear of handling them. Clearly, her confidence in his own abilities was far less certain. He shook his head as he clambered down from the curricle to look for the signpost that would reassure his passengers. This attempt to travel in the morning fog was a far greater folly than he had thought to take part in.

When they had first set out, he had not been able to see more than a few feet ahead of the horses. The fog had surrounded them like a wet cocoon, glistening in beads on the horses' broad rumps and dripping from their harness. He had needed to walk along at their heads, watching for unseen obstacles and listening for the occasional farm cart that would suddenly loom before them out of the gloom. He glanced down at his boots, encrusted beyond repair with red Taunton mud. At least under his care the carriage had suffered no mishap.

The girl had chafed at their slow progress, he knew, although she had made an effort to hide it. He had been able to observe her in odd moments when the fog lifted slightly, allowing him to climb back up beside her. Underneath her nervous anxiety he thought she was afraid. He suspected she had been awake all night, for he could see the shadows of fatigue under her eyes.

How he wished she would look at him with trust instead of the guarded expression that was always in those beautiful eyes! Miss Kendall, she had said he might call her, back at the inn. She and the lad had claimed to be cousins, both by the same name. He was not convinced, however. They had seemed so tentative. They hadn't even agreed on their destination when he had asked it.

"I may be in a position to offer you some further assistance," he had said earlier after rejoining them in the coffee room at the Ram's Head. He had felt far more confident then, freshly shaved, fed, and attired in a handsome ensemble that hadn't been slept in.

"You have done quite enough for us already, *my lord*," the girl had responded, without sounding the least bit grateful.

"We are already greatly in your debt, my lord," the lad had said with far more sincerity.

"I have at my disposal a curricle and pair," Brinton had continued smoothly, refusing to admit that the girl's attitude wounded him. "But before I offer you conveyance, I must inquire where your coach would have delivered you?"

"Brist—"

"Gloucester."

The two had looked sheepishly at each other, then the girl had turned to Brinton with a determined toss of her head.

"North," she had said in a tone that defied argument.

Brinton had carefully schooled his features to reveal neither surprise, skepticism, nor amusement. "It happens I have business that would not take me too far out of the way to accomodate you," he had responded. Somehow he had agreed not only to take the couple part of their way north, but to leave this very morning, while the fog was still virtually impenetrable.

Forgoing the races left him with extra money in his purse and an unfulfilled mission to acquire some prime horseflesh. Archie would let him know what he missed in Taunton. If he recollected rightly, Worcester's spring cattle fair was on Monday. Perhaps he would go there.

Brinton found the road marker at last and went through the motions of checking it. "We are only two miles from

Bridgwater," he said, returning to the carriage. "*If* you have enough faith at least in my ability to read signposts."

He couldn't resist darting a quick glance at the girl. She had the grace to blush at his remark, and the heightened color in her cheeks set off her eyes. Those eyes were stirring up the devil in him. He quickly reclaimed his seat and the ribbons.

Riding next to her was distracting, he had to admit. They both seemed to be making an excruciating effort not to touch each other—preserving the tiny space between them at all costs. This was difficult as they navigated the various dips and curves in the road that often came upon them quite suddenly in the fog.

Rafferty wondered impishly what she would do if he relaxed and allowed his thigh to press against hers. Would she not jump like a frightened rabbit? Perhaps it would distract her from her other fears and worries, but he stifled his urge to do it. Instead, he fixed his gaze straight ahead on the narrow tunnel of lane visible between the hedgerows.

"If it is any comfort to you, no one else on the road this morning could be making any faster progress than we are," he said. He could think of no other comfort to offer her, short of throwing down the reins and pulling her into a strong, warm, protective embrace.

Gillian heard Brinton's reassurance through a brain numb with fatigue. Her sleepless night combined with her anxiety over her uncle's pursuit and the frustration of their slow rate of travel had taxed her nerves to their limit. The added stimulus of dealing with Brinton's close presence had pushed her over the edge into her own personal fog of exhaustion.

She had not wanted to accept Brinton's offer back at the Ram's Head. She hated being in the position of requiring his aid yet again. He had looked elegant and aloof once more, neatly groomed and clad in immaculate cream-colored pantaloons and a bottle green riding coat. He had looked every inch an earl, and she still did not trust him.

Still, what alternatives had they? They had no funds to hire their own transport, even if there had been some available. They dared not reveal who they were, nor send home for more funds. Staying longer in Taunton would have been like the hare sitting still for the poacher to set his trap. Goaded by desperation, she had convinced the earl to set off at once, only to creep along at no better pace than a cautious walk.

The fog had enveloped them in a ghostly world limited to sound and sensation. The motion of the carriage and the constant creak of the harness formed a counterpoint to the rhythm of the horses' steady breathing. The sound of the animals' plodding steps was occasionally muffled by sodden drifts of spent apple blossoms, blown from trees unseen beyond the hedgerows, filling the air with their scent.

Lulled by the soporific effect of the rhythms on her tired brain, Gillian kept starting to drift into sleep. She caught herself slumping against the leather squabs, leaning perilously close to Brinton. She hastily pulled herself upright, hoping he hadn't noticed. *Two more miles to Bridgwater?* She tried to summon back her fear or frustration to keep her awake, but they seemed to have deserted her. Moments later Gillian was asleep, resting securely against Brinton's shoulder.

The isolation in which they traveled the last miles to Bridgwater began to break as the trio drew nearer the town. Brinton knew he must awaken Gillian, much as he might regret doing so. Sleeping, she looked like an angel, stirring curiously protective and noble feelings within him. A lock of hair had escaped her cap to rest wetly against his arm, but he was content to let it stay. He marveled at the sweep of her long lashes against her pale cheeks.

Driving had been more challenging with her slight weight against him, but he had enjoyed the closeness, no matter how unintended it was. He guessed she would be angry when she awoke—angry at herself and embarrassed. Perhaps he could forestall that if he could find an inn right away. The need for action would rob her of the opportunity to fume at him.

Even in the fog Bridgwater appeared to be a substantial town with a fine, wide central street. The road took them past the church in St. Mary's Street where the Duke of Monmouth had looked out toward Sedgemoor and failed to foresee his own doom. Beyond the church fashionable houses lined the street and the side roads as well. One was advertising itself as "The Monmouth Arms." Gratefully, Rafferty turned his horses into the stable yard and gave Gillian a gentle shake.

"Awake, Sleeping Beauty. Your castle awaits." When he saw her begin to stir, he addressed her in a firmer tone of voice. "Miss Kendall," he began, "we will stop here briefly to rest and dry ourselves."

Gillian straightened up and opened luminous eyes still clouded with sleep. The earl watched in amusement as realization of what had happened dawned in them and they then focused sharply on him. Gillian opened her mouth to protest, but the earl held up his hand.

"Think of your faithful cousin, riding in the back, with no doubt the greatest discomfort. We will not stay long. But for pity's sake, do not talk, do not remove your cap, and above all, do not look anyone in the eye—I mean, anyone." Especially the last, he said to himself, thinking of his own first meeting with her. If she were discovered now, traveling like this, the scandal would be beyond disastrous.

"Shall I stay in the stables with the horses, my lord?" The withering look she directed at him banished any remaining traces of the sleeping angel in his mind's eye.

"And leave you to your own mischief while we warm ourselves inside by the fire? I think not." Brinton tossed the reins to the stable hand who met them and clambered down. Let her think he didn't trust her. Had she no idea of the trouble she might find among the rough characters who hung about the stables? He only hoped she had sense enough to jump down by herself in a carefree fashion. They would all three of them have to be very careful to preserve appearances while they stopped here.

Gillian choked back her irritation at Brinton's high-handedness and clambered nimbly down from the curricle. It was quite unfair, she thought, how easily one could move about in breeches, even with an enveloping travel cloak.

She watched Brinton help her thoroughly soaked twin descend from the back of the curricle. Limp, wet blond hair hung over Gilbey's forehead and dripped onto his nose. Stiff and groaning, he looked truly pathetic, and she could not deny that it was her fault. She had shown very little gratitude for his loyalty and care thus far, she thought guiltily. Resolving to do better, she moved to her brother's side, offering a supporting arm.

Brinton quickly took a place at Gilbey's other side. Gillian made certain her arm was positioned where it would not touch the earl's, and she refused to recognize the frisson of disappointment she felt when he made no effort to alter the arrangement. With Gilbey limping badly, the trio crossed the courtyard and entered the inn.

They were in a central hallway that spanned the converted house from front to back. Its highly polished floor and pastel walls bespoke a standard of elegance still maintained despite the dwelling's lowered status. A graceful curved stairway with an elaborate iron railing began its ascent off to one side. Several doorways ornamented with fluted columns and classical pediments opened onto rooms that appeared for the most part to be empty.

"Not overbusy, I see," Brinton remarked with a note of satisfaction as the innkeeper and a porter appeared.

Gillian kept her eyes on the floor and said nothing.

"Aye, sir. 'Tis a terrible morning to be abroad, as you've no doubt seen." The man regarded them with obvious curiosity. He was thin and stoop-shouldered, with a small pair of spectacles on the end of his nose that gave him the look of a schoolmaster.

He produced the ledger book, and as the earl signed with a flourish, a huge smile lit his face. "We are honored to have your custom, my lord," he said with a deep bow. Gillian was afraid he would actually grovel.

Brinton ordered a private parlor with an adjoining room and was assured that there would be only a few minutes' wait. In the meantime his party would be served hot cider by the fire in the blue salon. Before the innkeeper left, he looked dubiously at Gilbey. "Is there anything else you require?"

"This gentleman was injured in an attack by footpads this morning in Taunton," Brinton said. "I believe his comfort would be vastly improved by a soak in a warm bath."

Gillian could not help lifting her gaze. She valiantly restrained her urge to kick Brinton. Their misfortune was just the sort of news loved by fireside gossips and could spread from this inn all over Somerset. Meanwhile, soaking her brother in a bath would delay them disastrously.

The innkeeper's eyebrows shot up comically, but he refrained from comment. "Certainly, my lord." He shepherded the travelers into one of the rooms off the hallway, shaking his head sympathetically. "I can have your wet garments spread in the other room to dry, my lord. And did you wish the young lad to be shown to the kitchen?"

Gillian's mouth dropped open, and she had to make a conscious effort to close it again. The man thought she was a servant! It was beyond too much.

Brinton had a devilish smile on his face as he replied, "That will not be necessary, thank you." The earl was already helping Gilbey remove his greatcoat so he might sink down onto the sofa pulled close by the fire. "The boy can stay and assist us with our wet things."

Gillian directed an accusing glare at Brinton as soon as the innkeeper was gone. "That fellow thinks I am your servant," she burst out, "and you deliberately encouraged him!"

Rafferty chuckled. "So I did. That does not sit well with you, does it? But think of this—who pays attention to other people's servants? If you are so determined to pass yourself off as a lad, you had best do all you can to avoid scrutiny. I suggest you adopt the role while we are here." He gave Gillian a sidelong glance and raised one dark eyebrow mischievously. "You may begin by removing my cloak."

"I will do no such thing," Gillian fumed. Her voice was tight with the effort not to shout. "There is no need for me to adopt such a charade when we are not in the company of others."

The rattle of a tray in the passage warned Gillian to say no more. Moments later a woman appeared, bearing the promised tankards of steaming, fragrant cider.

If the innkeeper looked like a schoolmaster, then this round woman looked for all the world like someone's cherished nanny. She beamed a delightfully benign smile on the gathered company.

"Welcome, welcome!" she exclaimed. "My lord, we are so honored by your visit! Here's just the thing to take the

chill off—our own local cider, as fine as any you'll find
served in Taunton."

Brinton had unfastened the closures on his cloak, and as
the woman approached with the tray, he swung the wet garment from his shoulders. "Here, lad. Drape this on that
chair by the window." He held it out to Gillian.

The aroma of the warm cider had triggered Gillian's
hunger, and she was feeling rather wobbly. She had no
choice but to step toward Brinton to take the cloak, however. As the earl dumped the heavy mass of wool into her
arms, she staggered under its weight.

"You brought some for the boy?" Rafferty cast an
offhanded glance at the woman's tray. "Good. I think he is
also in need of sustenance."

Once the tankards had been distributed and the woman
was gone, the earl exchanged his superior attitude for one
of solicitous concern. Setting down his own mug on the
small table beside Gilbey's sofa, he approached Gillian.
"Allow me to do you the service, Miss Kendall. It is clear
you need to sit down."

Before Gillian could realize what he was about, he was
gently unfastening her cloak. His fingers were sure and de-
liberate as they unndid the buttons, and a shiver ran through
her despite the warm mug clutched tightly in her hands. His
gesture was shockingly familiar, but her protest seemed to
be stuck in her throat. Before she could dislodge it, he had
removed the cloak from her shoulders and the moment had
passed.

"Sit," he ordered, and Gillian did so, selecting a chair she
felt was appropriately distant from the furnishings grouped
by the hearth. How could one man keep her so utterly off-
balance? He could be horribly unfeeling at one moment,
and remarkably considerate the next. He seemed to switch
from being aloof and annoyingly proper to having no regard for propriety at all. Beyond all else, Gillian thought he
seemed to delight in provoking her. Infuriating man!

However, she had to admit he was right about her posing
as a servant. Not only would she personally attract less attention, but as a lord's traveling party they would seem
more believable. Anyone making inquiries after a young

runaway brother and sister would never think to connect them with a pair of traveling gentlemen and their servant.

Gillian stared at the blue velvet drapes, lost in such thoughts. She failed to note a commotion and voices in the hallway until the innkeeper escorted another pair of travelers into their sanctuary.

"My deepest apologies, Lord Brinton," the innkeeper began. "The fire in the other parlor seemed to be smoking quite badly, and I thought perhaps you would not mind sharing yours with these good folks for just a few minutes?" He hurried on, perhaps fearing that Brinton might object if given the opportunity. "This is Squire Hammerton and his neighbor, Mr. Cornish. They live just up in Puriton; they are regular visitors here. I can certainly vouch for their character—they always pay their bill!" He giggled nervously and, after catching his breath, plunged on. "Squire and Mr. Cornish, I am honored to present the Earl of Brinton, and his companion . . . ?"

"Mr. Kendall," Rafferty finished with something less than his usual graciousness. He was annoyed by the intrusion and wondered cynically if the innkeeper even had another fire going in the other room as claimed. However, he had been left no polite choice but to accept the company thrust upon them.

The squire rushed forward to shake hands with the earl. "Honored, my lord—indeed, most generous of you!" He was a classic example of his species—round eyes looked out from a square, heavily jowled and rather florid countenance, set on a short, thick neck and massive shoulders. He was nearly of a height with Gilbey and the earl, quite dwarfing his companion by comparison.

Gilbey winced as the squire pumped his hand energetically.

"Mr. Kendall had the ill-fortune to be set upon by footpads in Taunton this morning," the innkeeper explained hastily.

"Footpads! In Taunton!" the squire exclaimed, releasing Gilbey. He peered at him curiously. "You were fortunate to escape worse injury, young man. 'Tis enough to make one stay at home!" He nodded sagely to the small assembly. "We are all well out of there, I must say." He launched into a description of the conditions he had found in Taunton, taking the opportunity to shed his coat.

His companion said nothing. He was a small man, apparently inclined to be taciturn or, as Rafferty surmised, he seldom found many chances to participate in conversations around the squire.

"Yes—we had our fill of the crowds and confusion," the latter continued with renewed enthusiasm, settling into a chair across from Gilbey's sofa. "No one knew if the race would be held or not. I couldn't brook no delay—I've got a special filly waiting for me at home." He winked outrageously. "My missus, you know. She finds she can't go long without my tender ministrations, if you take my meaning. That's not to say if they'd a barmaid or a chamber-lass as well-endowed as my wife, I wouldn't avail m'self of the opportunity." Hammerton lapsed into loud, coarse guffawing that totally obscured the silence of his audience.

Brinton dared not look in Gillian's direction. He felt somehow he should have been able to protect her innocent ears from such vulgar talk, but the squire, of course, had no way of knowing they were in mixed company. *Drat the innkeeper*, Rafferty thought. How long did the man need to prepare two private rooms?

"There's nothing to match the comforts of one's home, no matter what they say," the squire was rambling on again. "It makes you wonder why anyone would give it up. Why, there were two scapegraces spent the night in th' same taproom as Cornish and me, looking for a pair of runaways. Can you credit that? Footpads and missing persons!"

There was a subtle change in the room, as if a sudden noise had captured everyone's attention.

Gilbey shifted on the sofa, presumably to make himself more comfortable. "Were these Somerset people?" he asked with studied casualness. He was fidgeting with the edge of his waistcoat.

"Not at all, not by those accents," the squire answered.

"I meant, the missing persons—the ones they were seeking."

"I believe they were said to be Devonish. Ain't that right, Cornish?" Hammerton turned to his friend for confirmation.

"I believe the story was, a young lass and her brother from the South Hams had run away from their guardian."

"That was it—that was it!" The squire took over the narrative again. "And he a viscount! Imagine!"

"The guardian?" Brinton interposed.

"No, no, my lord. The lad. Such foolishness! Consider the trouble they might run against. Why, if a young gentleman like Mr. Kendall here can be accosted by footpads, just think what might befall two such young runaways!"

His ruminations were interrupted by a loud fit of coughing as Gilbey choked on his cider. Brinton knew then if he glanced at the girl she would be sitting as silent and pale as a ghost. He carefully kept his eyes on the squire.

"Think, indeed," he said encouragingly. "And why do you suppose a young viscount and his sister would show such poor judgment as to flee from their guardian?"

"Now that I couldn't rightly say," Hammerton replied, disappointingly. "These fellows had followed the trail to Exeter and then to Taunton, but lost track of them there. They were going to check all the northbound coaches this morning." He sniffed in disdain. "Imagine a viscount on the common stage!"

"Horrendous," agreed Brinton wryly. "Did you happen to learn who these people were?"

"They were little more than ruffians, I'd say," the squire replied honestly.

"I mean, the young runaways and their guardian." Brinton was finding his patience difficult to maintain. He caught a despairing glance from Gilbey.

"The Viscount Cranford, I believe," said Mr. Cornish, who had already proven he was a better listener than the squire. "The guardian was Baron Pembermore."

"You're certain of this?" Brinton's tone was laced with disbelief.

"Indeed," answered Cornish. "But it seems to me there was also some mention of the Earl of Grassington. I didn't catch the connection."

The Earl of Brinton set his cider down very carefully on the pedestal table beside him. He felt as though he had suddenly fallen over the edge of a very tall cliff.

Chapter Five

Rafferty knew his ears could not have deceived him. What sort of bumble-bath had he stumbled into? The Earl of Grassington was his elderly uncle, who should have been too preoccupied with marriage plans to get embroiled in any other folly. Cranford lands adjoined his uncle's in Devon, so there was a connection to the viscount, but could the lad truly be Cranford? Of all the titles in England the boy might have held, that one was almost too coincidental to be believed.

He had thought the viscount to be an older man. He tried to remember if he had ever met his uncle's neighbor. Could the lad have just recently come into the title? Had there ever been mention of a sister? The young earl rose and crossed to stand before the fire, staring into the snapping flames. He did not want the others to see his face, for he feared it would betray the conflicting emotions whirling through his mind.

Rafferty believed that the pair were siblings, at least. It would explain the resemblance between them and the unloverlike closeness he had noted. It hurt his pride a little that they had not confided in him, but, he reasoned, were he in their situation, he might not have done so either. At least there was certainly no marriage in the wind between them. A curious feeling of elation mixed with his other reactions.

He was horrified to think that any of these people were associated with Baron Pembermore, however. The talk bruited about London held the baron to be a scoundrel—a gamster and wastrel of the very worst sort, despite high connections. Could the man truly be the young pair's guardian? Was he the reason they were running away? How in heaven's name had his uncle come to be mixed up in the affair? Brinton struggled with these questions, aware that in the back of his mind a skeptical voice kept asking, *Is any of this story true?*

"Your rooms are ready, my lord." The innkeeper's voice cut into Brinton's thoughts.

Abruptly turning his back on the fire, the earl saw that cider was being served to the squire and Mr. Cornish and that the innkeeper was standing expectantly in the doorway to the hall, ready to lead his party upstairs. Rafferty willed an inscrutable mask of control to cover his features. He would fathom out this puzzle, but not yet.

The challenge of leaving the room without betraying her role kept Gillian from succumbing to the panic that had begun to surge through her. The squire and Mr. Cornish's tale had confirmed her worst fear—that, somehow, someone had indeed traced her and Gilbey to Taunton. Gillian had to assume that only the unforgiving weather and the extraordinary crowds had saved them from being found. What a mixed blessing that she and Gilbey had been prevented from taking their coach! She felt a warm surge of gratitude toward Lord Brinton for making possible their escape.

The earl, however, was impossible to read. She had watched him get up and move before the fire. He had moved casually, but she suspected that he had made the connection between his passengers and the Devonshire runaways. Was he shocked by what he had heard? Was he angry that they had deceived him? What would he do now? There had been no clue to his reaction.

Gillian gathered up the men's wet garments and her own, hoping the squire and his friend were not watching her. She nearly staggered under the weight of the coat and two cloaks as she followed after the others. She trailed slowly up the stairs, trying to avoid the dragging ends of the voluminous cloaks. Ahead, Gilbey limped along with his weight on Brinton's arm. The earl was coughing under the strain of assisting him.

The little procession entered an elegant room furnished all in Chinese yellow. Gillian dropped her burden onto the nearest satin-clad chair, longing to sink down on top of it. Her arms ached, and she felt exhausted to the very bone, but to sit without the earl's permission would be unthinkable in a servant.

Brinton needed a moment to recover and catch his

breath, but then he inspected the rooms and dismissed the innkeeper, requesting him to send up a hearty tea. As soon as the man departed, Gillian headed for the mate to Gilbey's chair by the fire. To her dismay the steps she had intended to be firm and purposeful faltered, and her knees wobbled. Her brother looked at her in consternation. Brinton was by her side in an instant, grasping her elbow and guiding her to the chair.

"I'm all right," she said, but her voice came out as a throaty whisper and there was a catch in it. *Oh, no*, she resolved, *not tears again*!

Brinton squatted in front of her chair, looking up into her eyes and taking her hands into his. He removed her gloves and began to rub her fingers, as if she were a child just come in from the cold.

"I—I just need to eat," she stammered faintly. The earl's motions were causing the most remarkable sensations to travel up her arms. In her weakened state she was afraid her body might begin to shake all over. She could not seem to unlock her gaze from his.

"Tea should be here directly," he said softly. He released her hands then and rose to pace away from the hearth and back again. He stopped and looked first at Gilbey, then at Gillian.

"I suppose that the name Kendall is as much a fiction as your relationship as cousins?" His tone was gentle but strained, leaving Gillian with the impression of tightly reined control.

She glanced at Gilbey and saw that he had colored to his ear tips. She knew that she was flushed as well, from the tingling in her face. How should they answer? Gilbey's eyes met hers and the twins stared at each other for a moment. Then Gilbey swallowed nervously and faced the earl.

"I suppose we should make a clean breast of things, my lord. We owe you that, for all your assistance—that much and a great deal more. Rest assured we will repay you."

"I have not helped you in expectation of repayment," Brinton said tightly. "However, I do feel I have a right to know whom I have been helping, and why."

Gillian toyed with the gloves in her lap. She could not bring herself to look at Brinton. Better to let Gilbey handle the confrontation, she thought. She was so tired, and she wasn't sure she could stand to see the look of disapproval that might come over Brinton's face when he learned their story.

Legally, she and Gilbey had no right to defy their guardian. Brinton might not see the justification for what they were doing and might even be angry that they had involved him. Yet, when had she suddenly become such a coward? She must have faced her father's disapproval a hundred times for various antics, and never had it bothered her. What made this so different? Defiantly, she lifted her chin and turned to the earl.

"Our family name is Kentwell," she began. "Gilbey and I are twins if you can believe it," she added with a brittle little laugh. "We live at Cliffcombe, in the South Hams, not far from Kingsbridge. Or should I say, we did." Emotion was threatening to defeat her brave attempt. "My brother is the Viscount Cranford," she finished quickly, looking away.

A wave of pain washed through her like a breaker tumbling stones on the beach at home. She had given up so much! She put a clenched fist to her lips and closed her eyes to banish the images of faithful servants and her dog, Hector, no doubt bereft and puzzled by her absence. She must not think of them. She must look only ahead.

The earl and her brother were shaking hands. "Not so well met as might be usual, eh Cranford?" Brinton said.

"Unusual circumstances, to say the least," Gilbey agreed. He aimed an encouraging smile at his sister.

"So, you have run away from home?" Brinton prompted.

"Yes," the twins replied in tandem. As they paused to see which one would take up the narrative, they were interrupted by a quick rap on the door.

"Devil take it," said Brinton under his breath. As he went to the door, he cast a meaningful glance at Gillian, who realized she ought to get up.

"What?" the earl fairly barked at the boy who stood outside. The lad held a bucket of steaming water in each hand. "Oh," Brinton said somewhat sheepishly, backing up. "Right through here—the tub is set up in the other room. Tyler will show you." He nodded pointedly at Gillian.

Gillian led the boy through, grateful for the earl's presence of mind.

"Just leave the buckets," she told the boy in a gruff voice. "I'll see to them." She escorted him back into the outer room.

Brinton tossed the lad a shilling and saw him out. As soon as the door closed, Gillian blurted, "Who is Tyler?"

Brinton smiled. "Tyler is my valet at home."

"And where is your home? We know as little about you as you know about us!" Her questions bore an undertone of resentment.

The earl parried deftly. "Let us not divert from the topic at hand, despite the interruption, Miss Kentwell. You have run away from your home in South Devon, a very drastic thing to do, and have run into nothing but trouble since." His eloquent, dark eyebrows rose in expectation. "Come now, Cranford, before your bathwater gets cold."

"Our mother died in childbirth when we were eight," Gilbey said, taking up the tale. "There were no other children. Then a year ago our father died. His younger half brother is our guardian, Baron Pembermore." Gilbey paused to look at Gillian, who nodded to him to continue.

She was watching Brinton's face as he listened, trying to interpret what she saw there. For the most part what she saw was an annoyingly handsome man, whose classically sculptured features hid what was passing through his mind. She thought she could detect a tightness to his jaw, however, and a slight narrowing of his eyes, as if he didn't like, or didn't believe, what he was hearing. Her heart sank.

"Our uncle has all but ignored us during this year that we've been in mourning," Gilbey continued. "We had settled back into fairly normal patterns at home, with the servants to attend our needs. We are almost nineteen, and in just over two more years will be of legal age." He cast a significant look at his sister. "Uncle William will interfere with us no more then," he declared staunchly.

"But you said that he'd ignored you?" Brinton questioned.

"We live quietly and keep to ourselves. Gillie does her music. I like to fish and fancy myself an artist. We favor long rides along the coast. Our headlands are rather spectacular—have you ever been to South Devon?"

"Yes," said Brinton. Gillian could see the corners of his

mouth had tightened, and the tenseness in his voice was unmistakable. Was his patience wearing thin?

"Five days ago our uncle announced that I am to be married," Gillian interjected. She could not mask the bitterness in her voice. "He had the arrangements well in hand."

"I imagine you took that rather amiss," the earl said with mock seriousness. He looked more amused now than tense. It was well his shins were not in striking range of Gillian's feet, for she had a stong urge to kick him.

"Truly," he continued more soberly, "I can understand how shocked you must have been, but there are still many arranged marriages these days. You are apparently of marriageable age, although I have to say, you do not look it. Was the match he desired for you so unacceptable? He did not propose to marry you off to a wife-beater, or some sort of rake-hell, did he?"

"No."

They were interrupted once again by a knock at the door.

"What now?" Brinton exclaimed in frustration. He opened the door quickly, and there, of course, was the woman with their tea. "Very well," he said ungraciously, "put it on the table there."

She entered the room and deposited the tray. "Forgive me, my lord," she said, seeing Gilbey seated by the fire still fully dressed. "Sir, Mr. Kendall's bathwater will be getting cold!" She was no doubt dismayed by the prospect of sending up more.

"He likes it that way," growled Brinton, all but pushing her toward the door. He gave her a half crown. "Thank you."

Gillian was already at the table pouring out tea when he turned around. He assisted her in setting out the enticing collection of breads, Scotch eggs, and potatoes, served with a few sausage links placed on the side. The aroma drew Gilbey away from the hearth without a word. They pulled up chairs and fell to ravenously, as if their earlier breakfast had never been.

After a pause of several moments, Brinton began again. "Surely you were not surprised to discover you must marry?" He sipped his hot tea and set the dish carefully back in its saucer.

"Of course not," Gillian retorted. She reached for another

split bun, weighing her words. Could she make Lord Brinton understand the horror she had felt over the betrothal? She must try, for it was clear that she and Gilbey still needed his help. They were only twelve miles from Taunton, for pity's sake, where their pursuers might still very well pick up their trail.

"My uncle could not care less whether or not I am ready to be a wife," she began again. "He pledged me to the Earl of Grassington without so much as consulting me, and then he all but expected me to kiss his feet in gratitude. Can you imagine? That I should be grateful to him for arranging to ruin my life!"

"Is the idea of the marriage so hateful, then?"

Gillian thought Brinton's eyes were watchful, and his posture seemed very stiff. "Grassington is old enough to be my grandfather," she persevered. "He does not socialize, nor is he known to travel. Although he is our nearest neighbor, I have met him only twice. To be forced to marry him is like a sentence to be entombed on his estate."

She paused, the color rising delicately in her cheeks with the passion of her remembered anger. "You must understand that, although I love the South Hams, I have desires. I would like to see London and something of the rest of the world. And I would pine for company, for people closer to my age, married to him." Overwhelmed by her distaste for the idea, Gillian abruptly got up from the table and moved restlessly to the windows overlooking the inn yard.

"Uncle William had the gall to sit in our drawing room and suggest that I should be pleased to be marrying an earl!" In the heat of the moment Gillian quite forgot that she was addressing one. "As if that were of utmost importance, or even highly unattainable!" She sniffed. "I am young, passable-looking, and the daughter of a viscount. My father left me a very generous portion. It is not outrageous to think that I might marry an earl—a young one—if I had that ambition."

Gillian spun around suddenly as if she had just remembered her audience. "But I don't care if I marry a title!" she burst out. "I want to marry a man—one I love and who loves me in return! Is that so terrible?" She stopped again to get herself in hand. Her voice shook a little with the effort it cost her. As tears started to well, she brushed them away in annoyance.

"Our uncle suggested that Gillian need only suffer Lord Grassington a little while, until he dies," Gilbey explained with a glance at his distraught sister. "After that she would be free to do as she pleased."

"I could not do that," Gillian whispered, staring at the two men still seated at the table. "The very thought is gruesome."

"Did you not consider that you might gladden his remaining years?" asked Brinton in an odd-sounding voice.

"No," she responded. "I thought every sight of me would just remind him of his numbered days." She shuddered.

"So you decided to run away."

"Not at first." Still battling tears, Gillian looked to her twin for help.

"We thought we could reason with them," Gilbey said. "Uncle William had this absurd notion that Gillian was 'sensible and biddable'. I don't know where he got that idea!" He threw an affectionate glance at his sister and smiled.

Gillian did not rise to his bait, however, saying nothing. Gilbey held out his handkerchief to her.

"I thought Uncle William would change his mind when he realized how opposed she was to his plan," Gilbey continued. "However, when I approached him, he just flew into a temper."

Gillian blew her nose and then stood behind her brother's chair with one hand on his shoulder, as if drawing support from the physical contact. "Gilbey even tried to approach Lord Grassington, but he could not see him."

"Why?"

"The earl wouldn't admit me—no reason given," Gilbey said.

"That was when I decided to run away," Gillian explained bitterly. "I do not think Uncle William will dare to follow through on his plan if he cannot find me."

"So you are planning to hide in Gloucester, or Bristol?" Brinton's disbelief was obvious.

Gillian's eyes lit with a spark of defiance she could not disguise. "Scotland," she answered. "We have an aunt there, although we have never met her."

There, it was out. Let Brinton think what he would.

Chapter Six

Leaving Brinton to digest what he had just heard, Gillian abruptly excused herself to go into the adjoining room and wash her face with Gilbey's bathwater. Over the remains of the tea, the earl and Gilbey faced each other.

"You agreed to this ridiculous scheme?" Brinton demanded.

"You do not know my sister. She would have undertaken the journey alone. I could not have stopped her. The best I could do was come along," Gilbey explained.

"You are also opposed to the marriage?"

"The very idea is an abomination!" Gilbey lowered his voice and leaned toward Brinton. "When I was at Grassington's, I overheard him talking rather loudly. He wants a new heir, and he thinks he's going to beget one on my sister. I tell you, he is so ancient, thinking of them sharing a bed turns my stomach!"

The young viscount thumped his fist on the table in a surprising show of frustration. "If I were of age, Uncle William would not dare to trade Gillian like a brood mare. Damn the man, and Grassington along with him! If she were your sister, you would understand."

Rafferty thought fleetingly of his own five sisters and allowed to himself that he did understand how Gilbey felt. If only he could fathom his own feelings as well! He could not seem to make sense out of all he was hearing. Somehow, the image of his elderly uncle with a young bride had not bothered him at all until now, when suddenly the anonymous young woman in question had Miss Kentwell's face.

The earl had a sinking suspicion that he was the other participant in the conversation Gilbey had overheard at

Grassington's. Hadn't his uncle told him quite pointedly that the object of the marriage was to get a new heir? The unpleasant scene had been interrupted by a footman, but Grassington had declined to be disturbed. *That could have been an unwanted visitor*, Brinton thought.

He desperately wanted to believe Gilbey's story. But the older earl had boasted about the willingness of his bride-to-be, and now the younger earl shook his head. There were plenty of female fortune-hunters who would tolerate the old man. Rafferty couldn't believe that his uncle would marry a young girl against her will. Nor would his uncle lie to him, he thought, no matter how much the man delighted in aggravating him. Was his uncle being deceived? Or, was he?

"I never took Grassington for such a lecherous blackguard!" Gilbey was continuing. "A trifle eccentric, perhaps, but this! His determination to bed my sister dashed any hopes we might have had about seeking an annulment after the marriage. Gillie could never keep out of his clutches long enough!"

Rafferty choked back his instinctive response to Gilbey's unwitting insult, producing only a small, strangled sound in his throat. Certainly the twins knew nothing of his connection to Grassington, and this was hardly the time to reveal it.

Gilbey appeared not to notice Brinton's reaction. "I pray, sir, that you will say nothing of this to my sister," he said, looking anxiously toward the connecting door. "She does not know that I overheard anything, and the matter is too indelicate for her ears. She may seem the worst sort of hoyden," he added, "but I assure you, beneath that facade, there lurks a very sensitive and innocent young girl."

The two men were polishing off the remains of their tea in silence when Gillian rejoined them moments later. Damp curls clustered around her freshly scrubbed face. Her smooth skin glowed, but she had not been able to erase the distress showing plainly in her blue-green eyes.

The silence between her brother and the earl seemed strained to her, and she wondered what they had been discussing while she was absent from the room. Had Gilbey learned anything of the earl's intentions? Should she just bluntly ask them?

She decided that it didn't matter. Reviewing her situation for Lord Brinton had revived her fears and desperation. With pursuit so close on her trail, all that mattered now was escape. Undoubtedly, Lord Brinton had saved them in Taunton, and they owed him a great deal more than the money he had spent on them. But if he thought they had time to spare sitting in baths, he could very well soak by himself. She and her brother would never reach Scotland if they could not outrun her uncle's hirelings. She, for one, was quite certain she would be relieved to quit Brinton's company. She had never before met anyone who so completely unsettled her. She was determined to get back on the road, without delay and without the earl.

Contriving to inject a note of brightness and energy into her voice, she addressed her brother. "Lord Cranford," she said, bowing to her twin with mock formality, "your bathwater has cooled considerably. How fortunate, then, that you shall not be wanting it, since we have not time to dally here." She cast a meaningful glance at Brinton. "Perhaps someone *else* can make use of it. *We* must be leaving."

She noticed that Brinton's dark brows arched in surprise, then smoothed back into a perfectly controlled expression.

"Exactly how are you proposing to do that?" he asked, his voice neutral and his hazel eyes unreadable.

"Well, I—I suppose that depends," she faltered. How difficult he made it for her to maintain her fragile confidence! "I thought, if we could just prevail upon your goodwill one more time, you might advance us funds for horses? Unless, of course, my brother is able to walk." She looked from Brinton to Gilbey and back, obviously at a loss and not liking it a bit.

Brinton smiled. "I appreciate your allowing me the chance to disassociate myself from your company. However, do you not think it would appear odd, and attract notice, if my servant and my companion left, and I stayed behind?" He glanced at their luggage in the corner where the porter had left it for them. "How would you manage on foot with those bags?"

Gillian flushed. "We would manage, my lord, if we had to," she answered stubbornly. "We dare not stay on here.

We are too close to Taunton and those who are apparently seeking us."

"You think you will get on faster without me?"

"It is thanks to you we are ahead of them at all, but we cannot afford to lose that advantage."

"So, you can be diplomatic when you choose! I suspected as much." Brinton turned his gaze directly into Gillian's face. "Let me be certain that I understand. You are planning to outrun these hunters for another three hundred miles, traveling, if need be, on foot, and dragging a portmanteau half full of books."

It did sound harebrained, put so bluntly. She was surprised that he remembered the books. The familiar despair she kept fighting began to settle around her heart. How had she ever thought she could escape by running away?

"Speed is not going to be your answer," the earl observed, leaning back in his chair. "You will have to use cunning if you hope to elude your pursuers." He looked thoughtful, as if engaged in a chess match. "We will leave together, as we came. I would suggest a change of route, however."

"What are you proposing?" asked Gilbey, who had been quietly observing the exchange between the other two.

"You have done nothing but head due north since you left your home, is that not so?" Brinton raised an eyebrow toward Gilbey, looking for his confirmation. "Your pursuers cannot hunt for you in every direction. Having lost you in Taunton, they may continue looking northward, hoping to stumble across your trail. We have changed the number of people traveling in your party. A change of route now would be another precaution against being found. I suggest we head east. We can turn north again at Glastonbury."

"A capital idea!" exclaimed Gilbey.

Gillian winced at the admiration in her brother's voice. Lord Brinton could suggest swimming to China, and Gilbey would probably embrace the idea with enthusiasm, she thought. The trouble was, once again, Brinton was right. They were better off playing the fox than the hare. Was the dratted man always right? He had taken complete control of them from the moment he had walked up to them in the inn at Taunton. Gilbey seemed in such awe of the man that he had almost completely lost his tongue. Even worse, her own brain seemed to have turned into mush. What on earth was the matter with them?

The earl was looking at her, waiting for a response. Grasping the back of Gilbey's chair like a lifeline, she raised her eyes to meet his.

"Just where are you proposing we end up?" she queried tentatively. She could feel her resentment toward him melting as her pulse quickened under his gaze.

Brinton was quite prepared with his answer. "Bath," he said, his hazel eyes never wavering from hers.

The route to Bath lay across the Somerset Levels, which stretched for miles to the east and north of Bridgwater. Heavy fog blanketed the open pastures, hiding the marsh-marigolds and half a hundred other wildflowers that filled the wet spring fields. The vast flatlands were prone to flooding, and large patches of water flanked the road and even crossed it in places, for only a few ancient channels provided drainage. The fog rendered both road and bogs invisible.

"Blast this weather!" Brinton exclaimed with surprising vehemence. His dark brows were drawn down in concentration, and his fatigue showed clearly. "I cannot for the life of me pick out the road more than a few feet ahead."

"If we find ourselves among the bulrushes, we'll know you've gone wrong," Gillian offered helpfully. She had agreed to go to Bath after a brief battle between caution and desire, for although she thought it best to part from the earl, there was merit in his suggestion to confuse their pursuers, and the chance to see the city was tempting.

"Young woman, unless you have a strong desire to join the otters and kingfishers, you might refrain from unnecessary comments."

"Do you not admire the water-ferns and iris?" she replied mischievously.

"Only from a distance."

Brinton did not take his eyes off the horses. His response was curt, but Gillian saw that the strain in his face had eased somewhat. She allowed herself a little smile of triumph.

Gilbey was once again perched precariously with the luggage at the back of the carriage, clutching the straps as Brinton eased the curricle through ruts and puddles. Occasional shadowy clumps of willows and alders loomed in the mist, but they did not serve to mark the way, for they grew as readily along the water as along the road.

The earl appeared to have all he could handle to concentrate on following the road and guiding the horses, who were fresh and resentful of the slow pace. But in truth, his mind kept returning to the questions that were bedeviling him.

Had he misjudged the twins? Were they sincere in their distress, or could they be merely playacting? He preferred to think the pair were innocent dupes in some scheme of their uncle's. Pembermore's reputation was undoubtedly black, but did the baron tend toward elaborate frauds, or just cheating at cards? Was his uncle the intended victim, or was the girl?

Rafferty smiled at the irony of it all. Here he was, helping his own uncle's intended bride to run away! What a scandal this would be if it ever came out! And he had placed himself squarely in the midst of it. If Archie only knew, his friend would think it all a huge joke.

He would be a fool to get in any deeper without learning more. In Bath he had a friend with whom the twins could stay while he tried to unravel the puzzle they represented. If the pair were truly going to Scotland, they would need to borrow more money than he had with him, and he could draw funds from the bank in Bath. He would have to wait, and watch.

Brinton and the twins had not been traveling through the wetlands for long when the fractious horses were suddenly spooked by a large, gray shape that soared silently across the road just in front of them.

"Whoa!" cried Brinton, struggling to keep the frightened animals in the roadway. "Easy, now. Let's not go for a swim."

As the horses ceased plunging, the carriage lurched, tipping at a crazy angle as one wheel sank deeply into the mud.

"Ho, what's going on?" called Gilbey from the back.

"What was it?" Gillian asked, grasping Brinton's arm as he coaxed the pair of bays to pull ahead.

"I believe it was a great heron," the earl answered, loud enough for Gilbey to hear. He was trying to keep his weight from sliding down the seat onto Miss Kentwell, who would surely be crushed or pushed out. He found it remarkable that she had not uttered so much as a single squeak of alarm at their predicament. Finally, to his relief, the horses moved forward, extricating the wheel and straightening the carriage.

"The fog makes everything so eerie," Gillian said softly. "We are near Sedgemoor, are we not?"

"We are," asserted Brinton.

"You can almost feel the ghosts in this weather!"

Ah, thought Rafferty, *so she does know something about history.* Aloud he said, "What ghosts?"

"Monmouth's army," she answered impatiently. "So many died here in his rebellion. Their blood must have soaked deep into these marshes."

"The Duke of Monmouth was a fool who had the right idea at the wrong time and went about it the wrong way," the earl said severely. *I hope I am not riding the same horse*, he added to himself. He transferred the reins to one hand so he could give hers a reassuring squeeze with the other. "You have a vivid imagination for events of more than a century ago. How is it you know so much about history?"

Gillian pulled her cloak closer about her, removing her hand from Brinton's arm as if she had only suddenly noticed it. "Our father was something of a scholar," she responded evasively. "He believed in the benefits of education and hired very qualified tutors for us."

Rafferty could sense her withdrawal and felt regret that his questions should cause it. Yet, there was so much he wanted to know about her. He tried again.

"You were allowed to sit in on your brother's classes?"

Gillian hesitated. If she revealed her full education, would he add "bluestocking" to the list of flaws he must already have noted in her? Still, she would not lie. Why should it matter to her what he thought?

"Our parents loved each other greatly. After our mother died, our father never really came out of mourning. I think he just found it easier to deal with Gilbey and me by treating us the same—same tutors, same studies, same freedom to do as we pleased." She looked at him shyly. "We studied history, geography, Latin, Greek, Italian, French."

He didn't seem as shocked as he ought to have been. "My sister Clemmy would envy you," he said quite seriously. "She always wanted to have such an opportunity to expand her mind."

"Clemmy?"

"For Clementina."

"And why could she not?"

"Oh, my father forbade it, I suppose. He was rather conventional and quite strict with my sisters. And then she was married after that. She is the eldest of my sisters and has been married for eleven years now. It seems quite amazing to think of it. She has three daughters of her own."

Gillian paused to consider what he had revealed. "Your father is dead?" she asked.

"Yes. I was sixteen when we lost him."

"I'm sorry. That must have been quite a blow—to you and to all of your family."

"I was angry for a while," he admitted with candor that charmed her. "I wasn't ready to become head of the household, and I didn't think it was fair. But I learned quickly."

"How many sisters have you?"

She watched his rather grim expression light up with a smile. Lord, he was handsome!

"Five," he answered, "more than anyone ought to be burdened with!"

"You do not sound as if you really mind them."

"No. If anything, I suppose I am overfond of them all, and I spoil them. But three are still unmarried, and husband hunting for them is not a job I relish."

Gillian's surprise at this remark was clear in her voice. "You do not seem to have objections to education for women. Why not allow your sisters to choose husbands for themselves?"

Brinton turned to her with an expression of mock horror. "What, have I been assisting a runaway radical all this time? Would you turn the world on its ear, woman?" He laughed.

Gillian was surprised at the depth of her disappointment in him. "Forgive me for thinking you might have an open mind. I see I am mistaken." She bit her lip, but she could not leave the subject alone. "But why not—" she began, only to have him stop her words with a finger laid gently against her lips. He had gathered the reins into one hand again, and the horses had slowed almost to a standstill.

"Now you are trying to make me out an ogre," he said, that enchanting smile lingering and the laughter still in his eyes. "Did I say that I would not allow my sisters to have some part in the choosing? Am I not helping you to defy the wishes of your own guardian?" His finger lingered at her mouth, brushing her lips gently before he withdrew it. "But truly, women are not practical creatures. You are ruled by your hearts, not your heads. And marriage is a practical matter. My sister Darcy, who I think is not even your age, would have run off with a poet she met last year if I had not intervened. They would have had to live on words instead of bread and meat like other mortals."

"But if they loved each other . . ." Gillian tried again, but Brinton shook his head.

"It doesn't signify. Love is a luxury possible only for those who have nothing to lose."

"Oh!" exclaimed Gillian in frustration. "You men think you know so much! I am sorry for you and for your poor sisters! If you had only known my parents—" She was interrupted by a yelp of protest from the rear of the carriage.

"I say! Must we stop? If I wasn't already thoroughly wet, this would do it! Or hadn't you noticed it's raining?"

Chapter Seven

The cries of street-mongers and the rattle of traffic on paving stones woke Gillian from a sound sleep the following morning. After staring at the sunlight leaking between the curtains of an unfamiliar bedroom window for a puzzled moment, she remembered where she was. Bath! She jumped out of bed and hurried over to let in the sights and sounds of the city.

As she watched the bustle in the street below her, Gillian thought back to her brief meeting with her hostess upon arriving the previous evening. Brinton's friend, Mrs. Alford, had received the twins cordially, especially considering the unexpected nature of their visit, but then they had been hustled off to their beds. Gillian now found herself wondering just why they had been sent up so quickly, and just how much longer Brinton had stayed before departing to his own rooms at the Castle Inn.

She was still standing by the window when she caught the rich scent of chocolate and heard a noise behind her. She turned to discover a little maid hovering in the doorway with a porcelain cup on a tray.

"Good morning!" Gillian exclaimed, smiling at the girl and advancing to accept the steaming cup. "And it is, isn't it? I do love chocolate to start off the day. Tell me, are the others up? Is there breakfast downstairs, or have I missed too much of the day already?"

The maid smiled timidly. "Oh, no, miss. We don't start too early. There's plenty breakfast all laid out. As for the others, I don't rightly know." She looked down quickly, shy again. Gillian guessed the girl was waiting to help her dress.

"I will confess that I do not . . . *did* not have an abigail to do for me at home," she began, wondering how to put the girl at ease. Then she stopped, considering for the first time the sad state of her and Gilbey's luggage and the fact that the house servants had surely been instructed to deal with it. There was no sign of her satchel in the room this morning. How shocked the maids must have been when they discovered the sodden, wrinkled mess of clothing stuffed inside!

She thought suddenly of her precious books inside the portmanteau that had gone to Gilbey's room. And what had become of the clothes in which she had arrived? Would she get them back? How on earth had Brinton explained her appearance to their hostess? She set down her cup and looked doubtfully at the maid.

"Your things is all in the dressing room, miss. Shall you be wanting the blue dress, then?"

Did she want the blue dress? Brinton had introduced the twins to Mrs. Alford by their real names last night, so Gillian knew she would be expected to appear as a properly turned-out young lady today. "Yes, the blue will be fine," she said, nodding.

She had brought with her only the smallest quantity of her own clothes, depending on the walking dress of slate blue *gros de naples* and a pale green muslin morning gown to fill her needs when she first got to Scotland. For a moment her confidence wavered, but she pushed her fears aside. They were in Bath, hopefully among friends, and altogether things could have been much worse. She resolved to trust Brinton and ignore her troubles for this one day.

A short time later Gillian descended and, after inquiring the way, strode energetically into the breakfast room. Gilbey was seated at the table and, to her surprise, Lord Brinton was helping himself to sausages at the sideboard. Upon her entry Gilbey stopped cold, a savory bun suspended in midair en route to his mouth. Brinton turned and stared in open admiration.

"Good morning, gentlemen," she said, smiling brightly for their benefit.

"Good God, I have a sister again," Gilbey said, struggling to his feet.

Bruton turned to him with a teasing look in his eye. "May I beg an introduction? I am sure I have not made this lady's acquaintance. Certainly I would remember such a vision of loveliness!"

Gillian blushed, but threw off the compliment with easy humor. "Serving butter with the sausage this morning, are we? Thank you, but that is a bit rich for my taste."

"Madam, you wound me!"

"You may roast me all you wish this morning," she declared, choosing a place at the table across from her brother, where she could turn her back quite deliberately on the earl. "Such a good night's rest has made me immune to your flummery. The sun is shining, and it is going to be a delightful day!"

The footman who had been standing so stiffly by the door hurried over to the sideboard to serve her, but Brinton firmly took the plate from him and silently dismissed the young fellow. The earl served Gillian himself, loading her plate with shirred eggs, toast, and a section of beautifully grilled trout.

Gillian did not see the exchange that took place behind her, so she was startled when Brinton placed the food in front of her, his sleeve brushing against hers. He was so close to her, she could make out the faintly musky scent of lime she remembered from Taunton.

"Perhaps the unaccustomed sunshine has blinded you to a compliment sincerely meant," he said reprovingly.

Caught off guard, Gillian looked up. Sparks were already racing through her veins from his proximity, and when she saw the warm look in his eyes, they all burst into flame at once. Her eyes widened in alarm at the sensation.

Brinton smiled and moved away. He took up his own plate and, to Gillian's dismay, sat down across from her next to Gilbey, where she could not avoid his disconcerting gaze. She bent her head to her plate, pretending to look for bones in her fish. Could he possibly sense her reaction to him? Did she somehow betray herself, or did men have some way of knowing?

"Gillie, you do look very fine this morning," her brother said, filling the awkward pause.

"You are too kind," she replied, finding her voice.

Bravely, she raised her head to address Brinton. "And how is it we have the pleasure of your company this early in the day, my lord?" It came out sounding like a challenge.

The earl leaned back in his chair. "I could risk another set-down and say that I simply could not stay away from your shining presence, or I could take the coward's way out and admit that the offerings at the Castle cannot begin to compare with Mrs. Alford's table."

Gilbey chuckled, and Gillian could not hide a smile. "Where is our intrepid hostess this morning?" she asked.

"Alice and I have been friends since childhood, and early hours have never agreed with her," Brinton informed them. "I am sure we will see her later in the day."

Gillian gave herself a mental slap for questions that were none of her business and changed the subject. "Upon your recommendation, my lord, we have changed our route and, one might say, have gone to cover here in Bath. We have you to thank as well as Mrs. Alford for a very comfortable night. But what would you suggest we do now?"

"I have business to attend here, and I think you may safely spend the day. It is a shame the shops are not open, for I am sure there are necessities that you have had to leave behind. However, we could tour the city a bit if that would please you."

"Could we?" Gillian's enthusiasm for the idea blinded her to any question about what sort of business Brinton might need to conduct on a Sunday. She turned to her twin. "Gilbey, do you think we would be safe? Is there anyone who would know us?"

"I don't recall that we have any connections in Bath. And who would suspect a pair of runaways to be taking in the sights?"

"Can we see the Roman antiquities? My father read to us about them. Can you imagine digging in the dirt and finding a head of Minerva! It gives me chills of excitement just to think of it! Does one have to take the waters to see the baths? And I'd love to see Pulteney Bridge—they say it is like a little piece of Italy."

Rafferty found Gillian's childlike eagerness a refreshing change from the studied boredom practiced by the *ton*. He gave her the wide, brilliant smile that lit up his whole face.

"What, not asking for the shops or the Pump Room first? But, of course. History and architecture it is." He turned to Gilbey. "Will your knee bear walking today?"

Gilbey thought that walking might relieve some of his stiffness, so after their meal the trio set off. They agreed that if anyone inquired, the twins were to pose as Brinton's visiting cousins from Devonshire.

It seemed as if the sun had drawn everyone in Bath into the streets. As the twins and Brinton progressed through Laura Place and across Pulteney Bridge, the pedestrian traffic on the pavements grew thicker and thicker, far surpassing the congestion of vehicular traffic in the roadways.

"If 'everyone of consequence' is in London for the Season, how can there still be so many people here?" Gillian asked Brinton playfully.

"Clearly, Bath hosts an immense population of inconsequential persons, including ourselves," Brinton replied, and they both laughed.

Gillian found she was quite enjoying herself, walking along with her hand resting lightly in the crook of Lord Brinton's elbow. Propriety had demanded that she borrow a shawl and bonnet from Mrs. Alford, so she felt rather stylishly turned out. The crowds had made it impossible to walk three abreast, and Gilbey had dropped behind them, stopping here and there to examine details of the scenery that caught his artist's eye. They paused along the Grand Parade for a view of the bridge. The sound of the river rushing over the rapids blocked out the city noises as they looked over the parapet.

"*Now* I can see something to admire in it," Gillian said, gazing back at the celebrated structure. "When we walked over it, it seemed nothing more than a charming street of shops!"

"If you ever travel to Venice, you will have had a preview of what you will see there," Brinton commented. His eyes were on Gillian, not the view.

"I will be happy if I can get to Scotland," she said sharply, turning away. She did not wish to be reminded of the uncertain future, or even the limitations of the present.

The earl stayed a moment, leaning casually against the stone baluster. Gillian could sense that he was still watching her. Then she heard him move, and he was beside her again, taking her hand and gently tucking it back in the crook of his arm.

"I did not mean to upset you," he said apologetically. "In fact, I was wondering if you might not be happy, here in this place, at this moment, on this day."

In this company, thought Gillian, but Brinton had not said those words. *I almost could be*, she added to herself. She did not dare to tell Brinton that, however. It alarmed her to think how much she was enjoying being with him.

They turned toward Bath Abbey, towering above the other buildings in this oldest part of the city. Prudence suggested that they avoid the services underway inside, but they found much to admire in its rich exterior, including the famous sculptured angels clambering up celestial ladders on the west front.

"They do not appear to have the least interest in interceding for us mere mortals, do they?" Gillian asked.

Brinton caught her reference to *Tristram Shandy* right away. "Your education is showing again, Miss Kentwell. Have a care, or someone may take you for a bluestocking!"

"In Scotland they are not averse to educated females," she said with a defensive toss of her head.

She started off ahead of the two men, but Brinton caught her hand before she had taken a second step. "Don't you know that I meant that as a compliment?" he said softly.

"Gillie thinks they read Laurence Sterne in Scotland," Gilbey teased.

"I have heard that they teach a good deal more than embroidery in their female academies. One day they will have women in the universities," she declared staunchly.

Looking down into Gillian's earnest face, the earl knew he did not want to talk about Scotland. He felt his emotions swirling in a confusion of warmth and sympathy that he thought he saw answered in the blue-green depths of her eyes. She made a lovely picture in her blue dress with the borrowed shawl and bonnet. She was charming and intelligent, and he wondered if, after all, his uncle had known exactly what he was doing in choosing her. If it was all an act on her part, it was a damn fine one.

He steered the twins up Union Street. "I judge the Pump Room will be too crowded to suit us at this time of day," he said to both of his companions, "but I believe it is required for all ladies to take in the shops on Milsom Street. Even, or perhaps most advantageously, when the shops are closed." *And we will be less likely to run into anyone who will wish to converse or ask questions,* Brinton added to himself. He hoped Alice was having some luck with the inquiries he had asked her to make for him while he kept the twins occupied.

In front of a milliner's window they halted. "Gilbey, look! There's a little cork riding hat almost exactly like the one I bought in Kingsbridge!" Gillian exclaimed. "Perhaps I was a trifle overhasty in consigning that hat to Hector's use, although it did sail on the wind just beautifully."

"Who is Hector?" the earl asked in surprise.

"He is Gillie's spaniel," Gilbey explained. "He got too old for hunting, but she liked to indulge his fantasies by throwing her hats out into the wind on the cliffs for him to chase. It's no wonder she hasn't a bonnet of her own."

"It takes a soft heart to be concerned about the fantasies of aging dogs," Brinton replied quietly.

Gillian turned to go on. "I believe in Scotland a lady may go out uncovered without causing a major scandal, Gilbey."

"Gillie thinks that in Scotland she'll be free to do anything at all that she wants," Gilbey explained. "She plans to dance barefoot in the streets."

"I'd like to know where she has gotten these ideas about Scotland," Brinton muttered.

The little group toiled up the hill, stopping for the earl to catch his breath partway up Bartlett Street, and soon they found themselves outside the Upper Assembly Rooms.

"From here we will go across to The Circus and The Crescent, which I know you will admire," the earl said. "By the time we make our way back down through Queen Square, it will be far less crowded at the baths."

"The Assembly Rooms are elegant," he continued, "but the best way to see them is at night, when the chandeliers are lit and the dance floor is crowded with Bath's best efforts at high fashion."

Gillian was looking at a broadside posted in the window. "There is a special assembly tonight," she remarked wistfully. "Do you suppose there is any way we could attend?"

*   *   *

Sometime later, Brinton stood at the window of Mrs. Alford's upstairs study with his back to the room. The slanting rays of the late afternoon sun flowed across the Aubusson carpet and up the side of the lady's elegant French desk, interrupted only by the earl's long shadow.

"It is absolutely out of the question," he stated in his most authoritative tone. The steel in his voice matched the rigid set of his shoulders as he watched the twins exploring in the garden below.

"What nonsense, Rafferty," Alice Alford chided, not even slightly intimidated by his imposing manner. Dressed in a becoming gown of apricot muslin, she was relaxing on an Adam-style sofa upholstered in pale blue damask that matched the paneled walls. Her dark locks were swept up into a chignon, with small curls framing her finely sculpted face. "Why should they not go? You have already paraded them about the city all day."

Brinton still faced the window. "It served to keep them occupied," he pointed out. "We avoided the fashionable times to appear at the most popular places, and no one recognized us."

"Or at least no one indicated so."

"Walking through town is quite a different proposition from openly displaying Cranford and his sister at the Assembly Rooms, where everyone is bound to take notice."

Mrs. Alford narrowed her eyes. "It is not like you to spurn a challenge, Rafferty. Last night you told me yourself that no one would suspect a pair of runaways to be touring around Bath, and certainly the same holds true in this! No one will suspect they are anything but what we say—cousins of yours from Devon. And as they are only on a short visit, it will cause no comment when they disappear again!"

Brinton turned from the window. "They are coming in," he warned. His expression was grim.

"I see you are bent on playing the stuffy earl this time," Mrs. Alford said. "You are denying Miss Kentwell the chance to be part of a little elegance and excitement—a chance that I suspect comes rarely to her."

"I rather thought I was protecting her," Rafferty responded, half to himself. He began to pace up and down the length of the carpet. "You don't know her. She has no interest in such things."

"And you know her so well?" Mrs. Alford's tone was light, teasing. "Is that why you asked me to see what I could find out about her for you? Tell me, if she has no interest, why did she ask about attending, and why are you so stirred up?"

"That was my mistake—I made the place sound more exciting than it is. She is just curious."

Alice Alford laughed. She sat up, carefully arranging the folds of her skirt and straightening the ribbon bow just under her breasts. "You know far less about females than you think you do, my dear friend, despite having five sisters."

She rose and, taking Rafferty's arm, began to walk with him as he absently continued to pace. "I think you know as little about yourself," she added gently. "I have never seen you in such a muddled state!"

Brinton abhorred the fawning attentions that would be focused upon him by all the unattached females in attendance at the assembly. Despite his denials to the twins, there was also a real risk that someone who knew him might be there. But he was not about to confide the biggest reason he wished to avoid going there. He did not want to see Miss Kentwell on display to such advantage. She was far too attractive, and he was already too much under her spell. In truth he, the courageous Earl of Brinton, was afraid—afraid of a mere slip of a girl.

They had just reached the window end of the room again when the door opened. The twins came in, their cheeks pink from the cooling afternoon air.

Their hostess detached herself from Brinton and came smiling toward them with hands outstretched. "Here you are, my dears! Did you enjoy my garden? It is a bit early in the season."

She led the twins to a pair of gilded chairs that faced her desk. "I have just offered to chaperone you at the assembly tonight, but Lord Brinton is being a terrible stick-in-the-mud."

"It does not seem very sensible to advertise your presence here."

"Does it matter if we are seen tonight, when we've been seen all over town today?" Gillian asked.

"It was, sir, your suggestion that we come to Bath," Gilbey reminded him. "You seemed to think that we would be quite safe."

Rafferty could see that he was outnumbered, but he was not yet defeated. "Pray tell us, Miss Kentwell, what would you wear?" He felt confident that this major obstacle would end the discussion.

"Oh." Her face fell, her disappointment clear as she seemed to search about for some reply. "I never gave any thought to that," she added, and at that moment she appeared very young indeed to the earl.

Mrs. Alford came to her rescue. "Have you nothing with you by way of a ball gown? Never mind. My women are skilled with their needles. We can fix up something of mine."

"But the time!" Gillian protested, despite the light of hope dawning in her face. "And what could Gilbey wear?"

"Lord Brinton will loan him something," Mrs. Alford said smoothly.

"Your faith in my wardrobe is flattering, Alice. I am not certain I even have suitable attire for myself," Brinton said stubbornly. "I came on the road expecting only to attend a horse race. The beasts seldom require formal dress."

"Oh, we will find something, then," the indomitable lady said. "I have my sources. I assure you, the evening will be a smashing success." With a toss of her dark head, Mrs. Alford rose and swept out of the room, ushering Gillian ahead of her.

Brinton and Gilbey were left staring at each other.

"Did you truly wish to go to the assembly tonight?" asked the earl doubtfully. He moved away from the window now and took the chair opposite Cranford.

"You must take into account that my sister and I are country rustics," Gilbey said, looking down at his hands. "We have been in mourning this past year as well, so we have not been much in company—especially such a glittering affair as an assembly at Bath."

"I'm afraid you will be disappointed. Bath in these days cannot begin to compare with London."

Gilbey smiled. "Are you warning me that there will be no one there but ape leaders and their mamas?"

"Not so bad as that." Rafferty laughed. "But the good company is likely to be thin, and I have no doubt that both you and your sister will be noticed and sought after."

"Well, come morning we'll be on our way again, with no one the wiser."

There was an uncomfortable pause. Rafferty realized he had not given much thought to the day to come. He had come to no conclusions about the twins or what he would do. If they had just a little more time . . .

Gilbey cleared his throat. "I find myself in an intolerably awkward position, Brinton, regarding tomorrow. You have my word that I will gladly reimburse all the expenses you are incurring because of us. To the point, would it be possible for us to borrow enough funds from you to see us to Scotland? While my sister's determination is no doubt so strong it would eventually get her there, I would much prefer to pay our way." Gilbey's pale skin had turned crimson to the ear tips. He jumped up and moved away from his chair, long strides taking him to the spot by the window so recently vacated by Brinton.

The earl was grateful he did not have to face the lad. Cranford had cut right to the heart of the matter, and Rafferty did not know how to answer. Did he believe the twins' story? It was time to place his bet, but he still did not know the odds. He did not care about the money—he could afford to cover his losses. But was he being played for a fool? If their story was a Banbury tale concocted to victimize him, he was loathe to go along with it.

"Well, Cranford," he said slowly, "let me see what I can do." He was not ready to make a commitment. How could he put the lad off? "I could speak to the bank in the morning after they open, but I think you will want an early start. I will be heading up to the fair in Worcester to see about buying some horses—perhaps you would care to go in that direction? There is a solicitor there through whom I might make some arrangement."

The answer was intentionally vague, and the earl watched Gilbey carefully to judge his reaction. The lad betrayed no sign of annoyance, however, but only turned toward Brinton with a look of gratitude and relief.

"I will appreciate whatever you can do, sir, as indeed I appreciate what you have already done. I must confess I have never felt so helpless in my entire life."

Chapter Eight

Gillian stood in her stocking feet between a matched pair of mirrors that hung in her hostess's Chinese dressing room. The gown she wore had been dramatically altered in the last hour.

"Now let us see—turn around a half turn and try a curtsy," Mrs. Alford said, studying her women's handiwork. The dress was exquisite: a dark green satin slip covered by an overdress of pale green English net, embroidered in silver and white.

"It is going to serve splendidly! It is just the right color for you, my dear; it suits you much better than it ever did me! We need just one more thing." Mrs. Alford turned to rummage in the drawers of one of the large lacquered wardrobes.

Gillian bit her lip and steeled herself to endure whatever further manipulations Mrs. Alford would require. The woman was obviously an expert, and what did Gillian know of female arts? She had already suffered the indignity of being encased in stays, although the corset was not terribly tight.

"Your proportions are excellent, Miss Kentwell, but I think we could do with bust improvers—you know, to improve the line of the dress? The neckline is rather deep and open."

Gillian shivered and hugged herself, not quite believing the elegant image she saw in the two mirrors. She dared not move, for she was surrounded by little piles of flouncing that had been sacrificed to shorten the dress. What would Brinton think when he saw her in Mrs. Alford's ball gown? Would the evening ahead be worth the agonizing humiliation she was subjecting herself to now?

Mrs. Alford was back in a moment. She reached down inside the low neck of the gown and Gillian's chemise to lift her breasts and put little rounded pads beneath them. Gillian blushed crimson at being handled so.

"There! You will be beyond perfect, my dear!" Mrs. Alford was beaming.

Gillian was mortified by the prominence her breasts had achieved with the help of the "bosom friends". It seemed every possible inch of creamy skin would be not only exposed, but quite literally held up for inspection. "Do you not think it is a bit, well, too much?" she protested, feeling very unsure of herself.

"Nonsense, my girl. You look magnificent, simply magnificent. Brinton may have flocks of admirers hovering around him tonight, but so shall you—I guarantee it!"

It hadn't occurred to Gillian that Brinton would, of course, be enthusiastically sought after by any female on two legs who wasn't blind. The image of him surrounded by eager, beautiful ladies made her suddenly even more unsure than she had already felt. What had made her think, even for a moment, that he would pay any attention to her?

"Of course, he is so handsome," she said distractedly.

Mrs. Alford smiled. "You must not mind about him—it is to be expected. He stands to inherit a great fortune to add to his own. It is generally accepted that when that happens, he will be elevated to a marquis, the first in his family. I'm afraid he finds it all a great annoyance—a 'faradiddle', he calls it."

She smoothed back a tendril of Gillian's hair, inspecting her charge with a critical eye. "You will cast all the other ladies into the shade, trust me. I cannot wait to see Rafferty's face when he sees you!"

Gillian was feeling the first flutterings of panic, however. A marquis! He had given them no clue he had such expectations. Was Mrs. Alford warning her away from him? And even worse, she and Gilbey were pretending to be his cousins! *I don't know how to act*, she berated herself. *Why did I think I wanted to do this? I am going to make a fool of myself again.*

Two hours after dinner the twins emerged from their respective rooms and joined Mrs. Alford in the entry hall.

Gillian found the transformation of her brother and herself nothing short of miraculous.

Gilbey looked resplendent in evening dress that appeared to fit him perfectly. A white embroidered satin waistcoat with a snowy white shirt and cravat contrasted against the deep sapphire blue of his coat. Tight black pantaloons flattered the shape of his legs. He even had evening slippers that appeared to be the right size. He seemed to have been struck speechless by her own appearance, however, and Gillian smiled.

She felt as though she was again in disguise. Her chestnut hair had been coaxed into becoming ringlets near her face, and bands of pearls and silver leaves twined through her tresses. Pearls at her throat and ears, courtesy of Mrs. Alford, set off the tone of her skin and matched the small pearls on the bands of green ribbon that trimmed her dress. The silver threads in the embroidery caught the light and sparkled almost as much as Gillian's eyes.

She did not mind that she wore the same white kid slippers she had walked in all day around Bath. There was no chance of borrowing shoes small enough to fit her, and she was determined to dance all night. She had resolved to enjoy herself despite the distraction of Brinton's presence, and despite any *faux pas* she might commit.

Mrs. Alford looked stunning in a gown of brilliant poppy red *crepe lisse*, ornamented with loops of gold braid and beading. Her dark hair was confined in a stylish toque with a cluster of matching plumes. She smiled warmly at the twins and sailed toward them.

"I shall be proud to present you tonight," she declared, adding with a little giggle, "even if we have created our own fairy tale!" She turned to Gillian and, taking the girl's gloved hand, pressed a small ivory fan into her palm. "You will be needing this, my dear. It can grow very warm in the rooms, even on such a cool spring night."

Gillian looked down at the fan, its carved leaves laced with satin ribbons. What should she say? Her mother had begun to teach her the rudiments of fan etiquette, but she had been only eight years old. She remembered nothing of what she had learned. What if she should send some sort of signal she never intended?

"You are so kind," she began. "You think of everything! I must confess, however, that my schooling in some of the finer arts has been sorely lacking."

"Ah! Even so. Do not worry, my dear; there are just a few points to remember, and all will be well." She quickly reviewed them and gave Gillian a brilliant smile. "Come now, our carriage is waiting. Shall we not conquer Bath tonight?"

The drive to the Upper Assembly Rooms was brief. The little party waited in a line of carriages for their turn to be dropped at the door. Then they were in, and Gillian had to admit that Brinton was right.

The rooms were elegant and somehow magical, with the chandeliers ablaze and all the people in their finery. Most of the men wore black, following Brummel's custom, but there were discreetly colored coats and some bright military uniforms scattered among them. The ladies' gowns spanned all the colors of the rainbow, although white was still predominant among the young.

Introductions began while they were still in the cloakroom. Mrs. Alford was obviously enjoying showing off her charges, and several young gentlemen asked to sign Gillian's dance card.

There was no sign of Brinton, however, until they reached the ballroom. A quadrille was in progress, and he was easy to see on the dance floor, partnering an equally tall and attractive woman in a rose-colored gown. He looked more handsome than ever, Gillian thought, in his black coat and pantaloons. They fit his muscular body like a second skin, and his shoulders had never looked broader. He moved with notable grace.

Gillian was so taken up with watching him, she hardly noticed when Mrs. Alford began to introduce her to Mr. Huntley, a short man with a thick neck and a stubby nose. He smiled politely as he reached for her dance card.

"They are lining up for the next dance; can it be you are not already promised, Miss Hopeworth?"

Hopeworth was the name she and Gilbey had agreed to use for the night. She was not promised, so she had no choice but to accompany the fellow onto the floor.

She soon wished she had not. She had the distinct impression that her partner was trying to peer down her bodice every time the dance brought them together. His rather protuberant eyes never seemed to stray from her bosom. His polite smile had become something a good deal more predatory, and he was perspiring heavily. As they progressed down the line, Gillian prayed for the music to end.

Inevitably, they arrived next to Lord Brinton and his partner, a young blonde dressed in daffodil yellow.

"Well met, cousin," Brinton said in a clipped, formal voice as the dance brought him and Gillian together.

His glance swept over her, taking in everything at once, Gillian thought, including her embarrassing décolletage and her undesirable partner. She could not detect a flicker of reaction.

"You must forgive me for not greeting you sooner," he added stiffly. "I had not realized your party had arrived."

Introductions were made, and then the couples moved on. That was all. Gillian felt oddly deflated, although she didn't know what she had expected. How could anyone impress the top-lofty earl? That she looked elegant in Mrs. Alford's dress was hardly significant.

Gillian had misjudged the earl, however. She and Mr. Huntley were not halfway back to the chaperones' seats at the end of the dance when Brinton reappeared at her side. She wondered how he had managed to dispose of his own partner so speedily.

"Allow me to escort my cousin, if you please, Mr. Huntley," he said. Although phrased correctly, it was clearly not a request. "I will be remiss if I do not greet the rest of her party."

Mr. Huntley looked annoyed. "I hope I may have the honor of another dance with you later," he beseeched her. With a wary glance at Brinton, he quickly pressed a hot, wet kiss on her gloved hand and fled.

"Oh, dear," sighed Gillian, giving her hand a little shake. Then she gave her savior a brilliant smile. "So you *did* see that I needed rescuing!" She laughed and playfully hit his arm with her fan. "You are always surprising me!"

"As you do me," Brinton murmured almost inaudibly.

A number of appreciative male eyes followed the pair's progress toward the side of the room. Gillian had no idea of the picture she presented, her face alight with pleasure and turned engagingly up to the earl's. When she and Brinton reached the chaperones' benches they found Mrs. Alford standing off to one side, engaged in conversation with some other ladies. Brinton coughed so discreetly, Gillian was not sure if it was intentional or not.

Mrs. Alford turned to them immediately. "Goodness, Lord Brinton, you naughty thing! Here you are finally! We have been here above half an hour, and you are just now coming to greet me!" She was addressing him much more formally than she had done at her home, Gillian noticed.

Brinton executed a graceful leg. As he straightened up, he gave Mrs. Alford a mischievous grin. "I don't know how I could have missed noting your arrival. I must have been terribly occupied. Can you possible forgive me?"

"Perhaps you can atone in some way," Mrs. Alford answered with a slow smile. Gillian was relieved that her hostess did not attempt to introduce her or Brinton to the other women.

The earl exchanged a few more pleasantries, then prepared to take his leave of them. "You will allow me to take you in to tea at the break," he informed Gillian. "It is safer if you do not have to converse at any length with strangers who might ask personal questions." Then drawing Mrs. Alford aside, he whispered, "Her dress is outrageous, Alice. What were you thinking? You knew we did not want to attract attention!"

If Gillian thought his severe tone might have subdued Mrs. Alford, she was mistaken. "She does look a picture in it, does she not?" the good lady purred. "She outshines everyone here. She cannot help being beautiful, Rafferty. It is good of you to notice!"

Brinton turned on his heel abruptly and stalked away, followed by Alice Alford's laughter. Gillian tried to muster her own spirits, but she apparently failed to mask her dismay. She felt the telltale blush burning her cheeks again.

"Never mind him," Mrs. Alford said reassuringly. She took Gillian by the arm and led her toward the benches, where there were now some vacant spots. "He can be an oaf and a dolt sometimes, like all men! You are a woman, an exceedingly lovely one, and do not forget that. You have every right to show off."

Gillian's next partner spent most of his time nodding his head to the rhythm of the music, apparently counting the beats to himself. Each time she attempted to make conversation, she had the impression she was interrupting and causing him to forget the next figure. When the dance ended, she suspected they were both relieved.

Mrs. Alford was again busily chatting, so Gillian simply stationed herself nearby and waited.

"They have played quite a few country dances, have they not?" she commented to a gentleman standing near her. "When, pray tell, do they break off for tea?"

The gentleman in question turned his attention to her with a smile. "They should be stopping soon. You'll see it is almost the end of the second set if you check your card."

Gillian nodded, embarrassed. *Of course.* Her dance card listed the dances in each set and indicated the breaks as well.

"You must be thirsty," the gentleman said, pursuing the conversation. "Have you already an escort for tea, Miss . . . ?"

Gillian realized then that she actually had four gentlemen hovering around her, and she had been introduced to none of them. Fortunately, at that moment Mrs. Alford came to her rescue.

"Excuse me, gentlemen." She was smiling politely, but her eyes were cold. "Do I know any of you?" She put an arm protectively around Gillian's shoulders.

At her arrival the small group began to melt away. Mrs. Alford turned a disapproving eye on her charge. "Miss K— that is, Miss Hopeworth, *must* you? It simply is not permitted to converse with those who have not been introduced." In a softening tone she continued, "I suppose it seems very rigid, but one has no other way of judging a stranger's character. You know, anyone at all can dress up as a peacock. It does not mean the person is not a poor jackdaw underneath!"

Gillian smiled sheepishly. "I am sorry, Mrs. Alford. I was entirely at fault; I was not thinking."

"Never mind, dear. Just do not make the same mistake again. Some men are only too willing to take advantage."

There were three dances left before the tea break and Gillian's partner for the next one appeared promptly. He was a confident, handsome young man, quite the opposite of Gillian's previous partners.

"You could not have been at the May Day fancy dress ball on Thursday," he said, staring intently down into her eyes. "You surely would have been chosen the May Queen. You are so tiny, I suspect you of being a fairy princess."

Gillian was fascinated by his method. His conversation was a steady stream of flattery. Meanwhile, he was dancing especially close to her, touching or brushing against her body whenever a figure of the dance gave an opportunity. His behavior was so outrageous that Gillian had to laugh.

"You are not going to dance with *him* again," Mrs. Alford observed after the young man had returned Gillian to her. Her indignant tone softened as she caught Gillian's eye. "I thought you might have to wipe the drool off his chin," she whispered mischievously, and both women lapsed into conspiratorial giggles.

"May I ask what is so comical?" Gilbey came over to them after returning his own partner.

"Nothing, nothing," Gillian assured him, "at least not to concern you. But I would dearly love to dance this next one with my own brother!"

Gillian relaxed and moved through the steps by rote, taking the chance to observe those around her. Mrs. Alford had been invited to dance, and flashes of her brilliant poppy color showed occasionally between the other couples. When Gillian did not see Brinton among the dancers, she began to scan the knots of people around the edges of the room. Had he changed his mind about taking tea with her? Had he left? Would he do so without saying good night?

Finally, she saw him, buried at the center of a group of simpering young women. *Of course.* She missed a move in the dance, and Gilbey glanced at her in surprise.

When the dance was done, Gilbey led her back to the chaperones' seats. "Mrs. Alford isn't here," he observed, sounding a bit at a loss.

"She was dancing." Gillian wondered how he could have

missed seeing her. Following the line of his gaze, she saw his eyes were on a striking young woman who had been part of their last set. She smiled. "She will be back at any moment, Gilbey. I will just wait here for her, if you wish to secure a partner for the last dance."

"You're a brick, Gillie," he said, flashing her a grin.

Taking a seat, Gillian scanned the room to see what had become of her chaperone. Absently, she tapped her closed fan against her lips. Where was Mrs. Alford? What should she do if someone approached her to dance? She checked her card to make sure she was not already promised.

Belatedly, she remembered Mrs. Alford's advice about the fan. "You must not touch it to your face." Guiltily, she jerked it down into her lap. Had she been looking in anyone's direction? Had anyone been looking at her? She had no idea.

In vain she searched the crowd for Mrs. Alford. Neither could she see Gilbey anywhere. The only person she recognized was Brinton, and he was making his way toward her. He did not look pleased.

"Cousin, would you walk with me?" he growled through clenched teeth as he reached her. His dark eyebrows were drawn down to an impossible angle. He maneuvered her away from the main crush of people, backing her into a space beside a statue. "Where is your chaperone?" he demanded in an angry whisper. "And what in the devil's name do you think you are doing?"

Without letting her answer, he continued. "First you are having conversations with all sorts of people you have not been presented to, and the next thing I know you are sitting by yourself, quite vulnerably, signaling every male in the room that you are available for kissing!"

Brinton had to have been watching her, Gillian realized in pleased surprise. She knew he expected her to be properly cowed by his great anger, but somehow, she could not quite control the corners of her mouth, which insisted on turning up. A little bubble of laughter welled up inside her, popping out as a giggle before she could stop it.

"Don't you think that is ridiculous?" she asked, her eyes wide. "Of course I meant no such thing! I was just thinking."

There was a dangerous glitter in Brinton's eyes. "Then, apparently, you should not think!"

"Oh, then I should no doubt be agreeably vacuous and silly," she assured him. "Either that, or else I would get in twice as much trouble as I do now!"

"Lord save us," Brinton replied, rolling his eyes.

Gillian laughed merrily, watching the earl struggle to keep his features from softening into a smile. The musicians were starting up, and for a moment Gillian's heart beat a little faster. Would Brinton ask her to dance?

"This is the last before tea," he said soberly. "Were you promised for this one?"

"No, my lord."

"Good. Then we can just wait it out and make our way toward the tearoom."

Gillian sighed. She had been spinning a daydream about what it would be like to dance with him, but now she told herself that she should have known better. With resignation she accepted his proffered elbow.

Brinton would not give in to the temptation to dance with Miss Kentwell. Just having her hand resting in the crook of his elbow was causing a tremor to pass between them. He could barely believe the exquisite little minx beside him was the same person as the ragamuffin lad whom he had assisted in Taunton. Even harder to believe were the raging emotions surging inside of him—jealousy of her various partners and a protective instinct that bordered on the ridiculous. He had not been able to keep his attention off her from the moment she had arrived, although he hoped his interest was well hidden. He was reacting like a father and a lover, when he was neither.

Slowly he and Gillian worked their way toward the octagon that connected the various rooms. Many other couples had the same notion, and the press of people was becoming almost a solid wall. Jostling bodies and sharp elbows were all around, and Brinton tried to steer a course that would protect Miss Kentwell from the brunt of the chaos. He could feel his breathing beginning to grow labored, and then came the familiar stabbing pain in the right side of his chest. He stopped and waited.

"Lord Brinton, you are looking terribly pale," Gillian said, her concern evident in her voice.

To answer, he would have had to speak, something that
he could not manage at that moment. He hoped the spasm
would pass, and they could continue toward the tearoom.
Instead, he clutched his chest and bent as the coughing
seized him. He felt someone pushing him, and opening his
eyes, he saw it was Miss Kentwell.

"We must find a clear space where you can sit down,"
she was saying. Alarmed by his coughs, people were making way for them as she pushed him toward a small anteroom. Blessedly, it was empty when they reached it.
Brinton collapsed gratefully onto a velvet sofa and Gillian
sat down beside him. She had kept hold of his hand.

"How can I help you?" she asked softly.

He shook his head, drawing ragged breaths. The warm
sympathy in her blue-green eyes would have made him
weak if he had not already felt that way. He knew he
should remove his hand from hers; he knew they should not
be alone together. But he did nothing. When he had regained his breath, he answered her.

"There is nothing you, or anyone, can do. It is just a re-
minder I live with." *You could help me by not looking at me
that way. You could help me by not being here, so close and
warm and desirable.* As he returned her gaze, he felt as
though everything around them fell away, leaving just the
two of them floating in an empty space together. As his body
recovered from the spasm, his discomfort was replaced by
other budding sensations he did not want to acknowledge.

"You said when this happened before that you are not ill.
What is it, then? What causes it?"

He wished she would not talk. Talking called his attention to her lips, which looked full and soft and inviting. The
urge to kiss them was growing stronger in him every moment. He knew he must not give in. With a supreme effort
he replied, his voice low and rough.

"It is a souvenir of Waterloo. It helps me remember how
fragile and fleeting our lives can be. The details are not
pleasant or fit for a young lady to hear."

"I know that war is ugly," she insisted. "I will not be
shocked. It does not distress me to talk about the human
body."

I don't want to talk about the human body, Rafferty

thought. *I want to feel one, yours, pressed close against mine.* The girl's scent was making him light-headed. For a moment he feared he would either throw himself upon her, or pass out. Surely it was a reaction to her, and not an after-effect of the coughing spell. He tipped his head back, fighting for control. When he straightened and looked at her again, her head was down, her eyes on his hand she still held in her lap. She began to stroke his gloved fingers absently, apparently lost in thought.

"You are very brave, to bear with it so well," she said. "Many people would feel sorry for themselves, instead of looking upon it as you do."

She abruptly lifted her eyes to his again, and he groaned inwardly. Had she any idea of what she was doing to him? Was she deliberately trying to seduce him? If she was, did that even matter to him anymore?

"That dress brings out the green in your eyes," he said softly, as if in a trance. It was not what he had meant to say.

"That is not all it brings out." Gillian giggled. Then she blushed crimson and put one hand to her mouth. "Oh, dear, I should not have said that! I think I keep company with my brother altogether too much."

Rafferty chuckled, and as he did, something inside him snapped. Hadn't he said life was fleeting and fragile? Shouldn't pleasure be seized when the opportunity came? Even as he struggled with his conscience, he felt his body subtly repositioning itself, and his head beginning to lower toward Miss Kentwell. Whether she knew it or not, he was going to kiss her, deeply and thoroughly. "You are an Original, Miss Kentwell—beautiful, intelligent, humorous—"

The door opened. Brinton froze instantly. Miss Kentwell jumped up from the sofa, and then he heard her voice, coming as if from a great distance.

"Gilbey! I am so glad it is you."

Cranford closed the door behind him and advanced into the room. "Brinton! Someone said you were ill."

Chapter Nine

Dawn was just beginning to brush the sky pink as Gilbey sat alone in Mrs. Alford's breakfast room. He washed down the sharp taste of pickled herring with a sip of tea and sighed, frowning into his cup. This morning he and Gillian were leaving Bath—with Brinton.

He really should have found a moment to tell Gillian of the plan he and the earl had made to go to Worcester, he knew. He had pushed off the task, certain that his sister would be angry because he had not consulted her. Now he was having his own doubts about the decision. He did not want to go. He hated not having any choice.

The young viscount felt trapped between his duty to obey his uncle and his desire to protect his sister. He did not blame Gillian for their predicament. It was Uncle William who had cornered them to the point where they felt forced to run away. But Gilbey felt uncomfortable flouting the law.

Now he was not at all certain he had done the right thing in approaching the earl for further assistance. Grateful for Brinton's help in Taunton, he had taken the man's intentions for granted; he had even defended those intentions to his sister. Had he been too naive? Last night when he had found Gillian and Brinton alone together, he would have sworn the earl was making advances toward her.

Did Brinton have the wrong idea about Gillian? She was running about the countryside without any female companion or chaperone and wearing men's clothing. Then last night, that dress! What might anyone think?

Gillie was so heedless of consequences—that was always the trouble. She never gave a thought to her reputation. Such things had not mattered so much when they were younger, or at home, but now . . . ?

Gilbey pushed another bite of herring around on his plate. He had grave misgivings about the day that lay ahead, but it was too late to change the plan. He would watch the earl closely.

Light, rapid footsteps sounded in the hall, and a moment later, Gillian appeared. "Gilbey! Everything is nearly ready, except that Mother's songbooks are not with our things. What could they have done with them? I have looked all through both of our rooms." In one brisk, efficient motion, Gillian scooped a plate from the table and moved to the sideboard, where she piled on liberal amounts of egg, herring, bacon, buns, and warm toast.

Gone was the elegant princess of the previous night. In her place stood the old Gillian, clad in Gilbey's cast-off clothing except for her own riding boots. She looked like a cross between an errant schoolboy and a stable lad who had mistakenly found himself in the house.

Gilbey opened and closed his mouth twice before he could get a response to come out. He did not know what behavior to address first. "Gillie, you are hopeless," he finally said, rolling his eyes heavenward.

"Whatever is the matter?" his twin asked innocently. She quickly sat down at the table.

"You shouldn't have searched through my room. What if someone had seen you?"

"No one did. You know I can't leave without the books. You'll have to help me look when we have finished eating." She began a vigorous attack on the pile of food in front of her.

Gilbey stared in silent disapproval until his sister looked up again.

"Well?" she challenged. "It is faster to take everything at once than to get up again for second helpings. We don't know when or where we will have another meal. I think we should make certain we are well-sustained, at least to start out!" With her mouth full of toast she added, "And the sooner we set off, the happier I'll be!"

Gilbey speared his last bite of food. Narrowing his eyes, he pondered his sister. Was she still so eager to leave Brin-

ton this morning? He thought she had enjoyed the earl's attentions last night, but he might be mistaken. After years of
close understanding, suddenly, lately, he was finding his
twin difficult to read.

When she met his gaze, he looked down hastily, inspecting the pattern on his empty plate. "I don't think ladies are
supposed to eat such quantities," he grumbled. "And I wish
you could leave off wearing those clothes of mine."

He earned a sharp look from his sister. "My, are we not a
bit stuffy this morning? As it happens, I hardly have a
choice about the clothes, have I, since we are traveling so
light. What does it matter, Gilbey, when we are by ourselves?"

He shifted uncomfortably. He had to tell her. "We will
be going with Brinton as far as Worcester."

"What!" Gillian threw down her fork with a resounding
clatter. "May I ask just when this was all arranged? No one
bothered to consult me! I have no intentions of going with
Lord Brinton, to Worcester or anywhere else!"

"Now, Gillie, is that right? Somehow that does not match
the impression I got last night!"

"What impression?"

Gilbey evaded her question. "I know I should have asked
you, but you were with Mrs. Alford when the subject came
up. We decided on this plan yesterday afternoon."

"What do you mean by 'the impression you got last
night'?" she insisted.

Gilbey sighed. "Last night coming home you had such
stars in your eyes, I thought you would follow Brinton to
the ends of the earth if he'd asked you."

Gillian heard him and answered without missing a beat.
"That is ridiculous!" She was not yet ready to admit other-
wise to her brother. "I am as set against going with him
now as I have been since the beginning."

Last night she might have been blinded by stars in her
eyes, but this morning she thought she was seeing quite
clearly. Brinton was far more dangerous than anything she
could have anticipated, for he seemed to rob her of all natural caution.

Even though his touch had triggered reactions unlike
anything she had ever experienced before, her walk around

Bath with him had not prepared her for the overwhelming assault on her mind and senses caused by his close presence at the assembly. She had completely lost all sense of herself with him last night. Gillian had disappeared—Scotland had disappeared. Escaping Uncle William and finding true love—all had been forgotten. Brinton had filled her being so completely that, even as she danced with other partners, she had thought only of him, imagining him in their places—his hands touching her, his eyes holding hers. When they had been alone in the anteroom, Gillian was quite sure that Brinton had been going to kiss her. If Gilbey had not interrupted, she would have allowed it to happen, and worse, she would have kissed Brinton back. Later, when finally they had danced together, the pure pleasure of it had made her giddy.

Obviously, the man knew what to do with women. The fierce, hot look in his hazel eyes and the way her body had responded to him both excited and terrified her. She could not control the sensations he set off in her body, and they frightened her almost as much as his power to cause them. It was not fair that he could make her melt with one glance from those fascinating eyes! No wonder the women at the assembly had flocked around him like moths to a flame! She felt shamed by her lack of resistance to him.

Certainly the irresistible force she was feeling had nothing at all to do with love. Love was what her parents had known—a gentle, romantic gift of one self to another. Love bound hearts together; her mother had left Scotland forever rather than be separated from the man she loved. Gillian did not feel that way about Brinton! She didn't even like Brinton, did she?

He had not tried again to kiss her, although some part of her had hoped all evening that he might. In truth, the earl had been silent and brooding for the entire carriage drive back to Mrs. Alford's. Had he somehow been disappointed? She had shaken her head as she pondered it later, lying in her bed. No, he had not even wanted to go to the assembly in the first place. She had been a fool to think anything at all about the time they had spent together.

She had awakened this morning, determined to act immune to Brinton's charm and appeal. She had thought it would not be difficult if she could avoid any more contact with him. All she and Gilbey had needed to do was get on their way early, without crossing Brinton's path again. Now, she found her plan thwarted before she could even put it into effect. *Confound the man!* Brinton had defeated her without even being present. She glared at her brother, the only available substitute.

"Really, Gillie, it is a sensible plan," Gilbey was saying. "Worcester is directly on our way north from here. Lord Brinton is going there anyway, so it saves us some expense."

"I do not think we should be troubling him any further."

"I had to trouble him, Gillie—I saw no choice. The meager sum we tried to leave with him to pay for our lodging in Taunton will not cover meals, fares, tips, tolls, and lodging all the way to Scotland."

"You didn't ask him to loan us more money?"

"If we were to send home for funds, to the servants or even to Mr. Worsley in Kingsbridge, then we should have to wait somewhere long enough to receive it. There would be a great risk that Uncle William would find out where we were, or that those ruffians he's sent after us would catch up to us. Brinton suggested that if we went with him to Worcester, he might be able to make some arrangement."

"Gilbey, we have already accepted a great deal of help from Lord Brinton," Gillian said carefully, trying to keep the edge of desperation out of her voice. "It is dangerous to be so indebted to him. We must break from him here; we really cannot go with him to Worcester."

"What else can we do?"

"We could ask Mrs. Alford to help us instead. She might loan us the fare for a northbound coach right from Bath."

"And you would still need tips, tolls, meals, and lodging all the way to Scotland," came a deep voice from the doorway.

Gillian spilled the tea she had just lifted to her lips. She glared first at the food on her plate, awash in brown liquid, and then at Brinton, who was leaning quite casually against the door frame.

"Don't you ever behave like a normal person?" she cried

in exasperation. "Some people knock and allow themselves to be announced."

Brinton grinned and advanced into the room. "Is that how they do it? The footman who answered the door was still half asleep. He looked immensely pleased when I said I would show myself in."

He leaned across the table and removed her ruined plate. "Allow me to get you another. It's the least I can do after startling you so." He turned toward the sideboard and added offhandedly, "You would have difficulty asking Alice anything this morning, I believe. She won't be awake for hours."

Gillian made a face at his back as he got her more food. Of all the rude and obnoxious things to do! She wondered how much of the conversation between her and Gilbey he had heard.

Even as she seethed with frustration, she found she was admiring the way his perfectly tailored clothes displayed the form of his body. *Treacherous thoughts!* As he turned around, she quickly averted her eyes, focusing on the flowers in the urn on the pier table. She looked at her plate when he set it in front of her, coloring a little when she saw the modest portions he had given her. Gilbey no doubt approved.

"You may have gathered that I have just now been telling Gillian about our agreement," her brother was saying.

"I hope it was not purely on our account that you are yourself arisen so early?" Gillian asked with cloying sweetness.

"I can see that she is quite taken with the idea," Brinton said to Gilbey. "And no, Miss Kentwell, fear not. I have business in Worcester that demands an early start this morning. My curricle with a fresh pair and an extra mount are waiting outside. May I ask if you will be ready soon?"

"Yes," answered Gilbey.

"No," muttered Gillian, reaching for a bun.

Gilbey rolled his eyes in answer to Brinton's raised eyebrows. "My sister is nearly ready, my lord. It is just that some important personal items have been misplaced in the house, and we will need a few minutes to look for them."

"Do you mind if I ask what is missing?"

"It is some small, leather-bound books," Gillian volunteered rather sullenly. "They are Scottish songbooks that belonged to my mother."

"Ah, the infamous books," replied Brinton. "They were not returned with your other belongings?"

"No. And I have searched our rooms quite thoroughly."

"It is an oversight, I am sure." He paused. "What of the library or the music room? Have you tried there?"

"There is a music room?"

"When you are finished, I would be happy to show you."

Gillian sighed with regret. If only they were not leaving! A music room could keep her content for days at a time. But was it wise to go anywhere with Brinton? His very presence was already affecting her as she had feared. What if he touched her, or spoke of last night? Still, she needed to find the books. She nodded.

Gillian needn't have worried about Brinton, for his conduct was quite unexceptional. He led her to the music room without so much as taking her hand. It was a small but pleasant room, with a window facing the garden as in Mrs. Alford's study. A quite new pianoforte occupied the center of the room, where it attracted Gillian's attention at once. As she tried its keys, Brinton looked about the room and noticed several small leather volumes stacked on the fireplace mantel.

"What about these?" Brinton asked, reaching the mantel in quick, long strides. "*Ancient and Modern Scots Songs? The Ever Green*, by Allan Ramsay? These look quite old."

Gillian left off playing to come to his side. He examined the books one by one and handed them to her. His fingers did not brush hers even accidentally, yet she noticed that her pulse quickened.

"Alice must have had the servants put them in here, thinking you might sing for us. Then we went to the assembly instead."

Gillian did not say a word, but stroked the smooth covers as if they were living things. When she had received the entire collection into her arms, she looked up at Brinton. "Thank you," she said softly.

He returned her gaze for a long moment, his handsome

features composed as nearly as possible into an expression of apology. "Last night was something of a surprise," he began.

Oh, Lord! So he *was* going to talk about it.

"I think it may have been so for both of us. If anything I did offended you, I must beg your forgiveness this morning."

What could she say? That she wished he had done more? Admit that she had been overwhelmed with passion herself? She took the coward's way out. "Why, Lord Brinton," she said with an attempt at coquettishness, "I don't know what you could mean. Of course there is nothing to apologize for. The assembly was lovely, and you were very kind to escort us there."

His dark brows drew down for a fraction of a moment, and his eyes narrowed. Then his face smoothed. "Well, then. I suppose that is to the good as we shall be spending much of the day together. I understand that you are not pleased with our plan to go to Worcester, but I must echo your brother's sentiment that it is a reasonable course."

Gillian thought of their journey to Bath and the closeness of riding in the curricle with the earl. She dreaded repeating the agony of such proximity for an entire half day to Worcester. "Very well. I shall be pleased to ride the extra mount."

"What?" Brinton was obviously taken aback. "I think not, young lady! It is most certainly out of the question."

Gillian's heart sank. Was he going to insist that they sit together? "I am perfectly capable of riding astride. I did it all the time at home. And you must admit I am dressed for it."

Brinton's gaze hardened, and his eyes raked over her. "Yes, you are certainly dressed for it, and I can well imagine you rode that way at home. Judging by what you have told me, you lived like a hellion, with no restrictions and no training or regard for proper behavior. I don't know where you come by that virginal innocence that shines in your eyes. But by God, you will observe at least a modicum of propriety when you are with me. I will not allow you to make an exhibition of yourself. You will ride in the curricle."

Gillian felt as though he had slapped her. Her mouth dropped open for a moment in shock and confusion. Then she closed it firmly as her anger took over. "I will not ride there if I have to sit next to you!"

"You needn't worry. *I* shall ride the extra mount. I trust your brother can handle the curricle." He stepped around her and moved decisively toward the door. "Now, if you would please get the rest of your things together? I wish to leave as soon as possible."

Gillian hurried through the door ahead of him. A lump in her throat made it impossible to say anything more. Today he was behaving so differently than last night! She thought she was relieved to be spared his close company for the rest of the trip. She was surprised to discover that beneath her hurt and angry feelings there was also disappointment.

Brinton had ample time to ponder his own behavior and feelings during the long ride to Worcester. The trio had left promptly and made good time, only pausing occasionally to rest or change horses. The earl noticed that Miss Kentwell made certain to avoid speaking with him.

Her power over him was awesome. She had made him lose control of his passions at the assembly, and when he had resolved to bury those under layers of cool civility, he had lost control of that as well. He did not believe he had ever been so openly insulting to a woman in his life. He had come to believe that Cranford and his sister were who they claimed to be, and it made it even worse that he had spoken so to a woman of his own class.

He did not know what to make of the rest of the Kentwells' story, but he was certain that the sooner he parted from them, the better. His attraction to the girl was undeniable, but where could it lead? If she was in truth affianced to his uncle, then she was already spoken for. If she was in fact running away from the betrothal, the scandal would be doubled if he were to attach her to himself! He couldn't understand why he was having such trouble resisting her. The chit acted like a hoyden and looked like mischief personified!

He didn't doubt for a moment that she might have had an equally powerful effect on his elderly uncle. Had she manipulated the old man into an engagement, only to break it off? Was she after the nephew, now, instead? He had shaken his head. Their meeting could not have been anything but coincidence. He believed the twins still had no idea who he really was. Whether or not they were truly being pursued, he could not tell. But the conversation he had overheard between them that morning confirmed that they at least believed it.

He had decided that he should fund the rest of their journey, if only to make sure they reached their destination safely. They were so young and naive. As soon as he parted from them, his life could return to normal. He would put the girl out of his mind, and if he heard later that his uncle's fiancée had run away to Scotland, he would act as surprised as anyone.

They arrived at the Worcester cattle fair at midday. Striped and colored vendors' awnings fluttered in the breeze, and a thousand sights and sounds both human and animal met the travelers as they entered the market square. Brinton stayed close behind the curricle, searching for a place to secure the horses. Finally, he spotted a farmer trying to ease his empty wagon out of a space, and within a few minutes both the curricule and his own mount were tethered to the same hitching block.

Brinton watched with a frown as Gillian jumped nimbly down from the seat of the curricle to join the two men on the ground. "You would do well to stay here in the carriage," he said in a low voice. "There are rough characters about and rough language not fit for a young lady's ears. It is also too warm to stay muffled up in your cloak, and any man worth his salt will see in a moment you are not what you seem."

"But I want to see everything! I won't be shocked by the language. I have spent enough time around our own stables to have heard it all by now. I will keep my cloak wrapped around me, I promise." She began to move with them along the pavement. "What are you going to look at first?"

"I am here to look at horses. Having missed my chance in Taunton, I am still hoping to acquire some prime blood to add to my stables."

"For riding? For driving? Gilbey and I can help you. We know a thing or two about horses."

"For breeding," Brinton said, arching an eyebrow in Gillian's direction. He had certainly never had a woman offer to help him choose a horse before.

They made their way slowly through the crowds gathered around pens of cows, hogs, and ponies. They passed by a gypsy who was attempting to hawk a sway-backed piebald amidst unhelpful comments from the onlookers.

"I suppose you are going to tell me I shouldn't consider that one," Brinton couldn't resist saying.

"Would I insult you so?" Gillian quipped back.

They stopped quite abruptly in a crowd gathered around a big Scotsman selling a gleaming chestnut stallion.

"Now there's a beauty," breathed Gilbey in admiration.

"He must be at least seventeen hands," Gillian added.

"Hm," said Brinton. "Makes you wonder why he didn't already sell this morning, before we ever got here." He was speaking in a low voice, almost to himself. "Let's take a better look." He began to search for a way through the crowd, but before he could move, a small, sturdy man in a tweed jacket and red waistcoat grabbed hold of his coat sleeve and pulled him back.

"Excuse me? Lord Brinton, I believe?"

Rafferty rounded on the man with a fierce expression that would have left most people quaking. He did not like having his coat sleeves pulled at, nor having his identity advertised in the marketplace to ruin his hopes of a good bargain.

"Ah, yes, 'tis you, my lord," said the little man, apparently quite unperturbed. "Thought as much when I first saw you riding in." He nodded toward the twins. "They with you?"

There was something sly about the man's approach that made Brinton wary of answering. Matching question with question, he summoned his most intimidating growl. "What is it you want? Be quick—I am busy here."

"Yes, o' course, my lord. A moment only." The man's rough accent contrasted oddly with his polite words.

Who the devil is this? Brinton puzzled.

"Such an odd coincidence, running into you, my lord. Not two hours ago I got a report about your uncle, Lord Grassington."

Damn the man! He was already making matters worse. This was not the way Brinton had wanted the twins to learn of his connection. "You had a report?"

"Seems your uncle's intended and her brother have run away from Devonshire. Twins they are, although a more mismatched pair I never heard of. The lad is tall and blond, while the girl is a little thing, short with reddish hair."

"What has this to do with me?"

"Seems the pair are heading north, maybe to Scotland, and we're to be on the lookout. Their uncle is paying handsomely to get them back." The man attempted to peer past the earl to get a better look at the twins. "Next thing I know, here you come, riding in with them two. Just seemed odd, you know. Worth a look into, no offense intended, my lord."

Brinton reminded himself to exhale. He could detect no reaction from the young pair behind him, and he hoped they all three could appear calm and unconnected. Even so, his words came out more forcefully than he had intended.

"If I thought it was any of your business, perhaps I would tell you that I have no connection to these people except that I rode in behind them and we are sharing a hitching block. Perhaps not. Why the devil I should tell you, I haven't the faintest clue."

"My apologies. I should have said sooner. I am employed by Bow Street, part of the northern network. Name's Orcutt. Considering that you're Grassington's supposed heir, I thought these matters might interest you. Don't mean to be impertinent, your lordship."

"Well, you are. You assume a great deal, Mr. Orcutt. I have little if anything to do with my uncle's affairs, and I care even less about them." Brinton tried to sound thoroughly bored. "If you'll excuse me, now, I came here to buy a horse. I do not appreciate the interruption. Good day, sir."

As Brinton hoped, Mr. Orcutt accepted the brusque dismissal, but the man did not go far. Brinton began to elbow his way back into the crowd, passing between the twins.

"He is still watching us," he said in a low voice, without looking at either of them. "We had best get ourselves out of Worcester as quickly and unobtrusively as possible. Can you get yourselves back to the carriage?"

Chapter Ten

The twins had no time to react to the shock of learning Brinton's connection to Lord Grassington. In one hurriedly exchanged glance, they communicated their unspoken misgivings and also their agreement that, for the moment, the Bow Street agent was a greater and more immediate threat.

They answered Brinton with an almost imperceptible nod, even as they started to move. Quickly they slipped into the crowd and made their way through the marketplace, taking advantage of the flimsy wood and canvas booths to cover their movements as much as possible. When Gilbey finally stopped, Gillian nearly crashed into him.

"I just want to reconnoiter," he explained. "See? There's the curricle just ahead of us." In the crowded marketplace they could see no sign of either Brinton or the Bow Street agent.

"I'd like to know what Brinton is doing," Gilbey said as he climbed up into the seat.

"I couldn't care less," Gillian replied as she clambered in beside him. "If this carriage did not belong to him, I would say we should set off in it right now without him!"

"Oh, that's fine! We are in trouble enough without adding theft. Besides, we wouldn't have the slightest idea where to go."

"Anywhere that is away from him would be a safe wager in my book! Grassington's nephew! He must have been delighted when he learned who we were. I admit that I don't understand why he didn't just serve us up on a platter to that Bow Street man."

"Perhaps he doesn't like his uncle! Or perhaps he is against the marriage. Did not the agent say that Brinton is

Lord Grassington's heir apparent? Brinton would be cut out of his inheritance if Grassington produced a son!"

"A son!" Gillian gave an involuntary shudder. The thought of sharing a bed with the old man had so appalled her, she had refused to even consider the possible consequences. "But Brinton assisted us in Taunton before he knew who we were. He couldn't have already known then, could he? I think it more likely that once he found out, he thought he could keep helping us, right into a trap. Was it not his idea for us to come to Worcester?"

"Yes. But then, as you said, why would he help us to escape that Bow Street Runner? That doesn't make sense."

"Well, I have it in mind to get back out of this carriage and walk away from the problem. We could disappear into the streets of Worcester and go back to making our own way north."

"The few crowns we have would not get us very far."

"We could earn more! We could perform some kind of work."

"Oh, right. And what might that be? No one would ever mistake us for laborers."

Gillian tossed her head and stared off at the buildings bordering the square. "I suppose you think we should just sit there waiting for Brinton. Well, I don't." Before her brother could so much as utter a protest, she jumped down from the curricle.

She did not get far. As soon as she landed, she crashed full-length against a tall man who had just come up on her side of the vehicle. It was Brinton.

"Where do you think you are going?" he ground out between his teeth, grasping her by the upper arms. "If you do not get back into that carriage this instant, I will throw you in bodily."

He stepped back just in time to avoid the kick she aimed at his shins, but his iron grip on her arms never loosened. He spun her around to face the curricle, speaking quietly into her ear. "I will, too, little witch, make no mistake."

Gillian put a foot on the step and raised herself up, her back as straight as a ramrod. No longer at a disadvantage in height, she shot a look of pure loathing over her shoulder at Brinton and, shaking off his hands, climbed into the seat.

The earl looked across at Gilbey. "We have to leave—now," he said, his voice low but filled with unmistakable urgency. "Follow me as closely as you can, and don't stop for anything until I do." Without another glance at the twins, he moved to unhitch the horses and mount up.

Gilbey hesitated, glancing at his sister. Then he flicked the reins briskly and clucked at the pair of bays who had been standing so patiently. Protest and rebellion were smoldering on the seat beside him, he could tell. He urged the horses to follow Brinton, nevertheless. Was there really any other choice?

Brinton led the twins out of the market square by the nearest street. They followed him through the traffic as best they could, squeezing through openings that Gilbey normally might not have dared to try. Worcester was busy and noisy. It was a relief when they reached a quiet back street in the shadow of the cathedral. Brinton reined in his horse beside the curricle.

"We cannot stay in Worcester, and the sooner we are gone, the better. I dare not stop now to call upon the solicitors through whom I had planned to borrow your money. We shall have to manage on the sum I had put by for horse buying. We'll go north, but we'll try to avoid the main roads and towns."

"You are going with us?" asked Gilbey.

"As I seem to be under suspicion, it seems best if I disappear for a time. I know this area, and we haven't enough money to split up."

"How did you get clear of Mr. Bow Street?"

Brinton laughed. Gilbey thought a devil seemed to dance in the earl's eyes for a moment. "Remember the gypsy we passed in the market, trying to pass off his ruined animal as a horse? I suggested that our Mr. Orcutt was bad-mouthing his reputation and trying to steal his business. I didn't think the gypsy would stand for that, and when I last looked, he had Mr. Orcutt backed up against the wall of the apothecary's shop, embroiled in a rather intense, er, discussion."

Gilbey chuckled appreciatively. Gillian was silent.

"I have no doubt that the diversion has gained us only a little bit of time," Brinton added seriously. "We are going to need food, but I think we will stop for it after we are out of the city."

"Where do you think he is taking us?" Gillian asked Gilbey a short while later. "I am quite sure we are not heading north." Anxiety had supplanted all other emotions in her voice for the moment. "What if Lord Grassington and Uncle William are waiting for us at one of these outlying taverns?"

"Grassington is too ancient and fragile to have come this far. As for Uncle William, I cannot say. I don't see how they could have arranged it, Gillie. When could they have been in contact? Quite frankly, I think you are sniffing the wind in the wrong direction, regarding your suspicions about Brinton."

"Surely you agree now that he isn't to be trusted?"

"Yes, but not in the way that you think. Gillie, have you not noticed the way he looks at you?"

"No, I have not." A telltale blush gave away the lie.

Gilbey kindly refrained from pointing it out. "Well, I have. I don't know what his intentions are, but I assure you I am keeping a close eye on him."

There was no trap awaiting them at the roadside inn where Brinton finally stopped to purchase food. He, in fact, went in alone, bidding the twins to stay in the carriage, where they were less likely to be seen. The saddlebags he carried in with him were bulging when he came back out.

"This should do us for a while," he said, slinging the bags up behind his horse's saddle. He gave the animal a pat and added, "Let's give these fellows a good, long drink, for they will be well-tired by the time we stop again."

"Exactly where is it we are going?" Gillian demanded, unable to stop herself. "I know by the sun and the position of the hills that we have not been heading north!"

Brinton raised his eyebrows. "Oh, you'd like to know that, would you? I think I might enjoy seeing how bedeviled you could become if I refused to tell you, but that would be most ungentlemanly, would it not?" He gave Gillian an extremely roguish smile. "As it happens, we have been heading west. We will be turning north shortly, heading for a place where we may hide ourselves and decide what to do next. We will have to provide our own accommodations, but they will cost us nothing."

"What on earth is that supposed to mean?" Gillian could not keep the exasperation out of her voice, even though she knew it gave him satisfaction.

"It means we are going to camp in the Wyre Forest."

The twins looked at Brinton as if he had quite lost his mind.

Two hours later, the three travelers found themselves on foot in the sun-dappled glades of the ancient forest. Following a rough track that was barely wide enough to accommodate the carriage, they formed a small procession under the lacy canopy of branches. Brinton led the way beside his mount, and Gilbey brought up the rear with the tired pair drawing the curricle. Gillian walked in between, entranced by the beauty around her.

Stands of firs splashed their darker green against the other soft colors of the spring woods—the infant greens and golds of the larches, birch, and beech trees growing among the old oaks. Clouds of white cherry blossoms could be seen in places, along with bright carpets of bluebells in the glades.

"Oh, it is so beautiful!" Gillian exclaimed, drawing a deep breath. "It smells so wonderful; do you not wish they could bottle a scent that smelled like spring woods?"

"You would never get me to wear it." Gilbey chuckled.

"Watch out for the mud!" Brinton called suddenly from ahead.

His warning came too late for Gillian. As she stepped forward, her boot sank into the soft edge of a muddy rut, throwing her off balance. She tried to save herself, but her counterstep struck deeper mud. Down she went with a little cry of dismay.

Gilbey had to halt the bays before their forward motion overran his sister sprawled in the mud. As she struggled to sit up, Brinton and his horse turned back to her, carefully skirting the treacherous patch.

"Miss Kentwell! Are you quite all right?" Holding the ribbons in one hand, the earl extended his other one to Gillian.

She ignored it. "I am still in one piece," she replied. "The mud is quite soft, although the ground beneath it is not."

Gillian felt shaken, wet, and thoroughly embarrassed. Part of her wanted very much to take Brinton's hand, to have him help her up, hold her and comfort her. Part of her wished the earth would open up and swallow her, or at least, failing that, perhaps it could swallow Brinton instead. She stared at his hand as if it were a hot poker.

"Please allow me to assist you," he said, still holding out his hand.

"No, thank you. You will only get mud on your gloves," she managed to say civilly. She looked down at herself, surveying the damage. Mud covered her front all the way to her waist. Her forearms were caked to the elbows, where she had caught herself as she fell. Her cap lay in the mud two feet away. Ironically, her cloak sat, clean and dry, on the seat of the curricle where she had left it in the warmth of the sunny afternoon.

"Gillie, you are a picture," her brother said, beginning to laugh. "I am glad you are not hurt."

"If you continue to laugh, you may be the one who is hurt," she replied, glowering at him. She began to look about for some less muddy spot to place her hand and get up.

"I hope this assisting you up out of roadways is not becoming a habit." Brinton chuckled. Before she could realize what he was about, he stepped closer and seized her by the elbow, hauling her to her feet.

He had caught her unprepared. Off-balance again, she tottered against him, and they stood frozen for a moment, staring into each other's eyes.

There was no escaping it. Gillian felt the wave of attraction rush through her more strongly than ever. Her face tingled, and she thought she must be blushing, but the sensation spread from her face to every part of her body. Could a person blush all over?

The earl's eyes were dark but brilliant, seemingly lit from somewhere within. She could see distinctly all the colors that usually blended into the smoky hazel that fascinated her. Did Brinton feel the same pull that she did?

Could a man tell if a woman wanted to feel his arms around her?

Brinton's horse jerked restlessly on the reins, and Gilbey coughed discreetly. Gillian realized with horror that she did not know how long she and Brinton had been standing there. Had it only been a second, or had it been more?

She jumped back from the earl, focusing her distress on the mud that now soiled his coat and gloves. "My lord, your coat! I tried to warn you . . . "

He reached up his free hand to soothe his horse, stroking the animal's nose with a slightly muddied glove, but he did not take his eyes off Gillian. "It is of no consequence, Miss Kentwell. A little mud will brush off as soon as it dries. I'm afraid your own circumstance is not so easily remedied. I believe we should make camp without further delay."

A quick survey of the surrounding area revealed a small clearing adjoining the shelter of a large beech tree. The men unharnessed the horses and secured them and the carriage close by, where scrubby brush helped to conceal them. They then tried to remove the evidence of broken twigs and branches where they had forced the bays to pull the curricle off the track.

The afternoon shadows were beginning to lengthen as Brinton turned to the twins. "I think we must risk having a fire. The air will be cold once the sun has disappeared. I doubt that Orcutt or anyone who works for him would have managed to track us here. We will need kindling and firewood, and if we can find them, stones to put around the fire to keep it contained."

He paused, looking dubiously at the twins. "Have either of you ever camped before?"

"No," answered Gilbey.

"Yes," replied his sister.

"Gillie, I don't believe you can count the night you and Mary Feathers spent in Chester Norton's orchard." Gilbey said.

Brinton's eyebrows went up like a pair of question marks.

"She was trying to help Mary run away," the young viscount explained. "Half the people from Prawle Point to Kingsbridge were out looking for them that night."

"Never mind, Gilbey," Gillian said impatiently. "We will just do as Lord Brinton bids us."

"I expect you are wet and uncomfortable in those clothes, Miss Kentwell. You may wish to find a suitably private spot in the bushes to change your apparel. But it is important for us to gather the firewood before it is too dark to see. I might add that darkness falls very quickly in the woods once the sun sets."

"If you won't mind a little mud on your firewood, I can wait," Gillian offered gamely.

The trio gathered what seemed to Gillian a tremendous pile of sticks and branches to fuel their fire. They discovered a source of stones in a nearby brook, where Gillian attempted to wash off a little of the offending mud. As they returned to the camp, Gillian stopped to retrieve some appropriate clothing from the bags in the curricle.

There was no need to be uncomfortable for the night, she reasoned, carrying the leather satchel and a pair of Gilbey's old breeches into the bushes. She shivered as she removed her upper clothing and unbound her breasts. Her flannel nightrail could serve for a shirt, and would be warmer besides. She had another waistcoat, although it probably would not button now. The boy's stable jacket she had worn in Taunton would have to serve again for a coat.

She sat down on leaves and twigs to remove her muddy boots and stockings, then quickly got up again to finish changing. The ground was damp, and there were probably insects crawling among the leaves. She felt absurdly exposed and vulnerable. Who was there to see her? Fallow deer? Foxes? She smiled at her own foolishness, but hurried nonetheless.

Leaving the satchel, she took her muddied clothes down to the brook and washed them. If she spread them near the fire, with luck they might be dry by morning. She sniffed. She could not detect any hint of wood smoke in the air and wondered why Gilbey and Brinton had not yet managed to start a fire. *Men!* They always thought they knew what they were doing. She picked up two more stones to add around the fire and started back toward the clearing, carefully holding the rocks and the wet clothes away from her.

She stopped before she reached the camp. She heard

voices, and they did not belong to her brother or Lord Brinton. Who could have joined them? Cautiously, she peered through the greenery.

"Cooperation is your best choice, gentlemen," she heard a man say. Her throat tightened, and her breath came a little harder. Had Orcutt managed to follow them, after all? She could not see well, but she did not think it was his voice.

"Throw your valuables into a pile just there, and we'll be off with no harm to you. Don't be foolish now."

Thieves! She shifted her position to try to see better. How many were there? What should she do?

In the deepening twilight she made out the figure of one man, a little distance from her, who appeared to be holding a pistol. Was there only one? But he had said "we."

"My watch was already stolen in Taunton," she heard Gilbey say. "So was my purse, and I have nothing else."

"Right, squire, we believe that." The low, growling response came from very close to Gillian, startling her further. She moved her head carefully, trying to see through the leaves. She discovered that another man was standing with his back to her, almost directly in front of her.

Were there only two? How dare they! Anger began to rise in Gillian as she thought of the losses she had already been made to suffer. With her heart pounding, she cautiously set down the rocks and the clothes she had been carrying. Any small sound might betray her presence. Crouching, she peered under the bushes and tried to gauge the distance between her and the thief with the pistol. He was pointing it at Gilbey and Brinton, who were standing together. If she hit him with a stone, would not the pistol discharge? Yes, but if she could manage to hit the pistol, or the hand holding it, the shot would be off. What about the other man then?

Gillian wrapped her fingers around the larger of her two stones, feeling its cold smoothness and trying to steady her nerves. Her throwing ability was respectable. Even if she missed altogether, the crash of the rock landing across the clearing would still serve to distract the scoundrels. Quickly she formed a kind of plan, reaching for the wet breeches with her other hand. Watching carefully where she put her feet, she stepped back from the brush to give her arm clearance.

Gillian threw the rock, sending a prayer along with it. At the moment she heard the report of the pistol, she burst through the bushes, flinging the wet breeches over the head of the closest robber.

Brinton and Gilbey reacted with admirable promptness. The earl rushed at the first man, who had lost the pistol and was searching frantically for it in the leaves. Gilbey dived toward the other man, who was struggling with the wet cloth over his face.

Gillian jumped nimbly back into the bushes, where she could stay safely out of the way. She watched Brinton dispatch the first man with a tremendous uppercut to the jaw. He retrieved the pistol and turned toward Gilbey and the other thief.

"Stop!" the earl commanded.

The two clearly mismatched wrestlers paused, and Brinton used that moment to wave the pistol. Gilbey sprang away from his heavyset opponent, moving to Brinton's side.

"Well done, lad," the earl said. Motioning with the pistol just as the thieves had done to him, he forced the heavy man to join his partner, who was sitting up and rubbing his jaw.

"Gentlemen—and I grant you the term is a gross misstatement—we ought to detain you and see you handed over to the local magistrate. For private reasons of our own, we choose not to do that. If you have any wits, you will gather them quickly and depart. I suggest that you put as much distance between us as you possibly can, before we change our minds."

The miscreants did not appear even slightly grateful, Gillian noted from her position in the shrubbery. The heavyset man helped the smaller fellow to his feet, and they both treated Brinton to a murderous glare before they began to move off toward the brushy area where the horses and curricle were concealed. A sudden shout from that direction revealed the unexpected presence of a third scoundrel.

"Pull it, boys! Shake a leg, or the devil take ye!"

The two thieves took to their heels. Exchanging a look of

misgiving, Brinton and Gilbey sprinted after them. A mo
ment later, Gillian heard curses and the sound of three
horses galloping off.

Gillian emerged from her hiding place and ran to catch
up with the others. The earl and her brother had not gone
more than twenty yards.

"Are they gone?" she asked, coming up behind the two
men.

"Oh, yes, they are gone," Gilbey answered, turning to
face her. "They have gone, and they have taken our horses
with them."

Chapter Eleven

A thick, quiet darkness had settled into the woods all around the clearing where Brinton and Gilbey had finally built their fire. As the last traces of daylight faded from the sky above, stars were just beginning to show.

Gillian had helped to place the stones around the firepit, but she was notably inattentive and listless. Now she sat apart from the men, staring silently into the crackling flames as the earl and Gilbey assessed their situation.

"They got the portmanteau, and they would have had your valise if they had not dropped it," Gilbey was saying.

"I think we will be sharing my meager wardrobe," Brinton agreed, nodding. "It was a most unfortunate turn of events. Had it not been for your sister's bold intervention, however, it could have been much worse."

Brinton thought Miss Kentwell was unusually quiet. She looked very lovely with the glow of the fire lighting her face. She also looked small and lost and very fragile.

"Miss Kentwell, I confess I am in awe," he called to her, "but I do not know if it is more in admiration of your pluck or fear of your possible insanity."

When he got no reply, he asked Gilbey, "Is she all right?"

"I think she needs to eat," Gilbey said in a low voice. "Now that I consider it, none of us has had anything since we stopped at Tewkesbury this morning."

"Perhaps if I take something over to her?" Brinton ventured. "You are looking a little the worse for your wrestling match with our large friend."

Indeed, Gilbey's pale skin was already beginning to look purplish along the cheekbone under his left eye. He shifted as if unable to find a comfortable way to sit and nodded.

The earl rose and went to fetch the saddlebags. "I thank God I had already taken these off my horse," he said, returning. "We would have gone very hungry tonight, indeed."

As he and young Cranford removed the contents from the bags, he added in a low voice, "I am afraid we ought to keep watch tonight. We can spell each other."

Gilbey looked at Brinton in alarm. "You think we might have more trouble?" There was a reproachful note in the lad's voice, although he made no further comment.

Brinton suspected there were a good many things the twins might be wanting to say to him by now. Neither had yet confronted him over the issue of his uncle, for instance. But then, they had all been rather distracted.

He shrugged. "It occurred to me that those thugs might come back. They were surprised and angry, and they ran off before they realized I had not, of course, been able to reload or prime the pistol." Gilbey was staring at him as if he, too, had only just realized it. "I don't suppose that you or Miss Kentwell had, in fact, a pistol in your baggage, as you intimated in Taunton?"

"No," answered Gilbey, with obvious regret. "Even if we had, it would be far from us now."

"I see." Brinton was studying Gillian again. "The books," he said suddenly, turning to Gilbey. "Which bag were they in?"

Gilbey groaned, which would have been answer enough. "The portmanteau. How I wish now they had been in the other."

No doubt that loss is adding to Miss Kentwell's misery, Rafferty thought, but he said nothing more. He divided the cheese, bread, and sausage and handed a selection of everything to Gilbey, tossing him an apple for good measure. Then he carried some food to Gillian.

"Eating cannot solve our problems, but at least it can help," he said, squatting beside her. "Not eating, of course, only adds to them."

She turned her head toward him without lifting it. "I am so very tired, and my head aches. Please leave me alone."

Brinton pried her fingers from where they lay folded over her elbow and gently pressed the apple he had brought her into her hand. Then putting his fingertips under her chin, he raised her head. "Your brother says you need to eat, and I agree. You will feel better."

For several moments he did not move. He was lost again, staring into her liquid blue-green eyes. They seemed huge and luminous in the firelight and overwhelmed his senses so that all other reality dropped away. He quite forgot how shocked he had been by her attack on the robbers. In the depths of those eyes, he could read her sadness and despair. He wanted nothing more than to gather her into his arms, to feel her and to give her his warmth and his comfort.

He knew he must not. He pulled back his hand quickly.

"I've brought you these," he said, his voice husky. He dropped her share of the food into her lap. "We also have chicken to finish roasting," he persisted when she didn't touch them. "You'll need something to drink; would you prefer claret, or ale? I am afraid those are the only choices."

She shook her head, and Rafferty felt the momentary frustration of a parent coaxing a recalcitrant child. He would not lose control of himself, however. He would get her to eat.

"If you do not begin to feed yourself, Miss Kentwell, I shall be obliged to assist you," he threatened. He found the idea rather appealing.

He raised an eyebrow suggestively. As he suspected she might, she straightened up immediately. Glaring at him, she bit decisively into the apple.

He smiled in approval. "Claret or ale?"

"Claret, I suppose."

"Good, then. We'll share it between the three of us. I should warn you, however, that this tavern is short of drinking vessels. We shall be forced to pass the bottle around like peasants."

Gillian raised the claret bottle to her lips for another drink. Even though it was almost empty, she still needed two hands to steady it. How was one supposed to take lady-like sips when the wine had such an unfortunate tendency to slosh pell-mell into the neck of the bottle all at once? She choked down a rather large gulp, and with a small cough handed the bottle back to Brinton.

Her brother had had his fill of both dinner and drink. The

men had said something about keeping watch, and Lord
Brinton had offered to take the first turn. Gilbey had
wrapped himself in his greatcoat and lay near the fire, already asleep, or nearly so. Was he not the
least bit bothered by all that had happened?

She doubted that she would sleep this night, unless the
wine wrought a miracle. Her eyes kept straying to the darkness beyond the fire's dancing shadows. The woods at
night seemed far less friendly than the flowering wonderland she had so admired that afternoon. Was it only because Brinton thought they needed to keep watch? Her ears
were fixed on the forest around her, but all she heard was
the innocent rustling of new leaves in the treetops and the
distant babble of the brook.

She pulled her cloak closer around her shoulders. Where
was Brinton? She felt a moment's panic before she realized
that the earl had moved away from the fire to bury the remains of the chicken they had eaten. He had already carefully repacked the saddlebags with the food they were
saving for morning.

She stared into the dwindling flames of the campfire.
Why had he hidden that he was Grassington's nephew? She
hated to admit she had begun to trust him. He had rescued
them so many times now, she was starting to think that
Gilbey must be right. Why else would he go to such lengths
to help them, unless he was protecting his interest in his inheritance? He had not planned to leave Worcester with
them, yet how quickly he had changed his mind!

Tears pricked at the back of her eyes, and she tried to
banish them, stifling a sniff. It was too ironic, being
stranded here with him. Everything had gone awry from the
moment she and Gilbey had left their home. Had she been
so wrong to challenge her fate? She had gambled, trading a
secure future of potential misery for nothing more than a
dream of freedom, love, and safety in a place she had never
even seen. Now the empty woods around her seemed to
mock her choice. She had lost everything. Here in this
wilderness, there were no links remaining to either the life
she had left behind or the one she had hoped for.

The tears in her eyes threatened to overflow, and she
brushed at them angrily with her hand. *Stupid chit!* she

scolded herself. *Sinking into a well of despair! Utter non-sense.* But despite her attempt to rally, she could not shake off the mood that gripped her. She jumped when she suddenly heard Brinton's voice beside her.

"I was going to offer you more wine, but I think you have greater need of this at the moment."

She glanced to the side without moving her head and saw that he was squatting beside her, offering his handkerchief. Somehow the very ordinary civility of his gesture pushed her tears over the edge.

"Too late," she replied in a choked voice as the flood began to cascade into her lap.

"Never too late," he said with a smile, and as he had done earlier, he lifted her head toward him. Very slowly and deliberately, he began to dry her tears.

"What is all this now," he said soothingly. "Can this be our intrepid heroine, turned into a watering pot? You must know that things are never, ever, as bad as they seem."

Despite the teasing edge to his words, his voice was deep and soft, comforting her like warm wine. His words and touches held an intimacy that she knew she should not allow, yet she seemed spellbound as he gently wiped the traces of moisture from her face.

"Is this the miss who spent a night in an orchard while all of Devon turned out to look for her?" His voice dropped to a whisper. "You must never lose hold of your courage. It is a very precious gift."

She felt his hazel eyes studying her. Did he truly think she was courageous, rather than foolhardy? Her tears had stopped streaming down, although she could feel them clinging to her lashes and lingering treacherously in her eyes. She could not seem to push any words out past the lump in her throat, however. She shook her head.

The fingers he had held under her chin moved slowly up to brush back a tendril of chestnut hair from her cheek. "Is this not the same fearless miss who throws rocks at villainous robbers and attacks brigands with wet clothing? You are not going to tell me you are afraid of the dark?"

In the flickering firelight he looked very much the rogue she had seen in Taunton. There was a glint of mischief in his eyes, and his unruly dark hair straggled over his forehead. The day's growth of beard shadowed his jawline and upper lip. His smile was infectious, and Gillian managed to produce a very small one of her own in response.

"Better, much better. You needn't be afraid, you know. Your brother and I will keep watch all night." His fingers trailed down from her hair to trace the smile on her lips.

His gentle touch sent fire racing through her veins so suddenly her breath caught in her throat, and her eyes widened in surprise. She realized that the ache of despondency in her heart was melting, rapidly giving way to a very different sort of ache. *No! Not again.* Yet she could not stop it.

Anxious lest he detect her reaction, she tried to find her voice. "But what would you do if someone came?" she finally blurted out. "We haven't any weapons! In fact, we haven't *anything*!—no walls to protect or shelter us, no beds to comfort our sleep—no table to eat upon, nothing to eat with! We haven't even any way to leave!" She looked down at her hands, clenched tightly in her lap. "It is my folly that has brought us all to this."

Brinton, who had dropped onto his knees when he first began his ministrations, now took Gillian firmly by the shoulders. "If we are here through anyone's folly, it is certainly not yours. Your uncle is to blame, and perhaps mine is as well—not to mention interfering Bow Street Runners, desperate thieves, and possibly even myself. Besides," he added softly, his eyes on hers, "you are wrong, you know. We have everything here we could ever need."

She looked at him sharply, wondering what he could mean and how she could continue to resist him. She believed he was toying with her, yet still she wanted desperately to throw herself into his arms. She could not allow herself to be swept up in his spell. Instead, she said, "Have we lost your wits along with everything else?"

He released her abruptly, leaving behind a burning impression of his hands that spread warmth to her very toes. He gave her a smile that seemed full of regret. "That might explain a great deal," he admitted.

Leaning his weight back on his heels, he said, "We are not so badly off as you might think. We have food and a warm fire and a fine night to camp under the stars. Had you noticed them?"

Gillian looked up at the display over their heads. The warm glow of the campfire did not reach the tops of the trees, which stood darkly etched against the velvet night sky. A vast array of stars stretched beyond, carelessly flung by some invisible hand. The beauty was both breathtaking and humbling.

The earl's tone became playful. "It is true we had our meal without utensils, but we have a handkerchief." He held it up and waved it about. "How civilized do we need to be?" He began to fold it, apparently satisfied that there would be no more tears.

"I am surprised that you should be concerned about our defenses when we have an ample supply of rocks," he continued brightly. "I would like to know how you came to have such an expert arm."

"Desperation," she replied. "That, or practice throwing hats." She summoned another small smile to hide her chaotic feelings. This unkempt and playful earl was so different from the stuffy authoritarian she had so disliked! "I must confess, I wish now that I had hit the fellow in the head! Gilbey and I had lost so much already . . . "

She paused, but the words continued to tumble out, as if there was no stopping them, now that she had begun. "We brought so little, and now everything is gone—Father's watch, our clothes, everything! All of my mother's song-books were in that portmanteau and my best shawl. It seems so cruel, and of what use are these things to anyone else?"

"I did not mean to make light of your loss," Brinton said soberly. "I would give anything to be able to restore them to you. But I did not want to see you so disheartened. You have more pluck than many men I know. You must not allow these setbacks to defeat you. Surely your memories of your mother, and indeed, of the songs in those books, are still safely locked in your mind and your heart?"

She nodded.

"One day you can buy yourself a new shawl, one that you may like even better, can you not? And do you not still have the few things that were in the satchel?"

She smiled a genuine smile, feeling a little foolish now in the light of his reassurances.

"There you are, Miss Kentwell. In the morning perhaps

you will even go so far as to sing a song or two for us when we set off again on our way." He rose, grunting as he straightened his long legs.

Gillian choked back a small protest. She did not want Brinton to move away from her, but she must not let him know that. She pressed her fingers against her lips to keep the whimper from escaping as he looked down at her.

The earl reached for her hand and pulled her up beside him. As they stood there for a few seconds, their hands locked together, Gillian thought the very air seemed to crackle around them. Then quite without warning, Brinton opened his arms and she went into them without a single further thought. He was so tall, her shoulder and head were against his chest. Above the pounding of her own heart, she could hear the rapid beat of his, close under her ear.

He closed his arms around her, cradling her, and she felt him nuzzling her hair. She felt small against the strong bulk of his body, yet she thought she had never experienced anything so delightful. She felt warm and protected. She had not the strength to deny herself this pleasure. Perhaps she would never meet another man with all the qualities she was discovering in Brinton. Whether her future lay in Devonshire or Scotland, she thought she would like to have this one moment to remember.

"I love the smell of your hair," he murmured. His voice resonated deep in his chest, and a shiver ran through her. The earl pulled his cloak around to cover them both as much as he could.

"Cold?"

She nodded, even though it wasn't true. Excited, yes. Frightened, yes. But she dared not tell him that.

He cupped her cheek with his warm palm, tilting her head back. "I can fix that," he offered, and his eyes searched hers, seeming to seek her permission.

She stared back in fascination. His eyes were shadowed by the angle of his face to the fire, but she could see clearly the small traces of care etched above his thick eyebrows and the fine lines at the corners of his eyes. In that small moment his face seemed unaccountably dear, and she wanted to commit every inch of it to her memory.

Something of her feelings much have shown in her face,

for in the next moment his lips descended to meet hers. His kiss was gentle, polite, experimental. Gillian kissed him back with her eyes wide open, not wanting to miss any part of the experience. The soft explorations of his mouth stunned her, however, and she found that she could not maintain her detached curiosity. His kiss filled her with pleasure, wonderment and longing.

It was Brinton who broke it off. "I should have known kissing you would be as different as everything else about you," he said with a wry smile. "Most young ladies of the *ton* close their eyes when they are kissed."

"And have you kissed so many ladies of the *ton*, Lord Brinton?" Of course, she supposed he would have. She had seen how the women flocked around him in Bath. But it was still oddly deflating.

He did not reply to her question. "Miss Kentwell, do you not think that by now we might call each other by our Christian names? We seem to have dispensed with almost every other social convention."

He was distracting her, fingering the curls of hair at the nape of her neck. "I'll tell you mine," he offered. One dark eyebrow rose persuasively.

"I already know it! It is Julian."

He laughed. "Minx! Have you remembered that all this time since Taunton? But that is not what my friends call me. My friends call me Rafferty."

"Rafferty!" She studied him, as if trying to decide if the name fit. "That sounds Irish."

"It is." His finger was tracing a line up her neck to her ear. It tickled and at the same time seemed to be flooding her body with waves of heat. "I was named for my father's rascally Irish batman, Rafferty FitzJames. He saved my father's life and was generally devoted to him, although he was constantly needing to be bailed out of one scrape or another."

The roving finger moved slowly around the edges of her ear and along her jaw, stopping at her lips. Brinton's voice was deep and soft, mesmerizing her. Was he trying to seduce her? Or was her own wanton nature creating these reactions to his touch?

"I remember FitzJames a little," Brinton was saying. "He used to tease me when I was small, and he was always say-

ing, 'Imagine me namesake, t' son of an earl!' Every time I
got into trouble, my father would blame it on 'the Irish in
me'—that was our little joke."

She twisted her head away from his hand. "I cannot
imagine you getting into trouble."

"Can you not? How little you know me! I think I am in
trouble right now, Miss Gillian Kentwell." His hand had
slid down her neck and was toying with the exposed, ruffled edge of her nightrail.

"Perhaps that is why I feel we should not be calling each
other by our Christian names," she said stiffly, fighting
against her own impulse to press herself against him.

He frowned. "Do you not consider us to be friends?"

"No." She tried halfheartedly to push away from his embrace. "I confess, I do not know what we are!"

"Then why the devil are you in my arms?" he teased
softly. His lips claimed hers again, and her last resistance
melted. As the kiss deepened, his gentleness became more
demanding, and she felt as if they were spinning, turning,
riding like a top on the crest of a huge wave. An unexpected weakness filled her limbs, and her knees seemed no
longer able to support her. Her mind seemed incapable of
further rational thought.

Brinton held her tightly against his body. She was aware
of his muscular hardness, and of the way her breasts were
crushed against him. They were tender from being bound
during the day under her clothes, but that had not prevented
her nipples from hardening into little pebbles that she
feared Brinton could feel right through her layers of clothing. She gasped when she suddenly felt his hand slip inside
her open jacket and waistcoat to fondle one through the soft
fabric of her nightdress.

"I didn't think those neck ruffles felt like shirt-linen," he
murmured against her hair, stroking her breast gently. He
sought her mouth again, taking advantage of her parted lips
in ways that surprised and shocked Gillian. How little she
knew of this business! How thoroughly aroused and helpless she was now.

Gilbey was sleeping soundly by the fire, and there were no
censuring eyes within miles of their lovemaking. She was so
awash in ecstatic sensations, she knew she would allow Brin-

ton to take any liberties with her that he desired. Each time he began a new kiss, he seemed to drink deeply of her, as if pulling her very soul from the depths of her toes.

Finally, Brinton lowered her to the ground. He pushed her into a sitting position and put himself several feet away. "Dear God," he said, obviously shaken. He stared at her, his eyes reflecting a glassy sheen of unsated passion, his hair and clothing in disarray.

Looking at him, Gillian wondered if she appeared equally disheveled and distraught.

We are staring at each other like children caught in a prank, she thought. Quite without her consent, the corners of her mouth began to turn up into a smile. It was silly. Were they not both adults? Why should they feel guilty? She had discovered such a remarkable mixture of rapture and contentment in Brinton's arms, she could not at that moment summon even the tiniest shred of remorse.

"Do not smile at me like that," the earl commanded sternly. The firelight danced over the angles of his face, creating a peculiar glint in his eyes.

"Why not?" Gillian's smile grew. "Is that also contrary to the custom, like keeping one's eyes open?"

Brinton growled and began to move toward her. At that moment Gilbey moaned and stirred. The earl froze. Two pairs of eyes fastened on the young viscount, who flopped onto his back with another groan and resumed his slumbers. His movement caused his coat to fall open, however, exposing him to the chill night air.

"He will catch cold," Gillian whispered dubiously.

"Yes, he might," Brinton answered stiffly, retreating to his former position. "Perhaps you should cover him." Glancing at her, he added, "Is he usually so restless? I am concerned that he may have suffered more injury in that wrestling match than he was willing to admit."

"Oh, I hope not," Gillian responded, her attention now clearly focused on her twin.

Brinton stood up. He offered his hand to help her rise, but this time he maintained a very proper distance between them.

Chapter Twelve

Brinton moved into the semidarkness under the branches of the ancient beech tree beside the clearing, trying to focus on his task instead of Miss Kentwell. He desperately needed to put some distance between her and himself. He scooped a handful of leaves from the soft carpet beneath him, crushing them in his fingers to see if they were dry enough to cushion her from the ground. He tried not to think of how her body had felt cushioned against his own.

From the shelter of the shadows he watched her move around the fire to attend her brother. The affectionate way she adjusted Cranford's coat and smoothed the hair away from his eyes sent a stab of longing through the earl. How often he had watched his eldest sister minister to her children with that same sort of tenderness! Perhaps it was time he began to think of settling down, after all, and siring offspring of his own. A vivid image of Miss Kentwell in his bed at home flashed unbidden into his mind. The full force of those innocent seablue eyes struck him as he pictured them fluttering open beside him, still clouded with sleep.

Devil take it! He turned back to his task, kneeling down to gather leaves. Whatever had possessed him to take her into his arms? She was supposed to be betrothed to his uncle! It was the worst mistake he had made yet, and he seemed to be caught up in an endless parade of errors that had started the first moment he had laid eyes on her.

He was still shaken by what had passed between them. He had never come so close to ravishing a woman in his life. Stopping when he did had required every ounce of willpower he possessed. He had never experienced that kind of overwhelming passion with anyone before. How had it happened? He had merely intended to comfort her.

Why don't you just admit that you are falling in love with her? demanded an aggravating voice in the back of his mind.

Brinton clenched his fist so hard that the leaves in it were crushed to a powder. *I don't want to be in love with her*, he argued. There was no place in his life for the luxury of such an emotion. He was the ninth deRamsay to bear the Brinton title, and the combined dignity of all the previous holders weighed heavily on him. His wife would have to stand beside him as a pillar of Society and even appear at Court. Miss Kentwell possessed rare qualities of courage and spirit which he admired, but he could not picture her as Countess of Brinton, even if she was the daughter of a viscount. He must marry a woman with the most sterling qualities—patience, diplomacy, and social expertise foremost among them.

What was he going to do? He had had no right to touch her. She was so young and inexperienced! He had not been content with an experimental kiss, a trifling dalliance like those commonly pursued in unwatched corners of all the best ballrooms. *Oh, no.* He had persisted, demanding more from her until their kisses had achieved an intimacy like a communion of their very souls.

Truly, he had robbed her. He knew he had awakened in her a response that was only a husband's privilege to uncover. He had thrown over the code of honor that had always been the center of his life. There was only one way to make it right.

With a sigh of resignation he gathered a last bunch of leaves into his arms and rose, turning back toward the fire. Miss Kentwell had sat down again, huddled in her cloak close to the warmth. She looked very small. What was she thinking? She was too innocent to realize the significance of what had happened, he was sure. Wasn't she?

The treacherous doubt stabbed him like a newly sharpened knife blade. Had she intentionally trapped him? If so, she must be feeling victorious, for he was as well and truly caught as a rabbit in a snare. Was that what her smile had meant? It didn't matter, he thought bitterly, for his course must remain the same.

He approached her, dropping his load of leaves beside her a little more abruptly than he intended. The stragglers flew up around them and a couple caught in the hungry fire, adding their smoky fragrance to the air as they flared and disappeared.

The girl turned to him, clearly startled.

"Sorry," he said, quickly trying to cover his feelings. "I think another armful or two should be sufficient."

"You truly do not need to go to so much trouble just for me," she said. She looked absolutely sincere.

"I do not mind," he mumbled and turned immediately to go back for more.

Coward, he scolded himself. He had never been one to shirk his duties, and he had never tolerated such behavior in the men he had commanded. But he had never offered marriage to anyone before. He was not sure what to say.

He returned slowly with the second load of leaves and arranged them with a great deal more care than he had the first batch. Finally, he sat down beside her.

"Miss Kentwell," he began, his voice deep and very serious. He could not seem to meet her eyes, nor indeed, to tear his gaze from his own hands clasped in front of him.

"Goodness, what is it?"

"Miss Kentwell, if our travels had not already compromised you, I am afraid my wretched behavior now most certainly has. The only thing to do, of course, is to offer you marriage."

He could sense her surprise even before she spoke.

"Lord Brinton, who is calling your behavior wretched? And explain, please, how I can be compromised over something that no one knows has happened?"

He looked at her in astonishment. Was she refusing him? He wasn't sure.

"Just think how pleased your uncle would be to discover that you had stolen his bride! The gossip-mongers, I am sure, would think it a great coup." She paused. "I do not hold you responsible for what happened between us, rest assured. How could I, when it must be obvious that I was a willing participant!" She looked down suddenly, and Brinton guessed that she was blushing.

"That you were willing does not excuse what I did," he said softly. "I have robbed you as villainously as those footpads in Taunton or the thieves we met here."

"How can you say so? You took nothing from me."

"Ah, but I did. Did you not find our kissing pleasurable?"

She raised her head and looked straight into his eyes, despite the blush that still colored her cheeks. "Yes, I did. I think I should be thanking you," she added with her disarming frankness.

He could not help smiling. She was so different from other women. "Do not thank me," he said soberly. "I have stolen your innocence. That sort of kissing—the discovery you have made should have been shown you only by a husband. Most certainly it should not have been by a man who has not even permission to use your Christian name!" He sighed. "It cannot be undone. The best I can offer you is a remedy after the fact."

She was silent for a few moments, and he waited for her reply. Finally, she said, "Is it always like that?"

"What, kissing?" He should have known she would say something unpredictable. "Not always. I will be honest and tell you that it is different with different people."

"Well, then. You have not robbed me of anything. I have still to discover if kissing would be so pleasurable with someone other than you, including a husband. Your offer is not necessary."

She turned to survey the bed of leaves he had made for her, and when he started to speak, she cut him off with a wave of her hand. "I doubt if I shall be able to sleep much, but I think I will try now. It would be a shame to waste all your efforts."

She gave him an expectant look, and he knew he had been dismissed. It was as if he had dropped a curtain between them and she had drawn it shut.

It seemed invasive to remain where he was, watching her try to get comfortable. He got up and fetched his spare coat from his valise to put under her head. Looking at her shape in the firelight, he was reminded of that first night in Taunton when she had slept on the floor by the fire with his coat as her pillow. God! Had it only been three nights ago? So much had happened, so much had changed.

He added some wood to the fire. As he stirred the flames, sparks rose into the night air, swirling and dancing rather like the confusion of contradictory reactions churning in his own heart.

He should be pleased and relieved that Miss Kentwell had disdained his marriage offer, he reasoned. Her refusal laid to rest his irrational suspicions that she somehow was trying to trap him into marriage.

Yet, he did not feel pleased or relieved at all. What kind of woman turned down marriage to the Earl of Brinton? He had never offered such a prize to anyone before. It was insulting to have it thrown back in his face. He recognized the signs of a bruised ego, however, and he smiled. *Only a very special sort of woman would do that*, he thought— *Miss Kentwell's sort.*

Part of him felt hollow and uneasy, as if he had somehow taken a wrong turn. Why did he feel such a painful sense of loss? Could he really leave her in Scotland and go on with his life? Scotland was still some two hundred miles away, or more than two days' travel from where they were now. Perhaps by the time they arrived there, his feelings would sort themselves out.

Quite remarkably, the dawn promised sunshine for a third straight day. A welcoming chorus of woodland birds greeted the sun's faint arrival even before the first rays could filter through the trees. Their noisy celebration ensured the arousal of the human intruders camped in their forest.

Gillian awoke stiff and cold. Groggily she laid out the travelers' breakfast of leftovers while the men were performing their abbreviated toilettes by the brook. She did not think warm ale was quite the thing to wake her up, but the beverage was wet and washed down the food more easily than she expected.

"We should have put these bottles in the brook," Brinton observed when he rejoined her. He was cleanly shaved and attired in a fresh shirt and pantaloons. He had changed his waistcoat, and short of his clothing being a bit rumpled, he might have been at home in London. Gilbey appeared a few moments later, cutting a respectable figure himself in attire that must have belonged to the earl. Gillian was impressed.

At length she got up and went to collect the clothes she

had laid out to dry by the fire all night. The lack of good hot water and strong lye soap had left shadowy mudstains on everything. She gathered them up with a sigh and, taking the satchel, retreated to her changing spot in the shrubbery. She hoped her cloak would hide the stains. She would be hard pressed to pass for even so much as a servant now. Ruefully, she thought that with her face unwashed and her hair uncombed, she probably would look more like a beggar!

When she rejoined the men, she was surprised to overhear the earl saying, "How are your ribs now, Cranford? Any better?"

"Just what is the matter with my brother's ribs?" she asked, planting her hands on her hips like a scolding mother.

The men exchanged a glance, and Gilbey shrugged. "That Hun I wrestled put an arm-lock around me that has left my ribs a bit bruised and tender," he said sheepishly.

"Are you sure they are only bruised?" she asked. "Does it hurt you to breathe?"

Gilbey assured her that no ribs were broken and declined her offer to bind them with strips torn from the dimity petticoat in her satchel. "Let me see how I go along," he insisted.

They left the forest and headed for the town of Bewdley, some two miles away on the river. Brinton carried his valise and Gillian's satchel, while Gilbey had the saddlebags slung over his shoulder. Gillian concentrated on keeping up with their long strides. She did not mind the exercise, which soon removed the stiffness and chill from her bones.

"We must make some sort of report," Brinton said dubiously. "The horses that were stolen belong to the inn at Tewkesbury, after all. If there's no magistrate available, I suppose I'll have to leave some sort of deposition. We'll have to hire transportation, and find someone to retrieve and store my curricle, as well. I don't know how long it will take."

It seemed unwise for all three travelers to be seen together in the town, but Brinton was loathe to leave Gillian alone. She insisted, pointing out that Gilbey would be far more help to him. But when the earl and Gilbey returned two hours later, they saw no sign of her by the hedgerow where they had left her.

"Where is she?" Brinton asked with an edge of concern in his voice. He quickly dismounted from the handsome bay saddle horse he had hired at the livery stable.

Gilbey winced as he more slowly swung a leg over the saddle of his own hired mount and lowered himself to the ground. "She's here somewhere," he said confidently. "Gillian!"

The earl and the viscount surveyed the open pasture that lay beyond the hedge, but they saw no sign of Cranford's twin.

"Gillian!" echoed Brinton.

"If I were you, I wouldn't make so much noise," came a familiar voice from above them. Gillian was calmly ensconced in the budding branches of a large oak tree nearby. "There is a curious bull at the other end of that field. He lost interest in me a while ago, but he is likely to come back to investigate you if you attract his attention." She flashed the men a charming smile.

"Are you coming down, or were you expecting tea to be served?" Brinton said with a frown. He spoke quietly.

"Do come down, Gillie," said Gilbey with a more urgent note in his voice. "We learned in town that Orcutt had been there, asking questions about us, checking whether anyone had seen us. We don't know if he might still be around."

"Do you need assistance?" Brinton asked.

"No," Gillian replied, demonstrating the fact by sliding off the branch she was perched on and beginning to climb down. When she arrived at the bottommost branch, she paused. Normally, with Gilbey or alone, she would have swung her body under the branch and easily dropped down. But to dangle herself in front of Brinton that way suddenly seemed like an extraordinarily wanton display.

"Oh, look!" she cried in her best imitation of alarm. "The bull!"

As the men turned away to look, she quickly dropped down.

"I don't see any bull," Brinton declared darkly.

"At least, not in the field," Gilbey said, giving his twin a penetrating glance.

"I do not know where he could have gone," she said innocently, "but I suggest we should not stay standing here."

Gillian could not hide her dismay when she realized there were only two horses.

"Orcutt's questions had, of course, stirred up everyone's curiosity," Brinton explained. "We had to make it clear that there were only two of us traveling together. The vehicles available were too slow for two men traveling by themselves in a relative hurry." He smiled. "I have gleaned from your brother that you are a tolerable rider," he continued, stroking the bay mare's neck.

"Tolerable!" Gillian looked at her twin indignantly. "I could probably outride you both!"

Brinton laughed. "Perhaps someday we can put that to a test. But today it is sufficient that you can handle riding astride." He positioned himself by the mare's stirrup, ready to assist Gillian. "Shall we?"

Gillian knew sitting in front of him would be a mistake. With his arms around her and his body pressing against her back, she would never be able to preserve the aloofness she was determined to maintain. But she realized with a sinking feeling that she would have to ride with Brinton. Gilbey's ribs were probably too sore to tolerate any pressure against them.

"I shall ride behind, thank you," she said stiffly.

"No, you will not," growled Brinton. "The back is too wide for you."

"Ahem!" interrupted Gilbey. "If we could get on with it? I have no desire to still be here at midday. Do you?"

They maintained an easy canter at first, striving to put distance between them and Bewdley. Gillian found riding behind Brinton no easier than riding before him would have been, for she could not hold her body stiffly away from his once the horse was in motion. She had no choice but to clasp her arms around his waist, and as the natural rhythm of their motion relaxed her, her slight weight pressed against his back.

The trio stopped to rest just beyond the village of

Billingsley in the shade of some trees where a brook crossed the road. While the men took the horses down the small embankment to water them, Gillian paced under the trees. Her thighs ached from stretching across the horse's wide back, but she was not about to admit her discomfort or change places with the earl. She was determined to walk off the pain and afraid that she might stiffen up if she stopped moving.

"That's not very restful," Brinton observed as he led his mare back up to the road.

"I'm all right."

The earl opened his saddlebag and took out a battered silver drinking cup. "Can I get you some water?"

She nodded, her throat suddenly swollen with road dust and thirst.

He filled the cup at the brook and returned to her, the dripping vessel in one hand and a daffodil in the other. His ungloved fingers brushed against hers quite intentionally as he gave her the cup.

She took it in both hands and drank greedily. "Thank you," she whispered when she stopped for a breath between sips.

"You are quite welcome," he said softly, laying the daffodil's great golden blossom against her cheek. With a teasing glint in his eye he said, "I can see you like butter."

Gillian couldn't help laughing. She ducked away from the tickling petals. "I thought that game only worked with buttercups!"

"Not so, dear lady." He took the cup from her hand and replaced it with the flower, closing her fingers around it. Without taking his eyes from hers, he raised the cup to his lips and drank deeply.

There was something dangerously intimate about the moment they were sharing. Gillian found herself easily caught up in the spell of his hazel eyes, and she was relieved when Gilbey's arrival broke it off.

"Found a straggler, eh?" her brother said, nodding toward the blossom in her hand. He wiped a drip of water from her chin with his coat sleeve.

"Lord Brinton found it," she said. Absurdly, she began to blush. She hoped he wouldn't notice.

"A lone latecomer," Brinton explained. "All the others have withered, but this one was trying valiantly to defy the passing season." He looked at Gillian. "It seemed appropriate."

His open expression altered abruptly, as if a mask had suddenly been slipped into place. He turned to his horse to put the cup away.

"Our horses will be worn out by the time we get to Bridgnorth. We will have to change them there, and see what other transportation we can hire. I also think it will be time for Gillian to resume her natural form." He looked at her, once again a model of politeness and control. "You have some appropriate clothes left in the satchel? Orcutt is looking for you disguised as a boy. We will need to throw him and any other agents he has notified off the scent any way we can."

Chapter Thirteen

Ominous clouds had begun to gather in the afternoon as the three weary travelers swayed and bounced in their hired carriage over the roads toward Shrewsbury. As darkness came, they had sought shelter at a farm and now prepared to spend the night in the farmer's barn. "She be dry 'n warm enough," the ancient owner of the barn assured them as they sat in his kitchen, eating bread and stew.

Gillian had shed her boy's clothing at the inn where the trio had stopped in Bridgnorth. The problem of getting out again unnoticed in her new identity had been solved by a quick exchange of confidences with a maid in the hallway. Gillian had convinced the maid to help her escape the dishonorable advances of a fictional gentleman by slipping down the servants' stairs and out the back of the inn. When Brinton and Gilbey left via the front, they had merely explained that their servant had already gone out ahead of them to prepare their carriage.

Sitting now in the cozy farm kitchen outside of Shrewsbury, Gillian felt awkwardly out of place in her elegant walking dress. Nonetheless, she was certain that the simple meal served by the farmer's wife was more delicious than anything she had consumed in weeks, possibly months. She was extremely grateful to sit on something that wasn't in motion and was more than ready to haul her aching bones out to the barn with Gilbey when they finished their food. Brinton stayed behind for a few minutes to talk with the old couple.

Gilbey led the way to the barn, carrying a lantern. As Gillian spread her cloak over a mound of sweet-smelling hay, her brother approached her.

"Gillie, have you confronted Brinton about his uncle?"

"About his uncle?"

"You know, about why he chose not to tell us who he was! About why he is helping us, or his feelings about the betrothal?"

"No," Gillian answered slowly. She smoothed a wrinkle out of the cloak and sat down on it. "There never seemed to be a good time to bring it up."

"You notice he has said nothing more about it himself, even though he must know that we heard Orcutt address him."

She could have asked the earl, Gillian knew very well. There had been opportunities, if not good ones—last night, for instance, or during their stops along the way today. Why had she avoided it? Was she afraid of angering him by bringing it up? Or afraid to hear what his answer might be?

"Perhaps we should both ask him together when he comes out," she offered without enthusiasm. She could not even begin to try to explain to Gilbey her hesitation. How could she explain what she did not understand herself?

The rattle of rain began then on the roof of the barn. From a gentle patter it quickly developed into a full-fledged roar. The twins heard Brinton's running footsteps and his "Devil take it!" just before the barn door swung open and he dashed inside.

"Shouldn't do that," he gasped, looking at the twins apologetically as he clutched his chest. He coughed and gulped for air. Finally, as the spasm passed, he sighed. "Sometimes I forget," he said. Still looking shaken, he sat down in the hay.

His clothes were wet. His hair was wet and dripped over his forehead. Although he brushed it back absently, it fell forward again, making him look rather forlorn and bedraggled. To Gillian he looked boyish and very vulnerable. At that moment she wished very much that Gilbey would say nothing.

Gilbey, however, wasted no time. "Brinton, my sister and I would like very much to know why you chose to conceal from us that you and the Earl of Grassington are related."

Brinton's shoulders seemed to sag. Gillian looked away,

then down, suddenly finding the toes of her slippers quite fascinating in the way they peeked out from under her skirt.

"Oh, that," she heard Brinton say. "Yes, I suppose I knew you would be asking me about that eventually." He paused, seeming to search for the proper words. "At the risk of offending you, I must say that at first I did not believe your story. Or at least, I was not certain if I did. The coincidence of our meeting in Taunton was rather remarkable, I am sure you will agree. And quite frankly, the story you told me directly contradicted what my uncle had said."

Gillian risked a glance in Brinton's direction. She found he was looking directly at her. In a soft, deep voice, he continued.

"Despite what either of you may think, my uncle is an honorable man. He told me himself that his bride-to-be was eager and willing. What was I to think when I met up with you two and learned that Gillian is supposedly this same bride-to-be, fleeing from a future that is clearly abhorrent to her?"

He did not wait for an answer. "I thought the best course would be to say nothing of my relationship until I could somehow verify one version or the other. You did not seem to know who I was, so I thought it would do no harm."

"I can see that you were in an awkward position," Gilbey said generously.

Gillian, however, was incredulous. "How could Lord Grassington have the nerve to make such a claim? It is absurd! He never even spoke with me!"

"You never met with him?" Brinton asked sharply.

"No! He is a most reclusive neighbor. I have met him only a few times in the past at obligatory social functions."

"I told you how he refused to receive me when I tried to call on him," Gilbey added. "We have had no direct contact with him at all."

"Uncle William," whispered Gillian with sudden, final comprehension. "He handled everything."

"I am afraid that must be so," agreed Brinton. "The baron must have told my uncle that you favored the match. It is not as inconceivable as you might think. My uncle is, after all, an earl, and exceedingly wealthy. He is also your nearest neighbor—your lands abut, I believe? For some, that is more than enough basis for a marriage."

"Not for me," Gillian said hotly. Then, suddenly shifting the focus of her thoughts, she asked, "I wonder how Uncle William explained to Lord Grassington my running away?"

"Perhaps he did not tell him," suggested Gilbey.

"But Lord Grassington is a magistrate! Could Uncle William have brought in Bow Street without his backing?"

"That is a good question," Brinton answered, rubbing his fingertips together thoughtfully.

"What made you decide to believe us?" Gilbey asked him.

To the twins it seemed a simple question, but Brinton hesitated. He got up and paced a few steps into the shadows, then came back into the circle of light cast by the lantern. "I am not aware that I ever actually decided," he said slowly. "While we were in Bath, I had some discreet inquiries made about you, but nothing confirmed or disproved your version of the story. I suppose our friend Orcutt helped to convince me."

He stopped, but Gillian sensed that he had left a great deal unsaid. "Even if you had believed us, it does not explain why you helped us," she prompted.

"At first it was only a gentleman's gesture to fellow travelers in distress," he said, adding with a small smile, "Perhaps there was a measure of curiosity as well."

Was that all it had been?

"When I learned your story in Bridgwater, I felt obliged to continue until I could get to the bottom of the matter."

"And now?" Gilbey asked.

"Now that we have come this far together, how could I in good conscience abandon you?"

Such a tidy answer, thought Gillian. Why did she feel such a sinking in her heart? What answer had she hoped to hear?

There was a momentary silence, filled only with the restless stirrings of the animals in the barn and the thunderous pounding of rain on the roof.

"Have you no qualms about crossing your uncle?" asked Gilbey finally. "It appears that he desired the marriage, regardless of the role our own uncle played in arranging it."

Brinton sighed. "No, for I believe the results of our actions will be in his best interest, as well as yours." He

looked at Gillian. "He wanted the marriage based on erroneous information. He would never force a young woman
into marriage against her will."

The earl turned his gaze toward the lantern, as if he
might find some sort of answer in its warm glow. "As-
suredly there is some scheme afoot. Pembermore must have
expected to profit by arranging the match, but for my life I
cannot see how."

Gilbey smiled. "We thought that, too, Gillian did an admirable job of browbeating our solicitor into trying to unravel that. Unfortunately, we could not stay to find out
whether he succeeded."

"You browbeat solicitors, too?" Brinton said, turning
back to Gillian with a low whistle. "What a versatile young
woman you truly are, Miss Kentwell!"

Gillian was not sure if he was mocking her now or simply teasing. She felt the color rising in her face and hoped
the lantern light was dim enough to conceal it. "I did not
browbeat poor Mr. Worsley, I merely reminded him that
my brother will reach his majority soon, and that Gilbey
will have more power and wealth than our uncle once that
happens. I simply suggested that Mr. Worsley should take
care to see on which side his bread was buttered."

"I gather that this solicitor serves both you and your
uncle? We may untangle this coil yet."

Gillian could not seem to shake off her low spirits or
soothe the undefinable ache she felt as the trio proceeded to
settle in for the night. She supposed she ought to feel relieved; she had not wanted to believe that Brinton was
moved to help her and her brother only out of interest for
his inheritance. Yet somehow, she must have been hoping
for something more—some revelation of a personal interest
in her and Gilbey's fate. Brinton's marriage proposal had
quite clearly been prompted by guilt and a slavish devotion
to duty. How right she was to maintain a distance from him
now! Obviously, a few kisses under the stars meant nothing.

Gillian wrapped her cloak around her tightly and tried to
get comfortable in her bed of hay. The barn was surprisingly warm, thanks to the body heat of the nearby animals
and the soft protection of the hay. She was exhausted, but

still she did not manage to sleep right away. Her mind was too full.

Later in the night she awoke to hear Brinton coughing. She heard him get up and move about. A little light slipped into the barn when he opened the door, and then it was dark again as he went out, closing it behind him.

Listening, she realized that the rain had stopped. She could hear Brinton's coughing continuing faintly somewhere outside. She fought the urge to go to him. *He does not need comfort from me*, she told herself sternly. She burrowed deeper in the hay, biting her lip. She would keep her distance. After a long while of waiting to hear him return, she fell back asleep.

In the early morning they took their carriage into Shrewsbury. The little city was already bustling with traffic rattling through the narrow cobbled streets, splashing muddy water onto unwary pedestrians. After parting with their vehicle at the busy Lion Inn, the twins and Brinton carefully made their way to the New Raven in Castle Street. There the earl booked outside seats on the next available northbound coach for "Mr. Bradbury and his niece and nephew."

When it came time to depart, their beefy coachman was only too happy to hand "Miss Bradbury" up, giving her a pinch and a lascivious wink. Brinton and Gilbey put Gillian between them to protect her from such depredations by their fellow passengers.

"I cannot see any advantage whatsoever to traveling in proper dress," the girl grumbled between clenched teeth, linking her left arm through her brother's with some idea of preventing him from tumbling off in the event of erratic driving by their coachman. She was intensely aware of Brinton on her other side, pressed against her by the crowding of other occupants of the roof seats. Finally, there was the crack of the coachman's whip and with a sudden lurch and a jingle of harness, they set off.

The day's journey was long and wearying, covering some ninety miles measured by the passing hours and stops at tollbooths, stops at inns, and the continuous march of mileage markers all along the turnpikes. At every stop

Brinton and the twins watched guardedly for suspicious strangers asking questions or any other indication that they were being sought.

Gillian secretly believed that it would be impossible for anyone not to remember Brinton if he were described to them, as he cut such a dashing figure. She prayed that Orcutt might not pursue their case, although even such a sheltered country lass as she was knew the reputation of the persistent Bow Street Runners.

Ignoring the unavoidable pressure of Brinton's body against hers used a great deal of her energy as the day progressed, added to her worrying about Orcutt. So did ignoring the behavior of their coachman, who seemed to relish every opportunity he had to handle her. She was relieved of that burden, at least, when they changed drivers.

The new coachman lacked the jovial good humor of his predecessor, but he appeared to find young women reduced to riding outside seats on coaches common and quite beneath his notice. Indeed, the fellow seemed interested only in speed. He missed no opportunities to spring the horses on straight stretches of road. His solution to deep mud was to run up on the roadbanks, tipping the coach so that passengers and luggage all hung in the balance for long seconds until the vehicle regained the flat ground and righted itself. Gillian found herself clinging to Gilbey with both hands, while Brinton held tightly to her.

It was dark before the coach stopped for the night at the Green Man in Preston. The sensation of tilting, rocking, and bouncing aboard the coach for an entire day followed Gillian to bed. There she dreamed that she and Brinton were careening down an unknown road in a coach with no driver and no horses.

No one questioned the identity of the northbound passengers in Preston, and the travelers started off again in the morning with somewhat lighter spirits. Another good day's traveling would see them to the Scottish border.

Their new driver was a singer with a taste for drinking songs and bawdy ballads. He encouraged the lusty enthusiasm of his rooftop passengers, inviting them to join him on the choruses. Their lively tunes floated out across the countryside as the coach bowled along, flirting with the Lancaster canal that danced close to the road at times and then lodged away, only to return again.

Time slipped by easily and they reached Lancaster itself by midmorning. Tucked between the canal and the River Lune, the ancient streets twisted haphazardly beneath the austere walls of Lancaster Castle, sitting grimly at the top of its hill. The coach rattled over the cobbles past the market square and pulled in at the Half Moon, where the horses would be changed for the second time and the passengers refreshed.

"I think I would prefer to walk a bit," Gillian said, and Gilbey concurred.

"My legs could use stretching, too," Brinton agreed, promptly joining them.

They strolled along the street near the inn, peering in shop windows. The innyard was bustling with activity and they had no desire to be in the way.

"Mmm. I may be more in need of refreshment than I thought," Gilbey said, stopping in front of a confectioner's shop.

Gillian had moved on to admire a display of ladies' accessories in the next window. A glittering array of decorated fans was artfully arranged against the drape of a Kashmir shawl. Among the fans were several she thought quite attractive. The one she most particularly liked was surprisingly ornate, its leaf of blush pink silk painted with garlands of flowers and inset with a panel of lace. Tiny silver spangles were scattered along the edge and strategically placed within the pattern of flowers and lace. The ivory sticks were pierced in a delicate design, further enhanced by touches of silver leaf. The effect might have been overpowering in a larger fan, but in this, the smallest of the fans displayed, it was quite taking.

As Gillian studied it, thinking back to the assembly in Bath, Gilbey and the earl caught up to her.

"I am surprised to think that these would catch your eye, Gillie," Gilbey said.

"Perhaps you underestimate your sister," Brinton said enigmatically. "Tell us, Miss Kentwell, which one do you prefer?"

For some reason the earl's question sounded to Gillian

like a test. "They are all quite lovely," she answered tentatively. "I suppose the choice depends upon the occasion for which it is intended to be used."

"Bravo," Brinton replied dryly. "That was an admirable effort to avoid answering. Perhaps you may yet become a typical coquette."

Gillian bristled. "I have no desire to ever do that! If you truly wish to know, I was admiring that tiny pink one with the lace. It would be very suitable for a ball or assembly."

Brinton's eyebrows shot up, and he smiled. "Ah, I am relieved. I was afraid you had given up your habit of speaking frankly."

Gillian felt her color rise and saw his smile turn into a grin. Why did he always enjoy needling her so?

"I quite agree with your choice," he went on. "It is diminutive and exquisite, much like the young lady who should carry it." In a single graceful motion, he captured her right hand and raised it to his lips, pressing a quick, courtly kiss upon it to emphasize the compliment.

Gillian was amazed that the back of her hand could burn so just from the pressure of that simple kiss through the fabric of her glove. She was even more surprised at Brinton's sudden change of behavior, although she told herself she shouldn't be. She thought they had both been striving to maintain a wall of indifference between them, yet here was Brinton, doing his best suddenly to tear it down again. How was she supposed to react?

Gilbey saved her the trouble by looking back toward the inn, where their coach could be seen standing in the yard. "I suspect we should be returning," he said. "It looks as though the change is finished and the other passengers are already coming back out." With a speaking glance at Brinton, he linked his arm rather possessively through his sister's and began to propel her back toward the inn.

"Oh, it is too bad," Gillian lamented, moving her feet reluctantly. "There is a bookshop just two doors farther up."

Brinton followed a few steps behind them.

"I never thought I'd see you interested in fans," Gilbey said, not troubling to hide his amazement.

Gillian frowned thoughtfully. "Nor did I. But lately I have come to realize that I am woefully ignorant of a great deal that I ought to have learned. Did you ever think that perhaps Father did not do so well by us, allowing us so much freedom?"

"What do you mean?"

"He seldom cared what we did. We took that indulgence as a sign of his love." She dropped her voice to a whisper. "But, Gilbey, I don't believe I know anything at all about being an adult. That scares me."

Her twin gave her a look that was hard to read, but he made no reply. They were approaching the busy stable yard of the inn, and it was no place for a private conversation. Quite suddenly, Brinton caught Gilbey by the coatsleeve, checking their steps.

"Look," he said softly, "there is Orcutt and another gentleman, talking with our driver."

Chapter Fourteen

"What are we going to do? We can't let them see us!" Gillian whispered in horror. She stepped backward, bumping squarely against Brinton and landing off-balance on the toe of his top boot.

"Whoa there," the earl said, grasping her by the shoulders and steadying her. "We may already be too late, but let us turn our backs and stroll casually away as if we have no connection with the place."

Gillian resisted looking over her shoulder with difficulty. "Do you suppose they will go away and we will still be able to claim our seats?"

"That's going to depend on what they learn from our coachman," Brinton answered.

"If they suspect we are passengers, they will no doubt wait for us to appear," Gilbey added gloomily.

"And the coach will have to leave without us," Gillian finished. "What then of our luggage?"

"One hopes they will carry it—what there is left of it—on to Carlisle, even without us. After all, we did book passage through that far," the earl replied. He glanced back, and his eyes narrowed. "I strongly suggest we start considering alternate transportation."

The twins followed his glance and saw their coachman climbing up to his seat, still shaking his head. Orcutt and the other man with him stepped back, but showed no sign of leaving the vicinity. The coachman cracked his whip and with a flick of the ribbons started the new team out of the yard.

"Time to shop," said Brinton, guiding the twins ahead of him into a concealing doorway.

As the coach rattled past, Gillian was absorbed in the

splendid variety of porcelain and pottery displayed inside on the shop's shelves. She had just picked up a porcelain candleholder when Brinton took it from her hands and replaced it on the shelf.

"We need a carriage, not a candlestick." So saying, he turned to the shopkeeper and, after a brief exchange of information, ushered the twins out of the shop. Hurrying them along the street, he said, "We are going to hire the fastest vehicle we can get from the stables at the Selby Arms. It is only a block from here."

"I would like to know how Orcutt turned up here," Gilbey interrupted. "He had to have already been here ahead of us, checking all the coaches."

"From Bewdley he must have gone to Shrewsbury, too," said Brinton thoughtfully. "But if he rode through the night, or even the next night, he could have gotten well ahead of us."

"Do you think that is another Bow Street agent with him?"

"Yes. I suspect that they use some message system, like carrier pigeons, to inform each other of developments in their cases. We used pigeons on occasion during the war."

"Ah," said Gillian. "That might explain how Orcutt already knew about us in the little time it took us to get to Worcester. I had found that rather frightening and inexplicable."

"It still does not explain why they assumed we would head north," Gilbey observed.

As they reached the corner, all three could not help an anxious glance back toward the Half Moon.

"Damn," said Gilbey.

"Indeed," said Brinton, hastening his steps. It appeared that Orcutt had caught sight of them, or at least he and his friend were heading in their direction. Gillian doubled her pace to keep up with the lengthening strides of her companions.

"We have two choices," Brinton stated, apparently quite calm. Gillian's own heart was racing with apprehension. "We can try to reach the stable at the Selby Arms before they come around the next corner and catch sight of us again, or we can look for a way to double back and hire transport at the Half Moon."

"I think we would be less easy to recognize if we split up," Gilbey suggested.

"A good idea," Brinton agreed. "If you will stay with your sister, I will try to get back to the Half Moon. You'll need to wait for me somewhere out of sight."

"Did we not pass an alley just before the china shop?" asked Gillian. "If it cuts through to this block, we can slip back that way. But we had better hurry."

Orcutt and his accomplice did not round the corner before their quarry gained the alleyway. The earl and the twins checked the street carefully before they emerged at the alley's other end. Brinton quickly made for the stable yard of the Half Moon, while Gilbey and Gillian scurried up the street to the bookshop, where they would wait for the earl.

"Don't stand right by the window, Gilbey," Gillian hissed as she pretended to peruse the pages of a book on self-improvement. "What if Orcutt should happen by and see you?"

"What if Brinton comes with the carriage and we don't see him?" her brother countered, but he moved away from the panes. Selecting a hefty volume on the art of trout fishing, he kept one wary eye on the street outside.

Gillian was intensely aware of the ticking clock at the back of the shop. It seemed as if whole minutes passed between each sharp click of the brass movement. She jumped and nearly dropped her book when the chime struck the half hour. Her heart had barely recovered when she heard Gilbey's terse report, "Here he is." The twins hastily left their books and hurried outside.

Brinton sat in the coachman's seat of a rather weary-looking barouche. The pair of horses harnessed to it were mismatched but apparently sound, Gillian noted as Gilbey folded down the steps for her. She clambered up, but just as her brother followed, they heard a shout from farther up the street.

"Hold there! Stop!" Orcutt and his fellow had come back around the corner and were running toward them.

Brinton slapped the ribbons vigorously and Gilbey

barely managed to fall into his seat as the carriage started up. They barreled up the street, forcing pedestrians to dodge out of their way. They rumbled right past the angry Bow Street agents.

Orcutt did not waste time shaking angry fists at them, however. As the barouche rounded the corner on two wheels, the hapless trio in it could see the two men racing toward the Half Moon, presumably to grab their mounts.

"They will be after us in a minute," Gillian despaired. "How will we ever outrun them in this?"

"This was the only vehicle the ostler would let me take without a post-boy," Brinton explained. "However, I did manage to contrive a small delay."

The twins were astonished to hear him chuckle.

"I found the boy who had charge of Orcutt's horse, and also his friend's. I told him those two were in the taproom up to their elbows in port and not likely to be out anytime soon, so he might as well unsaddle the beasts and put them to feed. I'm afraid I felt he deserved a handsome tip, to off-set Orcutt's displeasure when he discovers what I've done."

Gillian and Gilbey had to laugh, if somewhat nervously. The delay would help, but three people in a carriage could not move as quickly as two men on saddle horses.

"What will we do now?" Gillian asked apprehensively. "Even with the delay, we cannot possibly outrun them to the border."

"The regular north route follows the turnpike from here to Heron Syke near Burton and on into Westmoreland. But I've learned that there is another route, the Oversands Route, that runs from Hest Bank across the bay to Furness."

Brinton was silent for a moment as he guided the horses through an intersection clogged by a carter's wagon and a private coach. As they reached clear road, the animals surged forward, as if they could sense the urgency of their mission. Brinton raised his voice to carry over the noise of pounding hooves and rattling carriage.

"The Oversands Route is considered very hazardous because of quicksand and the fast change of tides in the bay. The drivers who use it know the route well, or they have to hire guides to take them across. Near the change of tide, it is not safe to start across. However, if the tides are in our favor, I thought it might be worth the risk to go that way. Orcutt might follow the other route, not realizing we'd have turned off."

"What if the tide has already changed?" Gillian asked quite reasonably. She nearly had to shout to be heard.

"Yes, what about that?" echoed Gilbey. "If we go that way and cannot get across, we would have to return to the other route, and could run right into Orcutt!"

"I asked in the stables if they had any idea of the tides," Brinton replied. "One fellow had just come up from St. George's Quay. He said the river was low, but he thought it was still dropping. If he is right, that is the best news for us."

Gillian considered the risks before answering. She was surprised to realize that she no longer resented the earl's leadership. It was a role he fell into naturally, she had come to understand, and she and Gilbey had fared well enough thus far by following his dictates. "We have to try *something*," she agreed at last. "I, for one, have no other ideas to offer."

"How far to the turn-off for Hest Bank?" asked Gilbey.

"It should be no more than two or three miles. That is why I think we have a good chance to lose Orcutt."

The road was good and the horses were fresh. In very little time indeed the barouche had crossed the canal beyond Lancaster. The little party of fugitives made good time until suddenly Brinton slowed the horses with an unmannerly oath.

Gillian and Gilbey peered around him to see what was wrong. Just ahead, a road crew of ragged men was making a passing effort to repair the highway. One man had just dumped his barrowful of stones, and the others were variously spreading these with shovels or breaking them up into smaller bits with picks and long hammers. Beyond them a lane branched off to the left, but the signpost was down, neatly laid by the side of the road

"How far to the turn for Hest Bank?" Brinton called. His casual tone betrayed not a hint of impatience.

"This be it 'ere, sir," one of the laborers answered, respectfully tipping his cap.

"Any chance we might possibly get by?"

Gillian marveled at his perfect control. Her own frustration at the delay was so close to boiling over, she knew she would have screeched like an old woman.

The fellow set his shovel against the banking and flapped his arms rather comically at the other workers. "See 'ere, let's let 'em through!" he called. One by one, the others left off their activity and took themselves out of the way.

The carriage bumped erratically over the broken bits of stone as Brinton eased the horses between the men and made the turn. He held the animals to a leisurely pace until they had progressed a little way down the road from the workmen.

Gillian peered back anxiously, trying to catch a glimpse of the road they had left. "There does not appear to be anyone following," she reported, letting out her breath.

"That is good," Brinton called back, "but that road crew may be a mixed blessing. With the signpost down, Orcutt may nip right past without noticing or realizing its significance. He may not know about the other route. But if he stops to inquire after us, the men will most certainly point out our way."

"Let us pray for the tide," Gilbey said.

They were headed now toward Morecambe Bay. As they topped a rise, the spectacular panorama of the bay lay spread before them. Miles of shining, flat, wet sand stretched almost to the horizon, where a thin, bright silver thread of water reflected the light from the overcast sky. Seabirds like tiny dots in the distance skimmed close to the sand, hunting for prey trapped in hundreds of pools and rivulets. To the north the misty hills of Furness and the lake country framed the view.

"The tide is definitely out," observed the earl.

The vastness of the sand beds impressed Gillian. She could imagine just how quickly the water might suddenly start to pour in again across such a huge, level area. "Let us hope we are not too late to cross," she added fervently.

The village of Hest Bank, grown up from the mere fishing village it had once been, clustered by the side of the Lancaster canal, which wound its way along the high ground above the beach and marshes. The grandly named Hest Bank Hotel was the headquarters for coaching activity and served also as a rescue station for travelers trapped in the bay by the tides. Brinton pulled in at the inn's stable block.

Gillian listened anxiously as the earl questioned the ostlers about attempting the crossing. It seemed to her that the four miles they had traveled from Lancaster had been the longest miles of her life.

"Can take two hours t' Kent Bank," one man said dubiously.

"You're close to bein' too late," said another. "You'll need a guide who don't need t' come back t'day."

"Is there anyone who would take us?" the earl asked. Gillian thought an edge had crept into his voice. "And will we need fresh horses?"

The first ostler cast a disdainful eye over their unimpressive equippage. "These should do," he said judiciously. "'Tis a light carriage. You're just up from Lancaster?"

"Yes," Brinton answered tersely. He waited without moving. Gillian found it impossible not to fidget and pace. It seemed to her that the more time they spent talking, the less likely it was that they would still have enough time to go.

"Jem Greenall might take ye over," one man said at last. "'E's in the tap havin' one afore 'e goes back."

Brinton wasted no time heading for the inn's taproom, but Gillian admired his restraint in not sprinting. She could see in the way he held his shoulders that he was suffering from the tension as greatly as she was, although he appeared outwardly calm. Knowing that somehow made her feel better.

Gilbey took her arm and matched his restless pacing to her own. Within a stone's throw of the stables a canal barge was being poled along the narrow water passage. Birds sang in the trees, and the world seemed slow and peaceful, utterly heedless of the urgency Gillian felt in her breast.

"Where is he?" she whispered to her brother as they walked. "Why doesn't he come back out?"

After what seemed an eternity, Brinton emerged with another man in tow. He nodded to the twins, who quickly joined him in front of the stables.

"Permit me to present Mr. Newcroft, who has agreed to

guide us over," Brinton said. "Mr. Greenall seemed in doubtful condition to guide anyone, but Mr. Newcroft has just brought over several vehicles, and he is anxious to get back while there is still time."

Newcroft was a beefy man in his mid-forties, with the roughened look of someone who spent a great deal of his time out of doors. Gilbey extended his hand for a hearty shake, and the four of them climbed aboard the barouche. Newcroft took over the driver's seat, and Brinton sat in front of the twins, facing them and the rear of the carriage.

"You gentlemen may have to walk alongside when we get to the beach," Newcroft cautioned as he started the horses.

"The devil!" exploded Brinton as they turned into the roadway. The others looked at him in astonishment. "I think that's Orcutt!" He pointed up the road to a pair of riders coming into the village at a distance.

As Gilbey and Gillian craned their necks to look behind them, Brinton was speedily extracting pound notes from his purse.

"Here, man," he said urgently, pressing the notes into the startled driver's hand. "You'll have to pay to get this rig returned to the Half Moon in Lancaster, and the rest is for your trouble. We're going to jump ship, but we want you to go on as if you still had us aboard. Think you can keep ahead of those horsemen until it is too late for them to turn back?"

Newcroft glanced in bewilderment at the crumpled notes in his hand and back over his shoulder at the two approaching riders, who apparently had not yet recognized the barouche. "I'll give it my best try, sir," he said.

"What exactly are we doing?" Gillian asked, not quite as puzzled as the driver.

"Do you think you can jump while the carriage is moving?" asked Brinton.

"Of course," she answered at once.

The carriage was already starting across the narrow canal bridge. Behind them, they heard a shout. Ahead of them, the road zigzagged abruptly before starting the descent to the bay. Stone walls lined both sides of the road.

"When we take the curve, we will have to leap onto the

wall and drop down behind it," the earl explained quickly. "There won't be much time."

The twins nodded. Gillian's heart was racing.

"Gilbey, you first, as soon as he's in the curve. I'll follow with Gillian." He paused, waiting for the carriage to slow for the turn. "Now!"

Gilbey leaped, and Gillian thought the image of him poised for that fraction of a second on top of the wall with his greatcoat flapping would be etched in her mind forever. He dropped from sight instantly, and then Brinton had her hand and was urging her to move.

"On three," he commanded. "One, two, three!"

It did not matter if the rocks at the top of the wall were stable or uneven, for they barely touched them. Gillian thought that she and Brinton in their travel cloaks must have looked like great, ungainly birds fluttering out and over the wall—that is, if anyone had been looking. She fervently hoped the back of the barouche had screened them from view as it rounded the curve.

She and Brinton lay sprawled in a tangle of long grass and briars. Her cloak was held fast by thorns in several places, and her skirt was hiked up to her knees, exposing her legs in their embroidered silk stockings. As she made a move to sit up and pull herself together, Brinton stopped her with a hand on her arm. Silently, he shook his head, one finger on his lips.

Listening, she heard the commotion of their own carriage passing another vehicle in the narrow lane. Then the other driver hailed the bridge, announcing his intention to cross even as he proceeded. Gillian heard muffled curses at the bridge and assumed they came from Orcutt and the man with him. Brinton grinned at her. He had not, however, removed his hand from her arm.

They lay still and silent for what seemed like interminable minutes, until they heard the clatter of horses crossing the bridge toward them and taking the corner a little too fast. Gillian shrank down into the brush, willing the riders not to glance over the wall and wishing for invisibility with all her heart. She only breathed once she heard the horsemen pass and continue on down the road, heading for the bay.

Even then, Brinton was cautious. He signaled her to stay as she was. Plucking his cloak from the clutch of the briars, he got to his knees and peeked over the top of the wall. Relief filled his face as he sank back into a sitting position. "I believe we are clear, at least for the moment," he said, and he gave Gillian a smile that would have melted the very stiffest resistance.

In that smile she saw a world of warmth and affection mixed with his relief. Under its spell for that moment, she quite forgot to be concerned about where her brother was, or whether her garters were showing.

"Pluck to the bone, that's my Gillian," the earl said softly, reaching with both hands to help her move. "Are you all right?"

She nodded, tugging her cloak free before she put her hands in his. He pulled her gently to a sitting position, then suddenly, somehow, she found herself in his arms. She was not even surprised.

His kiss was gentle and reassuring, demanding nothing, but it instantly rekindled her own desire to give. When he pulled his head away, she was not yet ready to make an end. She held her position, her head tilted up to him, her lips parted, inviting him back. He hugged her against his chest for a moment, then released her and scrambled to his feet.

"All this and such shapely legs, too," he teased, taking the edge off her disappointment. He reached for her hand and helped her up. At that moment there was a rustle of grass, and Gilbey appeared, crawling on his hands and knees.

"Oh, are we safe, then?" he asked, color flooding his face in embarrassment. He stood up hastily, brushing the grass and soil from his knees. "What do we do now?"

Brinton cast his smile on Gilbey. "First, we pray that our friends won't catch up to Mr. Newcroft too soon. They haven't a guide, so let us hope that they are not too familiar with the route. Picking their way should slow them considerably."

"Second, I suggest we eat! These acrobatic stunts have sharpened my appetite." The twins nodded in agreement.

"After that, we will hire mounts and see if we can make it to Scotland by nightfall. Are you up to it?"

Gilbey grinned and nodded some more, his blond hair falling forward over his eyes. As he brushed it back, Brinton thumped him enthusiastically on the back.

"Well done, old man," the earl said approvingly. He turned to Gillian and did not see Gilbey wince.

"You, Miss Kentwell, were also superb. I heartily commend you both for performance under pressure."

Brinton and Gilbey climbed over the wall into the road and reached back to help Gillian. When they were all in the lane, they began walking up toward the bridge and the inn beyond it.

"However did you think so quickly of what to do?" Gillian asked Brinton.

"One learns to react quickly when habitually exposed to danger. That is one skill that can be acquired in His Majesty's service."

"How did you know it would work?" Gilbey questioned. They had stopped to let a farm cart cross the bridge ahead of them.

"I didn't," the earl said, surprising them. "It was the only thing I could think of. A show of confidence is one of the greatest secrets of command, you will learn someday."

An hour later, the trio sat on their hired horses at the top of a steep slope overlooking Morecambe Bay. They watched with interest the tiny figures of two horsemen who appeared to be struggling in pursuit of a slow-moving barouche. The carriage advanced steadily in the direction of the Kent Estuary and the dramatic hills north of the bay. In contrast the men, who were leading their mounts, gave every appearance of studying the sand and testing their footing after every few steps. They were quite far behind. Out in the bay, small channels of water had begun to be evident, showing silver among the vast sand flats.

"Do you think the tide is starting to turn?" Gillian asked, her concern audible in her voice.

"I would say so," Brinton responded. "Are you worried about them?"

"They still have quite a distance to go."

"They'll be all right, Gillie," Gilbey reassured her.

"I agree, Miss Kentwell. They have some time left. If they should need assistance in the last few minutes, they will be near enough to the shore then to obtain it."

"I would love to see their faces when they finally discover they've been chasing after Mr. Newcroft," Gilbey said and chuckled.

The earl turned his horse's head back toward the road. "Fascinating though it may be to watch them, we have a much greater distance to travel ourselves, if you wish to reach the border by tonight. We should push on."

The twins reined their horses around to follow him.

"I would gladly trade almost anything for a pair of breeches right now," Gillian said, adjusting her skirt and looking enviously at the men. "You cannot even begin to imagine how appalling the prospect of so many more hours in this sidesaddle appears to me."

Chapter Fifteen

Softened to silver by the overcast sky, the brightness of late morning shimmered over a pleasantly rolling landscape. Frisky new lambs cavorted in the fields, and stone walls marched over the hills like solid columns of well-disciplined soldiers. Along the main turnpike to Kendal, however, chickens scattered and farmers gathered their flocks to the side of the road as the twins and Brinton charged through.

None of the three fugitives had any doubt that the Bow Street agents would try to catch up to them. That shared assumption spurred them along the roads without needing to be openly addressed. They raced against unseen opponents—the relentless clock ticking away the daylight hours, and their equally relentless pursuers, somewhere behind them. How far behind they could not tell.

There were frustrating delays. Slow moving drays and every plodding ox cart in Lancashire seemed to be on the Kendal road this one day. Gillian often fell behind, handicapped by her clothing and saddle. Nonetheless, the trio managed to cover the remaining miles in reasonably good time.

"How much of an advantage do you think we have gained?" Gilbey asked as they awaited fresh steeds in the yard of the Highgate Inn.

"Perhaps an hour," Brinton answered uncertainly. "Orcutt and his friend needed that long to finish crossing the sands from where we saw them. But once they discovered our ruse, they would have wasted no time setting off again. They'll have to come around from Kent Bank to rejoin the main road here, but I do not know how long that will take them."

The newest obstacle that faced the trio was the lack of another sidesaddle for Gillian. The Highgate had none available. The resulting quandary called for a quick consultation among the three travelers.

"I cannot say that I am sorry," Gillian said. "A walking dress is not made like a riding habit. Can we not hire another barouche? I suppose a post-chaise would be far too slow."

Brinton shook his head. "I am afraid that any carriage is out of the question. Our purse has a bottom, and we are getting ever closer to it. The fact is, we have quite a significant distance yet to cover today. If we were to travel by carriage the rest of the way, we most likely would have to forgo bed and board."

"What else can we do? I cannot ride astride dressed as I am. I was barely managing on the sidesaddle."

The earl studied Gillian thoughtfully, holding his hat in one hand and absently running the other through his hair. His scrutiny made the girl blush. "Perhaps you will get your wish for breeches, after all, my dear." He turned his speculative gaze to the stable boys bustling about the busy innyard. "I suspect we might obtain a set of used clothing, not far from your size, for a great deal less than the extra cost of carriages from here clear to Scotland."

"The change may help us to throw Orcutt off again," Brinton added. "He must know that our luggage is well on its way to Carlisle, and he will be looking for you dressed as you were."

It took the earl very little time indeed to find a young stable boy who cared more for some ready money than he did for his spare work clothes. Gilbey and Brinton waited while Gillian changed in an empty tack room.

"Brinton, I can't believe you are having my sister don the clothes of some stable lad," Gilbey protested quietly. "God knows when they might last have been laundered, or what vermin might infest them!"

Brinton grinned. "If that is your only objection, I think you should put your mind at ease, Cranford. This is a respectable establishment, and I doubt they would allow filthy habits among their employees, any more than you would among your own servants."

Gilbey reddened. "That does not put my mind at ease," he blustered, "for I am sure you know that is not my only objection. However, I suppose we have no alternative."

Gillian emerged, dressed in a serviceable pair of breeches, a shirt of coarse linen and a striped jean waistcoat, stockings, cap, and a wool coat patched at the elbows. Her cloak, dress, and petticoat were draped over her arm. She smiled mischievously and affected the swaggering walk of a young groom. "And what, my lord, did you wish to have done with the young lady's things?" she asked in an equally affected accent.

Brinton smiled, but did not laugh. "Why, we'll bundle them up in that cloak and secure them to your saddle, lad," he said with an attempt at a serious expression.

Gilbey laughed in spite of his expressed disapproval. "Really, Gillie, you look like the oddest creature that ever came down the 'pike. Could it be the half boots that spoil the effect? But you do sound just like our Jamie."

They continued heading north from Kendal through pleasant, fertile land, and gradually ascended out of the valley. As the road continued to rise, the fields gave way to low, stunted trees and a landscape of bracken and heather. By the time they began the long, steep climb up Shap Fell, the barren hills wore only wild heath and peat moss. Spring had been left behind entirely. A cold, raw wind was plucking at their sleeves, and the sky had become leaden. The moisture in the air felt like a wet hand touching their faces.

The twins and Brinton walked to ease the horses. By the time they reached the summit, Gillian's muscles were aching from the exertion, and she noticed Brinton was coughing. They stopped just long enough for the earl to catch his breath. She thought it a blessing to remount her horse as they began the slow descent on the north side of the fell.

The venerable Greyhound Hotel in the village of Shap offered a welcome respite as well as a change of horses. However, Brinton removed his cloak and put it around Gillian before they entered the inn.

"I don't need it," she started to protest, but Brinton hushed her.

"It is not for warmth, love," he said, "It is to cover you.

If they get a good look at you, you will find yourself in the kitchen, or worse, in the stables."

He appeared not at all uncomfortable with their situation. He obtained a table for them in an out-of-the-way corner and commanded tea and biscuits. While they waited for it, he made conversation.

"Did you ever read any of Defoe's accounts of his travels about the country? He came through this part of the fells, from Kendal to Penrith and went on to Carlisle, just as we are. If I recall, he described these mountains as 'full of unhospitable terror', ninety years ago. Perhaps he didn't stop here."

Gillian looked around her with renewed interest. "I never knew Defoe was a traveler. I wonder if . . . " She did not finish.

"What?" asked her brother.

"I was thinking that Father's library at home was so extensive, perhaps he had a copy. But it really doesn't matter, does it?" she finished sadly.

"You are not having second thoughts about what we have done, are you, Gillie?"

She shook her head slowly, looking down at her hands. She had twisted her fingers together into a knot in her lap.

"A touch of homesickness, perhaps?" asked Brinton. His voice was soft with concern.

She nodded. She had suddenly begun to feel so tired and blue-deviled. She knew she would never see her home again, but that pain was now familiar. Something more was troubling her. Brinton's gentleness made her heart knot like her fingers, and she realized it had to do with leaving him. At the end of this day, if all went well, they would reach the Scottish border. She could not turn back, did not want to turn back, yet every mile now brought her nearer to the time when they would part. How would she feel once he was gone?

"I would gladly loan you my copy," the earl was saying, and then he paused awkwardly. "That is, I could send it to you . . . " His sentence trailed off, much as her first remark had done.

She summoned a weak smile. "That would be very kind of you. I may have a great deal of time for reading!" Were they all feeling uncomfortable about the parting to come? No one smiled at the comment she had meant to be light-hearted. When the tea arrived, they drank greedily and in silence.

There was little conversation as the trio, refreshed and mounted on fresh horses, progressed towards Penrith. Gillian was grateful, for her horse was skittish and her mind was busy with private thoughts. She remembered the antagonism she had felt for Brinton when she had first met him, and the suspicions she had harbored. When had the last lingering trace of those feelings disappeared? For try as she might, she found she could no longer summon any such negative emotions.

She knew that her life and his had only intersected for this brief time. Yet she kept remembering the moments they had shared in the forest while her brother slept. What had possessed them to share such intimate passions? Would such a thing have happened with anyone else? She could not say, but the idea seemed absurd.

She glanced up ahead, admiring the way he sat his horse, tall and graceful. How broad his shoulders were! Those shoulders had gradually taken on the burden of all her problems. For every obstacle that had confronted them, he had found a solution. His resourcefulness, his controlled, thinking approach, the commanding quality that she had disliked in him at first—these were aspects of him that she realized now she had not only come to value, but to depend upon. She thought guiltily that she had actually come to depend upon Brinton far more than she did her brother.

Gillian's thoughts were pulled back by her horse, who slowed down whenever her attention wandered from guiding him. The hedgerows were growing lusher as the road led downward, and he seemed to take an extraordinary interest in the delicacies to be found there. But she knew she could not fault the animal. She was distracted and fatigued. The muscles in her thighs were becoming increasingly shaky and refused to maintain the firm command she knew the horse was trained to expect. She settled herself and tried to focus on getting to Penrith. However, the road ahead seemed to unwind in endless miles of repetition.

She tried to fathom what Brinton might be feeling. Yesterday, when she had resolved to be cold to him, he had behaved with polite restraint. This morning she had forgotten her resolution in her relief at escaping from Orcutt, and Brinton had kissed her—briefly, it was true, but tenderly.

As she thought over the past few days, she realized that while he seemed to delight in teasing her, using her Christian name and generally behaving in a most improper way, he had never done so in front of her brother. *Until today*, she thought with a small smile. Today he had called her "my dear" in Gilbey's hearing, and at Shap he had called her "love." Did that signify anything?

She shook her head. How could anyone understand such a contrary person? The twisted knot in her heart seemed to be pushing tears up into her throat. The fact was, she had come to care greatly for him. In the days and weeks and months ahead, she would feel a great hole in her life. She would miss his perverse teasing and the wicked smile he seemed to keep just for her. It was not going to be easy to be swept off her feet by some brawny Scotsman, with Brinton haunting her heart.

The three weary travelers crossed the River Eamont, and a mile farther came finally into "Red Penrith." As they progressed through the narrow streets, they could see by the fine buildings of red sandstone how the town had come by its nickname.

"Better from that than from all the blood that must have spilled here," Gilbey commented with a grim smile.

Gillian shivered, for his reference to centuries of warfare with the Scots seemed only too real to her here. Growing up in Devonshire, she had been removed from considering anything about it. She was shocked to realize the last bloody troubles with Scotland had occurred within the space of her grandparents' lives. What a profound effect this must have had upon their thinking! Perhaps it was not so difficult after all to understand why both of her parents' families had refused to accept their marriage.

Did people in Scotland still hate the English? Would her aunt turn her away? Even if she did find a welcome there, would she be able to be happy? She felt the blood rush into her face as she recalled her foolish prattling to Brinton about Scotland as they had walked in Bath. What a child he must think her!

She looked up beyond the buildings toward the high, wooded slopes of Penrith's Beacon Hill, standing sentinel to the northeast as it had for centuries. Its solid presence seemed to symbolize the hard wall of reality she had just come up against. It felt like a warning of things to come.

The cloud-capped ranks of the Furness Fells and the Cumbrian Mountains stretched spectacularly to the west and stayed in sight for many miles as Gillian and her companions continued on the road toward Carlisle. They could not sustain the bruising pace they had set at the beginning of the day's journey, so they did not linger when they changed horses in the village of High Hesket. But all three stopped abruptly when they caught their first glimpse of the Solway Firth and the distant, mist-shrouded hills of Scotland. The late afternoon sun had managed to cast a few slanted rays beneath the clouds that had filled the sky all day, tinting the scene with soft, golden light.

"Look at that!" breathed Gilbey in awe. "Doesn't it prickle the back of your neck to finally be within sight of it?"

"We are still a good twenty miles from our destination," Brinton said dampeningly, "but I agree, there is still something exciting about seeing it."

Gillian stared and said nothing.

"Our Gillian is overcome, I think," the earl added, smiling at her. "Did Caesar feel like this on the brink of victory?"

Gillian gave him a rather tenuous smile in response and then urged her horse back onto the road. Her lack of reaction bothered Brinton, especially after the odd attitude of brittle brightness she had adopted since Penrith. He let her move ahead so he could exchange a word with her brother.

"Do you think we are pushing her too hard?" he asked. "I thought she would be more excited."

"As did I," Gilbey agreed. "I am certain she is exhausted, but she does not want us to know it. I doubt either of us can deter her from continuing; she seldom sways from a course once she is set upon it."

"I have noticed that."

"Sometimes," Gilbey added slowly, "she has to preserve an illusion in order to keep going. I have seen her carry through that way many times, just when you would think she could not do more. It might be best if we pretend not to notice."

"If you think so," the earl agreed reluctantly. He decided to let the twins ride ahead of him, where he could keep an eye on Cranford's sister.

They managed to continue on for several more miles before Gillian's rigid pose began to give way. The girl might be plucky and stubborn, Brinton thought, but she was obviously suffering. He spurred his horse to catch up to Gilbey.

"Look at your sister," he said tersely.

Gillian looked round at that moment to see what was going on behind her. Her pinched, white face and slumping posture clearly betrayed what she had not been willing to admit.

"Tell her my horse picked up a stone, or whatever you must," Brinton told Gilbey. "We can stop by that grove of trees just ahead." He let the viscount go ahead to rejoin his sister, and watched the hurried conference between the two. He held his horse to a very slow walk.

The Kentwells waited for him under the trees without dismounting.

"Your horse doesn't act as though he'd picked up a stone," Gillian said, eyeing him suspiciously.

"I am not certain that he has," the earl responded half truthfully. "I would like to check him now, before there is a problem." He swung down from his saddle, realizing for the first time how tired he felt himself. He began appropriate motions to check his horse's feet, but he kept his eye on the girl. Was she going to stay in her saddle?

Brinton heard the creak of leather as Gilbey dismounted, and only then did Gillian follow suit. She slid from her horse with a graceful, fluid motion that did not stop when her feet touched the ground. As he watched, her slight form continued its descent into a small, crumpled heap beside her horse.

Brinton was beside her before her brother could even move. She lay absolutely still. "What the devil is the matter with her?" he cried.

There was a note in the earl's voice that made Gilbey look sharply at the other man. He saw no trace of anger there, however. If anything, Brinton's face showed anguished concern—even panic, Gilbey thought—in contrast to his sharp words. And that, in itself, Gilbey found extremely interesting. He had assumed that nothing under the sun could cause panic in the coolheaded Earl of Brinton. He smiled.

"She has fainted, man, that's all. She'll come round in a minute."

"Fainted! That's 'all'. Your brotherly concern is overwhelming," the earl said dryly. He gathered Gillian into his strong arms and carried her small, limp form to the grass away from the horses. "What in God's name would cause this? Is it exhaustion?"

Brinton knelt beside Gillian and raised her head gently so that it rested against him. Gilbey watched as the earl brushed Gillian's hair back from her face. Brinton looked up at him when he didn't answer immediately, and Gilbey was shocked at the depth of emotion he saw in the earl's eyes.

"She needs food, my lord," he said, stumbling into formal address in the awkwardness of the moment. As much as he had been wondering how things stood between Brinton and his sister, Gilbey had not expected such a sudden and dramatic revelation of the state of Brinton's heart. The man was clearly in love with Gillian. Gilbey felt as embarrassed as if he had walked in on them in bed. "I should have recognized the signs when she started acting oddly," he added quickly. "The exhaustion just makes it worse."

"We must still be at least five miles from Carlisle," said Brinton, looking thoroughly distraught. "What should we do?"

Gilbey could hardly believe that the great, resourceful earl was asking *him* what to do. He was extraordinarily pleased that he did, in fact, have an answer. Recalling what Brinton had said just that morning about the secret of command, Gilbey straightened his shoulders and looked confidently at the earl.

"We have to get some food into her. If you will stay here with her, I shall go back to the last farmhouse we passed and obtain something for her." He looked at his sister cradled against the earl and felt his confidence falter for just a moment. "She should be coming out of it. This has happened before, but it has never lasted for long."

"I'll stay right here with her," Brinton reassured him. "I am certain you are right. The exhaustion has hit her hard along with this. We should have stopped to eat in Penrith. After all, what has any of us eaten since Hest Bank this morning? Nothing but tea and biscuits at Shap."

Gilbey turned to gather the reins of his horse, nodding his head in agreement. He felt very much to blame, but there was something comforting about having someone else share the fault. He realized that he not only admired Brinton, he trusted him. As he mounted and turned his horse to go back up the road, he pondered what he had discovered. Brinton loved his sister. But how did Gillie feel about Brinton?

As Gilbey's horse pounded up the road, Brinton settled himself on the flower-strewn grass and gently laid Gillian's head in his lap. He stroked her cheek with the back of his fingers, feeling the softness of her skin in the hollow beneath her cheekbone. He closed his eyes for a moment as his hand lingered there.

He had known anguish before; he had held comrades in his arms as the life bled out of them. He was feeling anguish now, but the pain was different—there was a tender sweetness mixed into it that made it almost unbearable. It was not an anguish born of worry, for he knew that Gillian would quickly recover. It was the heart-rending pain of holding the woman he loved and knowing that he could not have her.

He could not stop himself from touching her. He searched her face for signs of awakening, but the long sweep of her lashes remained still against her cheeks. His fingers roamed, exploring the silky texture of her hair and tracing the graceful curves of her lips. It took all of his strength not to gather her up against his body in a crushing embrace. He forced himself to be content with looking and touching, savoring this moment with her like a doomed man at his last meal.

"Miss Gillian Kentwell," he said, smiling down at her, his voice a ragged, accusing whisper. "It seems, after all, that it is you who has robbed me, although you will never know it! I have lost the confidence I had in my future. I do not know, now, how I am going to live my life without you in it."

Chapter Sixteen

Consciousness returned to Gillian with an inevitable headache and an equally sharp realization that her cheek was resting against someone's thigh. *Not Gilbey's,* she thought, struggling to focus her mind. A faint, familiar male scent gave her the answer she sought. *Brinton's.* Shocked at the intimacy of their position, she sat up abruptly.

The sudden movement was a mistake. Her head reeled, and she very nearly fainted again. A gentle pressure forced her back until she found she was resting against the earl again, but at least now her head was against his chest. She opened her mouth to speak, only to find a finger placed lightly against her lips.

"Stay still a moment, little one." Brinton's deep voice was infinitely soft and very, very close to her ear. His fingertip traced her lips tenderly, then stopped.

A tremor ran through Gillian. She knew he had felt it when his arm tightened slightly around her. She hoped he would attribute it to her upset state. She closed her eyes and let her head lean against the comforting, warm solidity of his body.

"You fainted when you got down from your horse," he explained quietly. "Your brother has gone to get you some food."

She opened her eyes again. "Gilbey?" She was amazed to discover she had not missed him.

"Have you any other?" The earl was smiling at her.

"No." She answered his smile with a little frown and made another attempt to sit up. His arm held her back without the slightest apparent effort.

"Are you certain that you are feeling strong enough to

stir?" he asked. "You may rest here until your brother comes if you wish. I promise to behave myself."

"I am feeling better," she lied. He might very well behave himself, but that would not prevent her from having her own reactions to their close contact. She was quite sure that she could manage to sit up. He did not need to know that she felt as weak as a newborn and too shaky to stand. As he released her, she pulled away and repositioned herself on the grass at a safer distance from him.

They sat in silence for a few moments. Gillian stared pointedly up the road, watching for her brother. Finally Brinton cleared his throat and spoke.

"Even if you rode astride when you were at home, Gillian, you cannot be accustomed to staying in the saddle for so many hours on end. We have covered more than forty miles this way today, which is admirable. But I think we will have to procure a carriage when we get to Carlisle."

Gillian did not know how to respond. She did not like to admit how welcome the prospect of a carriage sounded to her. She was not even certain she would be able to remount her horse to finish the last few miles to Carlisle.

"How much farther to the border?" she asked hopefully.

"Less than twenty miles, I believe. I think we can reach Gretna Green before dark."

She sighed. "What of our finances, Lord Brinton? Did you not say there could be no more carriages? And what of Orcutt? Do you think we are still enough ahead of him to allow ourselves the luxury of slower travel?" She forced herself to turn and look at him.

He smiled. She wished he would not, for that smile softened the aristocratic contours of his face, and deepened the little lines by the corners of his eyes. It made him look just the way she wanted to remember him, and that caused her pain. The morning would come all too soon.

"You still do not feel that you could call me Rafferty?" he asked wistfully.

She shook her head.

"You wound me, but I suppose I shall recover," he sighed. He plucked a few tiny white flowers from the grass and began to toy with them.

"I have come to the conclusion that I must obtain some

funds in Carlisle if there is any bank still open or any solicitor whom I could approach. We will have to retrieve our luggage, also. We will just try to accomplish these errands as quickly as we can, and keep our eyes open. Orcutt is still behind us, but there is no way of knowing how far."

Gilbey returned a few minutes later, and as Gillian ate, Brinton quickly outlined his plan. Gillian found it difficult to choke down the bread and cheese her brother had brought her, for despite her hunger, her throat was tight. Finally, when she was finished, the men collected the horses. Gilbey waited beside hers to help her mount.

With Brinton's assistance, she got to her feet. Try as she might, however, she could not get her legs to do what she wanted. Her knees were bowed, and her muscles refused to support her weight. Her bones seemed to have turned to butter. By her third step she would have sunk right to the ground, had not Brinton slipped his arm around her waist. Then the earl slid his other arm under her knees and lifted her.

He carried her toward Gilbey as if she weighed nothing. "Cranford, if you will mount, I'll put her up in front of you. She cannot ride another mile. We shall have to lead her horse."

So Gillian rode into Carlisle sitting sideways in front of her brother. The feel of Brinton's hands on her waist as he had put her up lingered in her mind and on her body; his hands had felt as strong and warm as ever, but they had been shaking. She did not know why.

In Carlisle Brinton's plan was executed with military preciseness and efficiency. The twins used the last of Brinton's funds to hire a cabriolet and an extra mount, and managed to locate the coaching inn where their luggage had indeed arrived on the coach from Preston. They reclaimed the bags and proceeded to wait for the earl in an alley off English Street, watching for signs of Orcutt or his fellow agent.

At length, Brinton found them. He patted the pocket of his coat, nodding his head. "This should see us there in style and get me home again as well," he said.

Gillian winced guiltily. Not once had she considered that after traveling well out of his way to escort them, the earl would still have his return trip to make alone. Her heart, already heavy, seemed to sink her even further into the squabs. She remained exceedingly quiet as they proceeded toward Scotland.

The goal Gillian had struggled so hard to reach struck her as ironically unimpressive. The landscape near the border consisted of wild, flat, barren moors and peat-brown streams that appeared nearly black in the waning daylight. The border itself was the narrow River Sark, crossed by a small, single-arched bridge with a tollbooth on the far side, soon left behind.

As the travelers approached the yard of the infamous Gretna Hall Hotel a half mile beyond, the lamps were just beginning to be lit. A porter with a lantern hurried to meet them, along with an ostler and two stable boys. Once they had taken charge of the animals and luggage, Brinton gathered Gillian into his arms, not caring what impression her unseemly appearance might make on the people around them, and ignoring her small squeak of protest.

"We shall require a private suite with two sleeping rooms, dinner, and three hot baths," he said in his most commanding voice. "I hope we are not too late in the day?"

The effect of his request was quite satisfactory. The porter, nodding the whole while, ushered them into the building, summoned several servants and issued a quick flurry of orders. He then turned to Brinton with an extra nod at the small figure in his arms.

"Would you be needing a 'blacksmith', sir? I did not realize at first that you had a young lady. It's not everyone who brings their own witness along, of course," he added, looking behind them at Gilbey, "unless, uh, that is . . . which one is the bridegroom?"

Gilbey's face had turned the brightest red Brinton had ever seen it. "Neither," the young viscount growled. "The young lady is my sister."

The earl spoke up quickly before the trio found themselves in a different sort of misunderstanding. "That's right," he added, "and I am their uncle. We are on our way to Dumfries. We would like to go right up to our rooms, please. I will come down again to sign the register." He decided to overlook the porter's impertinence rather than attract any further attention. He raised an eyebrow at Gilbey to warn him not to say more, then followed a chambermaid up the stairs. He asked her to send a young woman to attend to Gillian in her bath.

Later, after all three had bathed, changed, and eaten a lavish dinner, Gillian retired, leaving Brinton and Gilbey to their own company and the bottle of port they had ordered to follow their meal.

"I have never seen my sister quite so done in," Gilbey said, accepting a glass from the earl. "She was every bit as wobbly as a new foal."

Brinton smiled at the analogy. "That she was. However, I am certain that she will be fully recovered in the morning. How are you faring, Cranford? It has been a difficult journey for you—first your knee, then your ribs."

"I'm better now, after soaking." A serious expression came over Gilbey's face. "I was going to say, we are indebted to you for hiring the carriage. In the morning I suspect both Gillie and I will be nearly as glad to have it as we were this evening. That strikes me as a singularly inadequate thing to say, however. We are indebted to you for ever so much more."

"You needn't say anything," Rafferty replied. "In fact, I would rather you did not."

Gilbey's gratitude, especially here, of all places, made the earl feel like a fraud. The porter's impertinent assumptions when he realized that Gillian was female had only served to remind Brinton of his own assumptions when he had first met the twins. Archie would never have made the ridiculous bet with him if he had not first planted the idea of Gretna Green in Archie's head. Without the added impetus of the wager, Brinton was not certain that he would have gotten himself involved with the young runaways at all beyond that first night.

"I have no wish to embarrass you," the young viscount insisted. "It's just that, well, I am sorry that we must part in the morning. I have never spent six days so completely in the company of anyone, other than my sister, nor have I ever faced such odd and challenging circumstances and obstacles." He paused awkwardly, looking down at the glass of port he held suspended between his knees. "Without you we would have been lost. I will gladly repay you the funds you have expended on us, but we can never repay the friendship you have extended. Have I at least a small hope that when I am back in Devonshire, our paths might cross occasionally, if you visit your uncle?"

Brinton swallowed, his throat suddenly thick. Cranford's earnestness touched him deeply, but he knew that he could no longer predict that part of his future. "I cannot say, Cranford," he replied honestly. "If my role in what we have done should ever become known, it is highly unlikely that I would find myself in Devonshire. The scandal would make me quite persona non grata in any place where my uncle has connections."

He hesitated, looking at the lad's bowed head. How much should he say? Should he confess his feelings for the viscount's sister? "I would venture to say that, in the six days we have traveled together, we have all come to know one another quite well. I shall miss both you and your sister."

Gilbey had been staring into his glass, swirling the contents around the sides. Now he looked up suddenly, meeting Brinton's eyes. The earl sighed and plunged ahead.

"As I believe you have guessed, my feelings for your sister have gradually surpassed those of mere friendship. I would be less than candid with you, Cranford, if I did not admit that those feelings are a great source of torment for me. Consider the potential for scandal that already exists from my limited involvement with the pair of you. How much greater would such a scandal be if my involvement were anything deeper? It is unthinkable to risk exposing her to such a thing.

"Of even greater concern, however, is the immutable fact that I would never be able to offer your sister the kind of life she has built her hopes and dreams around. How could I love her and deny her the future she desires? Clearly, I cannot. So I think it best that she should never know how I feel. Because I know you also value her happiness, I have faith in you to keep my confidence."

Brinton drained his glass. "Will you have another?" he asked Gilbey on his way to the bottle.

Gillian's twin shook his head. "I've had enough."

"How about to save me from drinking all the rest myself?"

"All right, one more," Cranford relented, holding up his glass.

By morning Brinton had decided to continue with the Kentwells as far as their aunt's. He had wrestled with his choice for a good part of the night, weighing the painful cost of prolonging his departure against the pain of not knowing if Gillian had safely reached her final destination. He owed what little sleep he had gotten to the quantity of port he had consumed, and he faced the day with a cheerful front to hide both headache and heartache.

"I realized I could not go on my merry way without knowing the final outcome of your journey," he explained to Gilbey and Gillian at breakfast. "It would be too much like reading a long, involved book, only to discover the last pages are missing."

Gilbey openly expressed his pleasure, but Gillian was uncharacteristically quiet. She had emerged from her chamber transformed back into the stylish young lady who had dined at the farm near Shrewsbury. In fact, Rafferty noted, her blue-gray walking dress had been pressed and mended, and she had taken the time to thread matching ribbons through her hair.

"It is an improvement over the rumpled muslin I wore at dinner, is it not?" she had asked them anxiously.

"You look every inch respectable this morning, Gillie," responded her brother. "The innkeeper's staff will never recognize you."

"Thank you so much," she answered dryly. "I am sure that's just as well. But I am hoping that perhaps Aunt Elizabeth will. People do say I somewhat resemble Mama."

"You far surpass mere respectability," said the earl. "Your mother must have been a very beautiful woman."

Gillian smiled, but without her usual radiance. It was not surprising, Brinton thought. With so much depending upon the reception she would receive at her aunt's, she undoubtedly felt nervous. He wondered if the twins had given any thought at all to what they would do if their aunt turned

them away. It was that nagging question, more than anything else, that had convinced him to stay the extra day.

After breakfast Gillian paced listlessly as the trio waited
for their carriage down in the stable yard. The earl stopped
her with a touch on her shoulder.

"You will wear yourself out before our day's travels
have begun," he cautioned.

The girl nodded, crossing her arms and hugging herself
as if she were chilled to the bone. She was clad once again
in her traveling cloak, its hood raised against the morning
mist, but its open front failed to conceal her gesture.

"Cold?" Brinton asked, painfully remembering another
time when he had asked her that.

"I suppose," she answered him distractedly.

The weak promise of sunshine seen at the end of the previous day had not been fulfilled; the morning was gray and
dark, the mist heavy but not quite rain. Still, the air lacked
the bite it would have held in earlier weeks. The earl suspected that Gillian's chill came more from her emotional
state than from any external discomfort.

"We will have them close in the front of the carriage," he
said, studying her. "That will help to keep out the damp-
ness, although I am not altogether convinced that will help
you."

She sighed and began pacing again. After one full cir-
cuit, she stopped beside him. "I should apologize for being
such a peagoose. I am never good at hiding my feelings.
Now that we have come so far, I am ashamed to admit I am
terrified."

"What? This from the woman who has braved robbers
and Bow Street and the rigors of traveling four hundred
miles?" He turned to Gilbey, who appeared quite at ease,
lounging against a hitching block. "Cranford, what are we
to do with her?"

Gilbey gave him a weak smile. "Why, Brinton, no one
has ever been able to do anything with her, that's just the
problem."

Brinton took Gillian's hand and linked her arm through
his. Following the invisible track she had already begun to
wear into the paving stones, he walked with her.

"Miss Kentwell," he admonished her. "You have come

Gail Eastwood

so far, I cannot believe your courage is flagging now. What obstacles have you left to overcome? A paltry few miles, and an aunt you have never met, the Countess of—what is it?"

"Aunt Elizabeth is Countess of Culcarron."

"Right. Now, I have come to know that you are a woman of rare determination. There is nothing that will stop you from covering those miles today, so that leaves only your aunt to overcome. You do not know that she will not welcome you warmly, but even if she should not, I have every confidence that you will win her over. Is she not your mother's sister? How much of an ogre could she be? You must summon the courage that has temporarily deserted you and hold up your head with confidence. You must sail up to her door like a proud ship under full canvas, not like the sad, shredded remains of a shipwreck."

"You are right," she sighed. "I shall try to do better."

It took the trio three hours to reach Dumfries. Mist obscured their surroundings and spoiled the views of the Solway and the Cumbrian Mountains to their south. Only the peculiar odor of turf smoke was distinct along the way, drifting over the hedges of privet and sweet willow.

They did not tarry, although there was much to admire in Dumfries. They hired a landau and sat back against the cushioned squabs of its closed interior, leaving the damp job of navigation to their postboy. They crossed the River Nith and soon found themselves following it northward into the hills. The mist seemed to dissipate, settling into unseen crevices and valleys.

Gillian's attempt to rally her spirits had succeeded quite well, Brinton thought with a peculiar mixture of heartache and satisfaction. He sat facing her and Gilbey, so he missed none of the expressions that flitted across her face. She peered out the window of the carriage constantly, only turning to him or her brother occasionally to comment on what she could see. For his own part, he preferred the sweet torture of watching her, although he, too, occasionally looked out at the passing countryside.

"Is this more like what you imagined Scotland would be?" Brinton asked her.

The smoothly rounded hills were gaining stature as the carriage continued northward, resembling waves in a rising, rolling sea. The touch of spring was slow here, and a pale, infant green was just starting to creep up from the valley meadows into the velvet patchwork of bronze and tan on the slopes.

"Yes," she answered, a little breathlessly. "Do you not find it beautiful?"

He had to agree that it was. He could easily imagine hunting grouse among these hills, or walking the hilltops just for the pure pleasure of the views.

For a moment he was seduced into imagining coming back here to visit her, but he knew that was a foolish delusion. He knew he was right to step out of her life—he could never force the requirements of his own future upon such a free spirit. There was something special between them—something very like love had actually started to grow. The only way to stop it was to cut it off completely at the root, before it was too late for either of them to recover.

The carriage halted quite suddenly. Brinton stuck his head out to discover what was the matter.

"We've come to the split at Carronbridge," their postboy called back from his perch on the lead horse. "Would you wish a quick turn up the road, to see the Duke of Queensberry's estate?"

"No," replied Brinton after a confirming glance at his companions. Despite the pleasures of the beautiful countryside, there was tension within the carriage, and a trace of strain could be discerned in both twins' faces. All three travelers knew that they were now within minutes of arriving at their destination.

The landau began to move again, following the other road up out of Nithdale. The land to the right gradually began to drop away into a ravine, and the carriage turned left up a steep drive lined with trees.

Gillian and Gilbey craned their necks to catch a first glimpse of Carron Park. Through the trees and mist, it appeared like a pink toy castle. The house itself was of modest proportions, as the trio discovered when the landau pulled up to the door. Its stables and outbuildings had been cleverly designed to appear as integral parts of the turreted structure. A double stairway led up to an imposing entrance, but a smaller door set between the stairs was opened by a bewigged footman as the passengers stepped down from their carriage.

Brinton stayed behind a moment to attend to the unloading of their luggage, so he did not see the diminutive, gray-haired woman who emerged from the doorway. When he turned around, she was already there, inspecting the twins who stood silent and still, quite as if rooted to the ground. The first thought that flew into his mind was, *Why, she is no bigger than Gillian.*

"Lady Culcarron?" he inquired with well-schooled courtesy. When the woman nodded, he continued. "May I beg leave to present your niece and nephew?"

"Hmph," she said unencouragingly. "You may, but first tell me who the devil *you* are."

The earl was so surprised that for a moment no sound came out of his mouth. Lady Culcarron's voice was distinctively low, and her gruff manner was completely at odds with her delicate appearance. Quite from nowhere came the sudden question whether this would be Gillian in thirty years. Brinton consciously closed his mouth and smiled. He was quite sure he could detect a small gleam of mischief and curiosity in the countess's eyes.

"I am Julian Rafferty deRaymond, Lord Brinton, at your service, my lady. I am pleased to present your nephew, the Viscount Cranford, and your niece, Miss Gillian Kentwell."

At the sound of her name, Gillian seemed to suddenly revive. "We must beg your forgiveness for arriving at your doorstep in this fashion," she began. "There was no time—"

"You may come in," her aunt interrupted. "It is too damp to stand out here conversing in the drive."

The trio followed her inside, entering a modest antechamber with a tiled floor and dark, paneled walls. Several doors opened off it and a small stairway led upward against the wall to the right. A variety of trunks and boxes were stacked near the entrance. Silently, the countess led her guests up the stairs.

"You are very kind to receive us," Gillian began again. "I am sure it is a shock to have us descend upon you so—"

"It is all right, child. We were expecting you."

The countess had stopped in front of a massive pair of double doors in what was obviously the main reception hall. Gillian stopped also, but Brinton guessed it was more from the shock of surprise than to avoid a collision. He and Gilbey halted just behind her.

"You were expecting us?" the twins echoed in unison.

The countess pressed her lips together and closed her eyes for a moment, as if shutting off any further response. She inclined her head toward the doors in front of her.

Gilbey stepped ahead and, pushing down the brass handles, swung the doors open. He and Gillian preceded their aunt and Brinton into the room, where they came to another sudden halt.

"Uncle William," breathed Gillian.

Chapter Seventeen

The twins stood frozen in stunned disbelief. Gillian was certain that her heart had stopped.

"It cannot be," she moaned softly.

Lord Pembermore sprawled casually at one end of a rosewood sofa in the middle of Lady Culcarron's drawing room. His spindly form appeared quite at ease, his long legs stretched out and crossed at the ankles, and his elbows stuck out to either side of him, looking rather like crow's wings. He was sipping tea from an absurdly small cup while he balanced the saucer in his other hand. When he looked up, a slow, satisfied smile spread across his face.

"Well, well," he exclaimed heartily, fitting his teacup into its saucer. "So you are finally arrived at last! You have had a long journey and, I'm afraid, all for nothing." He rose from his seat and began to walk toward the twins.

Gillian took an involuntary step backward. She had been merely numb with horror at the first sight of her uncle. Now, the addition of sound and movement to the nightmare set off quite another reaction. All the emotions she had felt during the interview with her uncle the day he had announced his plan came boiling back to her at the sound of his voice.

She had been disgusted by his transparent attempts to win her and Gilbey's cooperation that day. He had cajoled, flattered, and threatened. He had tried to sever the twins' loyalty to each other, and he had lied. She had felt betrayed, but worse, she thought she had felt true hatred for the first time in her life.

Now the bubble of anger and revulsion inside her rose up into her voice and burst out in anguished denial. "No!" she cried, balling her hands into fists. Her nails dug into her

palms. "No!" she cried again, and this time the sound rever-
berated through the room. "Not here! You cannot be here!"
Her voice dropped off to an agonized whisper. "Not this. It
is too much to bear."

Lord Pembermore stopped in midstride and raised his
quizzing glass to examine his niece. "I can see that I have
surprised you," he said with the contrived smoothness she
hated so much. Gillian shivered and began to feel sick.

Gilbey glared at his uncle and put an arm around
Gillian's shoulders. "Stay back," he said angrily. "I tried to
warn you of what could happen, that first day, but you
wouldn't listen. You wouldn't listen two days later when I
called on you at Brentwood, either."

"Yes, it seems I did rather misjudge your sister," the
baron sighed, drawing his brows together. "Such a great
deal of trouble—trouble and expense. But then, you both
seem to have underestimated me, as well." His smile returned. "You were very foolish to try to defy me, Gillian.
Did you really believe you would succeed?"

He reached a hand out toward the girl's face, and she
struck his arm away furiously.

"Don't touch me," she hissed, shaking with the force of
her anger. "You have no right." Gilbey steered her toward a
chair.

"*Au contraire*, my dear," Pembermore answered calmly,
eyeing her coldly and rubbing his arm. "As your guardian, I
have every right."

"I believe even guardians have some limitations," Brinton said, stepping forward at last. "Their fitness can be
challenged in a court of law, for instance."

Lord Pembermore looked at him with obvious surprise.
"And who might you be?" His eyes narrowed. "We have
met before, I think."

The earl sketched a bow. "Lord Brinton," he said tersely.

Recognition dawned in Pembermore's face. He looked
quite pleased. "I recall you now, Brinton. You are Grassington's nephew! How interesting that you should arrive
with these two. Have you been escorting my nephew and
niece? I really must thank you for delivering them safely."

A small cry of protest escaped from Gillian's lips when
she heard her uncle's words. Must he twist everything to

his own purpose? What could Brinton possibly have stood to gain to rescue her and Gilbey from so much, only to deliver them to her uncle? He could not have known her uncle would be here, could he?

At Gillian's reaction the baron paused, seeming to warm to his idea. "Why, I should think your uncle will be more than pleased, Brinton," he added, grinning broadly. "Perhaps he will ask you to stand with him as his groomsman at the wedding."

The earl growled and looked as if he were about to seize Pembermore by the throat.

"Gentlemen, please! Shall we not all sit down?" Lady Culcarron interrupted. "More tea will be here momentarily, and rooms are already being made up for my new guests. I believe we have a great deal to discuss."

Gillian watched as the male members of the little gathering selected seats at their hostess's insistence. Only after they had done so did the countess seat herself, choosing a wing-backed chair between Gillian and the fire.

For a moment Gillian studied both her uncle's and Brinton's faces in turn. Lord Pembermore's bore an uncanny and, to her mind, regrettable resemblance to her father, rather like an artist's cruel caricature, even though the two men had been only half brothers. Just now the expression registered on it seemed to her to reflect great disdain and a rather supercilious hint of triumph.

Brinton's, on the other hand, was closed, betraying absolutely nothing. She had to stifle an urge to go to him and beat on him with her fists. She was upset and confused, angry and very much shaken by what had occurred. It would have helped so much to have some sign of what he was thinking or feeling. How well she recognized by now the mask of utter control that had dropped down over the earl's handsome features. How much she hated it at this moment!

A loud pop from the burning embers in the hearth punctuated the fleeting silence and brought Gillian out of her thoughts.

"Better," pronounced Lady Culcarron, surveying her separated guests. The rattle of dishes at the door announced the arrival of a footman bearing the supplemental tea tray, and silence resumed for another moment while the countess supervised the distribution of its contents. Once the tea and cakes had been served, she sat back and folded her hands in her lap.

"Lord Pembermore, it seems you were correct in your assumption that the twins were coming here. Now that they are here, pray tell, what are your plans?"

Gillian's heart sank, for it seemed apparent that her aunt intended to turn them over to her uncle. Her mouth was dry, and despite the long hours that had passed since her last meal, she could not bear the thought of eating. The tangy lemon smell of the little cakes gracing the plate beside her did not tempt her, but only added to the queasiness she was already feeling.

She thought the tea might help. She attempted to raise her cup, but that was a mistake. Her hand shook excessively, and the scalding tea sloshed into her saucer and splashed onto her dress. She hastily replaced the cup and, setting it aside, brushed at the droplets on her skirt. As she glanced about to see if anyone had noticed her clumsiness, she noted Gilbey wolfing down his food as if he had not eaten in days. *How can he?* she wondered. Was he not as upset as she was?

"Naturally, we shall not remain here imposing upon your gracious hospitality," Lord Pembermore was saying to her aunt. "I have every intention of taking them home straightway and proceeding with the marriage. If anything," he added, aiming a malicious look at Gillian, "we shall speed up the usual procedure, perhaps applying for a special license."

"Never!" Gillian exclaimed, leaping to her feet. She glared at her uncle. "I will never go back with you, and I will never wed Lord Grassington. I would sooner die in a workhouse!"

"Now, now, my child, that is a bit extreme," the countess said mildly. "Please sit down again." She looked from one twin to the other and back again. "I would like to hear what the two of you had planned to do once you reached here."

Gillian and Gilbey looked at each other.

"Gilbey," directed their aunt. She pointed to him with the piece of lemon cake she had just picked up.

"We were hoping you would take Gillian in," blurted Gilbey. "She hoped to start a new life here. I was to return home."

"I see," said Lady Culcarron.

Gillian did not see how her aunt could see at all. Put so bluntly, her well-intended plan sounded distressingly presumptuous. Gilbey's three spare sentences didn't even begin to explain anything!

"Why did you choose to come here, to me?"

"We had thought to get beyond the reach of English law," Gilbey began gamely enough. He cast a despairing glance at his sister, who straightened her damp skirt and nodded.

Gillian knew Gilbey could not explain her reasoning beyond the obvious point of legal jurisdiction. "It wasn't Gilbey's idea to come," she said earnestly, defending him. "He knew he could never have stopped me, so he did the most sensible thing under the circumstances." She sighed, hoping she could make her choice sound sensible. "Our mother used to talk about Scotland a great deal, you must understand," she continued.

"No doubt filling your head with romantic rubbish," commented Lady Culcarron. "And?"

"Well, she used to talk about you, Aunt Elizabeth. I know it sounds impertinent, but it made me feel as if I knew you. And she had these wonderful old collections of songs, and we used to sing them together sometimes. . . . I foolishly tried to bring them with me."

She paused, looking down at her lap, staring beyond the small, wet tea stains to the days just past. Did anything really matter now? She had lost so much more than just the books, and all for nothing.

"I just always thought I would like to come here one day," she finished, unable to keep the bitter disappointment out of her voice. "It seemed like the perfect solution."

She thought she could not bear to hear her uncle's barking laughter, and surely he would laugh. "Uncle William, how did you know we would come here?" she demanded. She had to know how they had failed. She sat ramrod straight, her hands balled at her sides.

Lord Pembermore positively smirked. "Did you think

Mr. Worsley would not mention that you had been to call on him? He is my solicitor as well as yours, after all. He was most surprised when I told him the full extent of your reluctance to go along with the betrothal. It seems you had left him with the impression that you were putting together a list for the announcements! It did not require great mental acuity on my part to guess where you were heading, once I learned whose address he had supplied to you.

"I dispatched some fellows to try to track you down, and I even engaged the services of Bow Street, but you have obviously managed to elude them all. I sailed from Plymouth on the first northbound ship I could book, precisely to cover such a possibility. As the wind and tides were quite favorable, I have been enjoying your aunt's hospitality for two days now."

Two days, thought Gillian despondently. *Plenty of time for him to pour whatever stories he pleased into Aunt Elizabeth's ears.*

"Lord Brinton," said the countess. "You have remained silent. I feel justified in asking what role you have played in all this? Do I understand that it is your uncle who wishes to marry my niece?"

Brinton cleared his throat awkwardly and glanced at Gillian. He had easily read her despair and confusion. He could see that his aloofness wounded her, and that recognition deepened the agony in his own heart. To hurt her was torture, but worse, that his behavior could do so proved she held at least some regard for him. If only he were able to offer her the kind of life she wanted! If only their two uncles did not stand in their way!

He wanted nothing so much as to go to her and offer compassion and comfort, but he did not dare. He had seen immediately that any hint of the affection he had for her would only give her uncle another tool to use against her, and possibly against himself. Lord Pembermore was clearly a ruthless, deceitful, determined man. If Rafferty and the twins were to extricate themselves from the tangle they were now in, they would have to proceed with caution and ingenuity. There had not yet been time to consider this new turn of events, and the earl did not wish to show his hand. Unfortunately, concealing his thoughts and intentions from

Pembermore meant, for now, concealing them from Gillian as well.

"My involvement in all this was, unbelievably, quite accidental," he said, getting up from his chair. He walked away from the gathered company, his hands clasped behind his back, and approached a small cabinet displaying upon it a black Grecian urn. The vase depicted what appeared to be a quartet of semiclothed lovers pursuing each other in perpetuity. The earl stared at it briefly, considering what else he should say. Pacing back again, he paused, facing the fire in the grate rather than any of his audience.

"Cranford and Miss Kentwell ran into some difficulties with which I was able, by chance, to assist," he said truthfully. "I had no idea who they were. As I was heading north myself, we decided to travel together for part of the journey. We ran into some further difficulties, and finally it just seemed appropriate to see them all the way here."

He gave up staring at the fire and looked quite intentionally at Lord Pembermore instead. "As for my uncle, I am not privy to his current state of mind," he added.

The baron opened his mouth to make some remark, but the twins' aunt spoke first. "What are your plans now that you are here?" she asked the earl.

Brinton faced her and made a little bow. "That is a very reasonable question. We are all literally strangers who have descended upon you without notice. I hope you will accept my apology. My original intention had been to go home."

"And now?"

Clearly, Lady Culcarron was not going to allow him to avoid answering her question. He sighed. "Now, I really do not know."

As the earl took his seat again, the countess surprised him by chuckling. "I am not at all surprised," she said. "We seem to have reached a stalemate."

Her gaze swept over the group gathered in her drawing room before she went on to address them. "I hope that you, Gillian, have learned that running away is seldom the solution to problems. On the other hand, Lord Pembermore, you may rest assured that I will not permit you to abscond with my unwilling niece out from under my own roof.

"All of you have chosen to descend upon me at an exceedingly inopportune moment, just as I was preparing to embark upon some travels of my own. But as you have come to me, I reserve for myself the right to make a decision as to what will be done. The problem demands appropriate consideration, and we are not going to solve it this day. I will sleep on it, and I suggest you do the same. We must call a truce for the time being."

She stood up, achieving an impressive amount of dignity for someone of such small stature. "I have no doubt that our new arrivals are travel-weary and would like to freshen themselves and rest between now and dinner. I shall expect and will tolerate nothing less than civil behavior at my table."

She turned to the twins and Brinton. "Maxwell will show you to your rooms. You have only to let her know if there is anything you require. We dine at seven." Addressing the baron, she added, "You may avail yourself of my library, if you wish, Lord Pembermore. I have a number of letters I must write before we reconvene." She shooed them toward the door with a fluttering of fingers, then folded her hands in a precise little gesture of dismissal.

Gillian hung back, signaling the men to exit ahead of her. "Aunt Elizabeth, could I ask for just one word with you in private?"

"Just one word, Gillian?" the countess asked, raising an eyebrow in a dubious expression that was suddenly rather reminiscent of Brinton. A momentary stab of fresh pain struck Gillian, who felt the loss of his presence keenly.

"I would expect that you might wish more than one word with me, niece," her aunt continued. "For two days I have endured your uncle's blathering about how irresponsible and disobedient you are—how wild and unmannered, selfish, unmanageable, and in fact, how altogether unmarriageable you are. I am aware that there are at least two sides, if not more, to every story." Smoothing her skirts, the countess sat down again, bidding Gillian to follow suit with a simple nod of her head.

The young woman arranged herself carefully on the square satinwood chair opposite her aunt. Her mind was whirling with a jumbled multitude of thoughts and warring emotions. Above them all she recognized a clear imperative not to waste this opportunity to speak with her aunt. She must be articulate and controlled, "a proud ship under full sail," as Brinton had said. If her behavior showed that she was not as her uncle claimed, would that not be the best possible defense?

She squared her shoulders and lifted her head. Her aunt was watching her, waiting. Gillian swallowed and managed a tentative smile. "Well," she began, "I must admit I would welcome the opportunity to discuss my predicament with you, Aunt Elizabeth. I am aware that I owe you some further explanation, especially since I was the one who involved you without either your consent or knowledge. But I will confess that I asked to speak with you just now over something much more mundane. You see, we have managed to bring very little with us." Here her voice quavered, and she paused for a moment to reestablish her control.

"I gather this was part of the 'difficulties' Lord Brinton mentioned?" questioned Lady Culcarron.

Gillian nodded. "I . . . I really have nothing suitable to wear to dinner, just this dress and an extremely rumpled muslin." She looked at her aunt uncertainly, not quite able to summon the confidence that Brinton would have counseled.

"That is nicely spoken, Gillian," her aunt said with a curt nod of approval. "I am pleased to see that you can exercise such rigid control when it is important to you. But I imagine that you are thoroughly exhausted and that you have been through quite an ordeal. You need not force yourself. You forget that I have already seen how you reacted when you discovered your uncle here. Are you not angered by what he has been telling me?"

The countess placed her hands together, aligning the fingertips precisely. "I will tell you, the more he said, the more I thought of your poor dear mother. You have no idea how much I loved her—how much I missed her! Our father ranted so after she ran off with your father—he called her all the things your uncle has been trying to call you." She smiled. "Probably a good half of it was true, and I expect that may be so in your case as well! When I saw you standing in my drive, it was as if she had come home at last."

Lady Culcarron looked up, and Gillian could see mois-

ture in the older woman's eyes. Quite suddenly, the girl
knew she had found a new ally.

"You are so very like her; has anyone ever told you?"
Her aunt sniffled. "Unmarriageable, my foot! I know men.
Dressed properly and presented in London, you would have
suitors falling all over each other, just as your mother could
have had. It would be so even if you were the worst hellion
that ever set foot in Almack's, and I can assure you that
you would not be." She stood up. "Come here, child."

Gillian obeyed. Tears were pricking at her own eyes as
her aunt enfolded her in a strong embrace. She had walled
in her need for a mother's compassion, confidence, and
companionship for so long. Could she dare to hope that she
had found it now?

"Look at us, dissolved into a fine pair of watering pots,"
sniffed the countess. She put Gillian at arm's length and
smiled. "We must find something for you to wear! It should
not be difficult, I'd say, if you look at us." She took
Gillian's hand and squeezed it affectionately.

Gillian came down to breakfast the next morning in a
simple, old-fashioned round dress of pale sea green muslin
that was stunningly becoming. She had doubted the wis-
dom of appearing at her best on this particular day, fearing
that somehow it might only aggravate her uncle's state of
mind. However, the satisfaction of catching Brinton clearly
admiring her looks in an unguarded moment, and the obvious pleasure she was affording her aunt made the effort
worthwhile.

The declared truce still seemed to be in effect this morning as the little group enjoyed a hearty meal in Lady Culcarron's breakfast room. Lady Culcarron was continuing to
play the diplomat as she had the previous night, and Gillian
could almost believe that all was right with her world. She
tried to focus on the enticing scents wafting from the table
and the gentle light reflecting into the room from beyond
the windows, where morning mist on the eastern hills had
been set glowing pinkish gold by the sun. She needed only
to look around the table to be reminded that the peaceful-
ness was all an illusion.

Even in its morning softness the light of day revealed

clearly how her uncle's face differed from her father's. Harsh lines of dissipation and the puffiness around his eyes and jaw bore witness to a life spent in pursuit of bodily pleasures rather than sober scholarship. The set of his mouth betrayed a sour existence of fleeting satisfactions and starvation of the soul. Gillian suddenly felt pity for him rather than hatred.

The light was far kinder to Brinton, softly illuminating his fine skin and the handsome planes and angles of his face. He was immaculately groomed this morning, of course, but as she looked at him she remembered the roguish charm he had when he was not, and how his rough shadow beard had felt against her skin that night in the forest.

Brinton caught her looking and smiled, but she found that no comfort. His very presence seemed to emphasize the uncertainty of her situation and her own confusion. Neither he nor her uncle should have been there at all. She had steeled herself for parting with him, yet he had not gone. *Why had he stayed?* She had been shocked to realize that her aunt's depiction of swains groveling at her feet in London held no appeal for her because she could not imagine wanting someone else. Only Brinton. *Rafferty.*

To distract herself, she split a scone and spread creamy butter on it. Her gaze slipped to her aunt, who was chatting lightly with the men. Gillian wondered if the countess had suspected there were feelings between her and Brinton. The good lady had asked so few questions about their involvement! Her cheerfulness this morning seemed almost forced. What had Aunt Elizabeth decided to do? When would she tell them?

Gillian had not long to wait. When everyone had finished their meal, the countess assembled them all in the library. Only Gillian chose to sit down. Brinton moved casually to stand by her chair, and Gilbey stationed himself on her other side. *Like flanking guards,* she thought, suppressing a hysterical giggle. She tried to calm herself. All her muscles had become tight with tension.

"Sleep and some time to consider have led me to a decision about our problem," Lady Culcarron announced. "As I said yesterday, you have reached a stalemate. I believe that the only solution is to clear the board and reset the pieces. I mentioned that you have caught me at an inopportune time. I was expecting to leave today for London. The grand-daughter of a good friend is celebrating her betrothal, and at the end of the Season I planned to go abroad. Had any of you arrived just a few days later, I would not have been here at all."

The countess paused and looked at the twins. "Some-times I believe that God does have His hand in our affairs, after all," she said softly. Then she continued in a stronger voice. "Obviously, I have had to modify my departure time somewhat, but I am still going to London. I have decided that Gillian and Gilbey shall go with me. I expect that you, Pembermore, will want to join us. As for you, Brinton, you may of course do whatever you wish."

A stricken silence filled the room, followed immediately by a babble of questions and protests from the men. Gillian sat frozen in her chair, gripped by panic as real as what she might have felt if an unburst artillery shell had suddenly landed in the library. *Return to English soil, with Uncle William? No!* She could not begin to fathom what her aunt had in mind.

Chapter Eighteen

"I say, Miss Kentwell, how are you finding London? Have you had time yet to form an opinion of us? Miss Kentwell?"

Gillian felt the warmth flood her face as she realized she had not been paying the slightest attention to the young man who was addressing her. She hoped he would assume she had not heard him due to the noise around them rather than her own preoccupation.

After little more than a week in London, she still was not used to the crowds and the noise of the city. Typically, Lady Fletching's at-home was proving to be a rout, attended by vast numbers of the *ton* curious to see their hostess's newly completed refurbishments. The house was indeed magnificent, with softly polished marble floors and a mixture of classical decorations, but Gillian could hardly wait to leave. She was finding that the social whirl of town life had little appeal for her. In truth, she had been growing increasingly preoccupied with each day that passed since her arrival.

"I am truly sorry," she apologized to the young man. She did not wish to be rude. "You were saying . . . ?"

She and Gilbey had already endured endless rounds of shopping, visiting, sightseeing, and entertainments in their first week here with their aunt. They had been introduced to what seemed to be hundreds of people whose names Gillian could not remember, including the young man now attempting to converse with her. What had increasingly distracted her was that all week, anywhere they had gone, there had been no sign of Brinton.

He promised, she reminded herself each day. *He said that he would be here. Do I still believe him?*

She had not realized at first how much his promise had meant to her. That fateful morning in Scotland, she had agreed to go along with her aunt's plan only after the countess had privately explained something of her motives and had given Gillian a dozen assurances that she would not allow Lord Pembermore's plotting to prevail. Brinton had declined to travel to London with the rest of their small party, saying that he had matters to attend to first. He had promised, however, to see them there. Gillian had clung to that promise as to a lifeline. The prospect of seeing him had sustained her through all of the activities that she had faced in this first week, but now her hope was fading, buried under the weight of continuing disappointment.

"I asked if you had yet formed an opinion of London in the short time you have been here, Miss Kentwell," the young man in Lady Fletching's hall repeated, smiling. He had stylishly cropped brown hair and was pleasantly attractive in an ordinary, unmemorable sort of way, except for rather highly placed eyebrows that made him appear constantly surprised.

Gillian hesitated for a fraction of a moment. While she might not recall this fellow's name, she remembered painfully the several faux pas she had made in Bath, and, for her aunt's sake, she did not want to make similar errors here.

"London is so vast and so varied, it is hardly possible to have only one opinion of it," she responded cautiously. "I can say that I am not yet accustomed to the crowds. Is it always like this?"

Her companion laughed. "That is the aim. When it is not, the event is considered a failure, and the hostess is disgraced."

"But that seems—" Gillian stopped herself before she could blurt out "unfair and unkind." How could a hostess be held responsible for the whims of other people? She realized, however, that it might be offensive to say so.

"Have I shocked you so easily?" The young man chuckled, mistaking her dilemma. "I wonder what you will think of the rest of our London ways, once you have discovered them!" He fixed a more serious look upon her. "The only way I can be sure of finding out, Miss Kentwell, is to ask if you would care to drive in the park with me later in the week. Am I too bold?"

Gillian blushed, not from maidenly modesty, but from embarrassment at the awkward situation. Would he not be insulted if she declined? Yet how could she accept when she didn't remember who he was?

"Perhaps I should seek your aunt's permission?" he asked.

She nodded, seeing his offer as the perfect solution. Lady Culcarron knew him. She seemed to be acquainted with an amazing number of people for a Scottish lady who claimed to venture into London only occasionally. She would, no doubt, give permission for the outing, since her intention was to expose Gillian as much as possible to the *ton*.

The countess had assured Gillian that attracting some eligible suitors was the most likely way to foil her uncle's plans, and that being placed on exhibit was the usual procedure. Tonight the countess would display the twins in a box at Covent Garden, where Gillian could at least look forward to seeing the play. Tomorrow night they were engaged for the gala ball that had brought her aunt to London. By some unknown sleight of hand, her aunt had also already obtained vouchers for Almack's for the next Wednesday night. Gillian sighed. It would all be so much more bearable if only Brinton were there.

The truth was, she missed the earl intensely. His desertion from the battlefield hurt her. She had counted on his support in her struggle against her uncle, although she did not know exactly what she had expected him to do. After the adventures they had shared on their perilous journey, she had looked upon him as a special friend and ally. Apparently, the time they had spent together meant nothing to him—just a quick, easy friendship as soon forgotten as formed. She ought to accept that, she knew, and consign their friendship to the rubbish heap along with her lifelong hopes and dreams.

The crowd in Lady Fletching's hall had progressed an inch at a time toward the exit they were all seeking. Gillian observed that what someone had said in jest was probably true—people did spend more time awaiting their carriages than socializing at these overpopulated functions.

"Was that young Lord Rochley I saw you talking to?" With what Gillian considered rather suspect timing, Lady Culcarron appeared at her side just seconds after the anonymous young man had departed.

She gave her aunt an indulgent smile. "Aunt Elizabeth, I must admit that you have introduced us to so many people, I simply cannot remember them all. Is that his name? I could only recall that we had been properly presented."

"He is a fairly eligible *parti*, my dear—the younger son of a marquess, with a handsome allowance and a good relationship with his older brother. Do you like him?"

Gillian avoided answering. "He wishes to take me for a drive in the park later this week."

"Oh, that is delightful, my dear! Did you agree?"

She shook her head. "He is going to approach you about it, Aunt Elizabeth. I didn't know how I should respond when I couldn't remember who the devil he was." Gillian clapped a hand over her mouth as soon as the words slipped out. "I do apologize, Aunt Elizabeth! I think I have not yet recovered from spending so much time with my brother and Lord Brinton!" She felt the inevitable blush creeping up her cheeks.

"I begin to think that is much truer than I realized," said the countess thoughtfully.

A few hours later, Gillian sat at a mahogany dressing table in a bedroom of her aunt's rented Mount Street town house, putting the finishing touches to her evening toilette. She wore an elegant and very new evening dress of cream figured crepe over a satin slip of pale green and an underslip of white Urling's lace. The low-cut bodice featured a stomacher of emerald green satin, which emphasized her tiny waist.

The abigail her aunt had hired for her stood behind her while Gillian fussed halfheartedly with the placement of a curl by her left ear. An evening at the theater required an early dinner, and there had been little time to get ready between the afternoon calls and the meal. Now it was very nearly time to go.

Gillian frowned into the looking glass. She had tried to banish Brinton from her thoughts, but somehow the effort had only made her think of him more. *You are being per-verse, just like him*, she scolded herself silently. She had told herself a dozen times to forget about him and enter into her aunt's scheme with greater interest. *You could find someone else who is far less aggravating*, she had argued with herself, but she remained unconvinced.

Her maid set a garland of white crepe roses in her hair. "Miss, if you would only smile, you will see that the effect is quite charming," she suggested.

Gillian groaned inwardly. She would be expected to smile and do the pretty all evening.

There was a knock at the door, and at Gillian's response, Lady Culcarron sailed in, resplendent in a gown of silver tissue trimmed with jet.

"Are we quite ready to sally forth?" the countess inquired, surveying her niece. "You look lovely, my dear, except for that face. We are going to see the Bard, not an execution. Do you not think you will enjoy the evening? *Measure for Measure* is one of my favorite plays."

She reached for Gillian's hand and raised her from her seat. "Come now," she coaxed. "I know that being here is not what you had hoped for or expected, but if you give yourself some time to accept the change, you will see that all may still turn out all right. Did you think you could only find love in Scotland? There are many who might not wish to admit it, but people fall in love anywhere, even right here in London!"

She gave Gillian a sad little smile. "I actually met my husband here, although I was not in love with him at first. Our love grew slowly, as we came to know one another. And because it grew slowly, it developed very deep roots and wide-spreading branches." She paused and looked out the window. "Since his death not a day has gone by that I have not missed him."

Gillian touched her aunt's arm in a shy gesture of sympathy. "Love can be very painful, I know. I saw what it did to my father, after my mother died."

"That was love, but he quite forgot that he had you and Gilbey. I know your parents' love was well-rooted, but it certainly never reached out to anyone beyond themselves."

Lady Culcarron pressed her lips together in a gesture Gillian had come to recognize. The subject was closed.

With a sigh the young woman moved to the bed to retrieve her reticule and fan. Did the pain she felt over losing Brinton's companionship mean that she had been in love with him? Then why did she also feel so angry?

The Royal Opera House at Covent Garden was large and spectacular, designed to resemble a Greek temple on the outside, and equally grand inside. The twins could not help but be impressed as they ascended the great stairway, set between rows of Ionic columns and illumined by hanging Grecian lamps. Swept along with the other patrons, they caught only glimpses of the statue of Shakespeare in the antechamber and the Shakespearean scenes painted in the recesses of the main lobby.

"When you said we were coming to see the Bard, I thought you were referring to the playbill," Gillian teased her aunt when they finally found their box and settled into the chairs. Her spirits had been somewhat restored by the contagious excitement and glamour in attending the theater, and she had resolved not to let the remains of her megrims ruin the evening for the others.

As she looked around, admiring the cut-glass chandeliers suspended between the boxes, she realized that the horseshoe design of the theater put the patrons on display to each other quite as effectively as it enabled them all to see the stage. She did not intend to look for Brinton, but she could not help a quick scan of the box seats where he would be most likely to sit.

What she found were many curious eyes upon herself and Gilbey, as new arrivals to town so late in the Season. She felt an urge to hide behind her chair until the program began. Once the curtain rose, however, she focused all her attention on the stage. She hoped that the other patrons would also become more absorbed by the performers there than by those in the audience.

She was quite astonished when, at the intermission bell, Gilbey leaned over close to her ear. "I see Brinton," he whispered excitedly.

Gillian truly did not know whether she wanted to look or not. The pain and anger in her own heart mixed with an aching hopefulness that thoroughly confused her. Clearly her twin looked forward to a reunion with the earl. With a small gesture Gilbey pointed across to a box that was noticeably more crowded now than it had been when the curtain rose. Brinton was standing there amidst an entire flock of young beauties.

Gilbey's enthusiasm was uncontainable. "Aunt Elizabeth, may I beg your leave to go extend our greetings? I have spotted Lord Brinton in one of the other boxes."

Lady Culcarron looked at Gillian. "Do you wish to go also, child?"

When Gillian shook her head, the countess gave Gilbey her permission to go without them. "I can see that Lord Brinton's clutch of hens has quite caught your brother's eye," she said wryly. "I wonder who they all are?"

"Well, I do not," Gillian said crossly, trying to wrestle down the ugly, searing jealousy that had gripped her at the sight of them.

Even if Gillian had wanted to observe the scene in the other box, she would have found it impossible to do so, for within minutes a steady flow of visitors was passing through her aunt's. Introductions to yet more people acquainted with the countess, and reintroductions to people Gillian had already met, kept her quite occupied and distracted from her own emotional state. It was a shock, therefore, when she looked up in the midst of an inane conversation about the weather to see Brinton looming over her, awaiting his chance to speak with her.

Her conversational partner apparently took the hint when Gillian suddenly blushed and stopped speaking quite in midsentence. The portly, middle-aged gentleman made his excuses and quickly yielded his seat to the earl.

"How do you do that?" Gillian hissed, not sounding nearly as annoyed as she wished.

"Do what?" asked Brinton innocently, settling into the chair beside her.

"Make people do what you want without even saying a word?"

"Do I do that? If so, I can think of any number of people who seem to be immune to my power." He was smiling at her, the warmth in his gaze melting her anger and jealousy, rekindling her aching need for him in their place.

"To start with, my mother and sisters," he said, continuing to smile in exactly the way she had tried to memorize when she had thought she was never to see him again. "I lay the blame on them for my inability to arrive in town any sooner."

"And why is that?" she inquired in a tight voice. His power over her was absurd. She had so longed for his company, but now that he was here, she was not sure which torture was worse—missing him or being with him.

"They all wished to come to London with me, but they could not be ready on a day's notice. There were bags to pack, and arrangements to make . . . " He hesitated, then reached over to take her hands. "The play will be resuming in just a few minutes. We have so little time to talk like this. I want to know how you are faring. You look absolutely stunning. Are you enjoying London? Have you been getting out? And what of your uncle?"

She shook her head. She could not begin to answer. Did he really care to know? Were they not two quite different people sitting here than the ones who had raced over hundreds of miles of road? He looked so elegant in a velvet evening coat of deepest corbeau, black pantaloons, and snowy white cravat, waistcoat, and stockings. She supposed she, too, looked more elegant—how far from the young runaway dressed in a stable boy's castoffs! They were in a different world now. She hoped the misery she was feeling did not show in her eyes.

"You are kind to inquire, Lord Brinton. I know you have guests who are probably awaiting your return."

A puzzled look crossed his face, then he brightened and actually laughed. "Goose! Is that what this is all about? Do you not realize that I have been dragged here this evening by all the females of my family? They and their friends are likely to suffocate me. Finding you here has been my reward, for I had thought I would not see you until tomorrow!"

"Tomorrow?"

"At the ball? You do recall Lady Darley's ball for her daughter, the event that brought your aunt all the way from

Scotland? Did you not receive the note I sent around this afternoon?"

"No," she said stupidly. "We did not have time to look at the cards that came this afternoon."

"Well, when you read it in the morning you will learn that I have finally arrived in town, and that I am looking forward to seeing you at the ball." He pressed her fingers ever so slightly, sending heat waves racing up her arms. "I am even so bold as to request a dance saved for me. But now that I am here with you, I shall be even bolder, and ask if I may take you in to supper tomorrow night? Can you stand that much of my company?"

She could not maintain her resistance in the face of his self-deprecating humor. She nodded. "I thought you were not coming," she finally managed to croak out. "I did look for you, at first, but we have been here now for more than a week."

He looked stricken. "I always keep my promises. I am truly sorry. The delay was unavoidable. Have you not been enjoying your visit? I hope that you will allow me to show you some of the sights. There is so much to see and do. There is so much that must be new to you!"

What could she say? *I could not enjoy it because you were not here?* No. Finally, she simply smiled and said, "I think I will begin to enjoy it more after today."

The warning bell rang, and Brinton was forced to take his leave. Gillian turned her attention to the performances with a considerably lighter heart. Brinton cared. He had not abandoned her. Perhaps their friendship could survive in London, after all.

Chapter Nineteen

Gillian was astounded to discover that it required an entire afternoon to prepare for a ball of the magnitude of Lady Darley's. Her aunt patiently explained that extra time was necessary to allow for possible disasters, but Gillian wondered how anything could go wrong. Every item to be worn, from gown to gloves and slippers, had been fitted, checked, and rechecked at least twice if not a dozen times.

Clad in her chemise and a soft muslin dressing gown, Gillian paused by the bed where her evening finery had been carefully laid out. The ball gown of sheer white net over a gold satin slip was so exquisite, she could not quite believe she would be wearing it. She reached out with reverent fingers to touch the gathered fall of lace that trimmed the décolletage. The short, puffed sleeves, the waist, and the exposed hem of the satin slip were decorated with loopings of green ribbon, gold cord, and pearls, discreetly accented with small white satin roses.

Beside the dress lay her new white kid gloves and the gold satin slippers she had begged her aunt to allow instead of the more usual white ones. The effect would be completed by an additional extravagance she and Lady Culcarron had not been able to resist, a mantelet of dark green velvet, lined in gold satin to match her slip.

Gillian discovered that she was quite looking forward to the ball, now that she knew Brinton would attend.

"Miss, if you would come sit by the fire, I'll dry your hair," her abigail interrupted gently. "When that French hairdresser arrives, he'll want it a bit damp, I expect, not wet like it is now, and besides, you don't want to catch a chill."

Gillian obeyed, giving the girl a grateful smile. The

young abigail was busily patting the moisture from her curls when there was a knock at the door. Gillian held out her hand for the towel and continued the task herself while the maid went to answer.

"Ooh, miss, there's a package come for you," the maid said, forgetting her more formal speech in the excitement of the moment. She returned bearing a small box that looked suspiciously like a fan case. It was tied with satin ribbon under which had been tucked a small card.

"Miss Kentwell, best regards, Brinton," read Gillian. Very proper, betraying nothing. What else would one expect from the earl? She had handed back the towel, but she noticed that her attendant stood transfixed by curiosity. She untied the bow and opened the box.

Wrapped in a piece of silk inside was a beautiful little fan very like the one she had admired in Lancaster. She lifted it out and opened it, catching her breath as the firelight reflected off the silver spangles and brought a soft glow to the pale pink silk. It had to be the very same one. She recognized the pattern of the lace and the delicate painted flowers. Brinton had to have gone back to Lancaster to purchase it, for she doubted there could be two so exactly alike.

"Ooh, miss, it's beautiful!"

"Yes, it is." Gillian held it in front of her, positioning her thumb and other fingers as her aunt had schooled her. She had been practicing and had reached a level of competence that would have surprised the young girl who had fumbled so in Bath. She hardly believed that she could have changed so much in less than three weeks' time.

However, Brinton could not know that. What did his gift mean? Was it proper for her to receive it? She was not sure, but he had certainly managed to please her. She closed the fan and hugged it to her for a moment before returning it to its wrappings in the box.

Not far away in Grosvenor Square, Lord Brinton was preparing for the ball at home in his London residence, a spacious mansion carved out of three town houses purchased and combined by his grandfather. The earl closed his eyes and concentrated on staying perfectly still while his valet eased a razor along his jawbone. Tyler was an excellent barber, but Brinton knew his own tense nerves could affect the outcome of the man's efforts. He was grateful that his rooms were peacefully located on the floor above those of his sisters, for he could imagine the bustle of activity that was no doubt taking place in those rooms below.

He had not expected to be nervous. He had surely attended a hundred such balls, and his only concern had always been to honor the usual niceties of proper behavior without creating an impression of interest in any of the inevitable husband-seekers. He had faced battles with more confidence than he was feeling this evening, and it was all because of Gillian.

When Lady Culcarron's drawing room doors had opened to reveal Lord Pembermore in Scotland, Rafferty had silently renewed his commitment to Gillian's cause. No matter what he had to do, he vowed that she would never be forced to marry his uncle. When the countess had announced her intention to take the twins to London, however, he had understood at once that her plan was to find Gillian a more suitable mate. At that moment of realization, his resolve had turned in an entirely new direction. Suddenly, he had faced the prospect of seeing Gillian in a conventional marriage with someone else, and he had known then that he could not bear to see anyone in that role but himself.

He loved her. That was one part of her dream that he could at least offer. He would overturn both uncles and wage a campaign to win her himself. If he failed, only then could he find some way to live with his loss.

Sending the fan had been his opening move. Had he done the right thing? How would she receive his gift? He felt as uncertain as a green schoolboy.

"Ahem." Tyler's discreet throat clearing brought Brinton back to the task at hand. The burly valet was as tall as his master and looked like a big farm laborer someone had dressed as a valet for a joke. Standing with his arms folded and the razor dangling casually between his fingers, he flashed a grin at the earl. "I've been finished for five minutes," he teased.

"You have not," protested Brinton. "But I apologize for being a bit distracted."

"A bit!" snorted Tyler. "It has to be a woman—it always is. But this looks serious. Very serious."

The earl nodded. "Possibly incurable," he responded with a sad smile. He allowed Tyler liberties that no other servant would dare to presume because he considered the man his friend. But he was not yet ready to open his heart and confide his hopes. Tonight would be a test of sorts, possibly a turning point. He would learn whether Gillian was at all receptive to his suit, and she would meet his mother and sisters.

As dinner proved to be a rather lengthy affair, Brinton and his family arrived at the ball much later than he had hoped. He was impatient with the usual ritual of depositing cloaks, being announced, and greeting the hostess. He was eager to find the twins and their aunt.

"Lady Darley," purred his mother while he fidgeted beside her. "You were so kind to add us to your guest list on such short notice. We would have been devastated to miss your ball just because we arrived in town so late!"

He nodded and uttered something similar, trying to stop his eyes from scanning the ballroom with its lavish decorations. His heart rate seemed to triple when he caught sight of a very short person with chestnut curls, dancing gracefully in a white and gold dress.

He had not believed possible how much he had missed her from the morning he left Scotland. He had hired a gig and retraced much of their journey, stopping in Lancaster to purchase the fan, and returning to Bewdley to recover his curricle. Thoughts of her haunted him on every road he traveled. He had proceeded to his primary estate in Lincolnshire, to pack a suitable wardrobe for London, and had then been required to go to Southampton to inform his family of his plans.

The brief moments he had spent last night with Gillian at the theater had stirred up fires he had banked from necessity. As he glimpsed her now moving through the lively figures of the cotillion, he could feel them burning again hotter than ever.

Brinton waited while his younger sisters made their curtsies. Once he had escorted them and his mother to the chaperones' area, he was free. He quickly sought out Lady Culcarron. The dance was just ending as he made his bow, and he looked up in time to see Gillian's partner returning her.

She looked stunningly beautiful, he thought. Her curls framed her face, and the pearls at her throat seemed to emphasize the perfection of her skin. Her cheeks were flushed, and she appeared happy and breathless, no doubt from the dancing. There was no way for him to judge if she was pleased to see him.

"Lord Brinton, good evening," she greeted him, offering her hand very properly. "How nice that you could be here. I have not forgotten that I promised you a dance." She turned away before he could search her eyes for a clue to the feelings behind her words. Fishing in her reticule, she drew out her fan and proceeded to use it, cooling herself vigorously.

The countess made some comment, but Brinton barely heard it. Gillian was using his fan, the one he had sent her. It did not match her dress at all, yet there she was, using it to chase the heat from her skin and looking up at him with laughing blue-green eyes. The smile he gave her started in his heart and spread slowly outward.

"Would you care to step outside?" he asked woodenly, yet what else could he say? He wanted to sweep her off her feet and carry her bodily to the nearest bishop. Wouldn't the gossip-mongers love that? Instead, he offered his elbow and sedately crossed with her to the doors that opened onto the Darleys' terrace.

They walked outside through the intersecting circles of light created by flickering torches flanking the doors.

"I have to thank you for the fan," Gillian whispered, standing on tiptoe to reach his ear. He knew that she had no inkling of how that would affect him. "I cannot believe you went to the trouble to go back and get it for me."

He felt intoxicated by her presence. His better judgment warned him that they should go back inside, but instead he found himself steering her toward the darkest corner he could find.

"Do you still like it?" he asked hopefully.

"Oh, more than ever," she breathed.

When she turned to him with such a look of delight, he could not help himself. He bent his head down to meet her lips with a gentle, exploratory kiss that quickly deepened as he felt her respond.

"I missed you," he murmured softly.

His emotions began to spin him out of control as his joy and his love for her combined with his physical desire. He pulled her tightly against him and rocked her with the urgency and passion of his kisses. He almost didn't hear the laughing voice that called him back from the brink of disaster.

"Should have known you'd be getting yourself in trouble out here, old man."

By God, it was Archie.

Rafferty eased Gillian back against the stone balustrade for support before he released her. The look he exchanged with her in the dancing shadows told him that they both knew the interruption was for the best.

The torchlights made Archie a mere silhouette. "Expected to see you in town much sooner than this, Rafferty! 'A few days,' we said. Thought you'd changed your mind about coming!"

"It's a long story, Archie," said the earl, tucking Gillian's hand into the crook of his elbow. "I just arrived yesterday and only had time to send you a note."

He inspected Gillian and even in the dim light recognized the unmistakable dazed, ruffled look of a woman who had just been thoroughly kissed. She could not go back to the ballroom looking like that! Her aunt and everyone else would be scandalized. And he needed to introduce her to his family.

"I have spoiled your hair, love," he said, turning to face her and touching the disarrayed curls behind her neck with a gentle finger. Someone had artfully gathered up her back hair and fastened it with a tortoise-shell comb, but the shortest tendrils had easily escaped. "Can you repair the damage?"

"I think so." She reached up with both hands and attempted to tuck in the offending curls without removing the comb.

The motion produced a wonderfully provocative effect with the low neckline of her gown, and Brinton directed a fierce look at Spelling when he caught him staring.

Gillian sighed. "It won't do. You will have to help me." She turned to offer her back to him.

The earl swallowed as he admired the curve of her shoulders and the delicate nape of her neck. If only she knew what she was asking! He longed to let his fingers explore in her hair, but what he had in mind would not have been helpful. "I'll try," he said gamely, summoning his most rigid control. He removed his gloves and tried to smooth the disobedient locks into place with slightly shaky hands. The softness of her hair tickled his fingers and challenged his restraint almost beyond endurance. His attempts to discipline the errant tendrils met with little success.

"I am afraid it all needs to be redone," he admitted with a sigh, "although I must say that I rather like it as it is."

At least they could return now with some degree of decorum. She no longer displayed the bright, dreamy look she had worn after he kissed her. It was a shame, really. How he had loved seeing her with that look!

He offered his arm again, walking her across the terrace and back into the light. Spelling followed close beside him.

"Lucky devil, Raff!" Archie said in his ear as the earl handed Gillian through the door ahead of him. "Who is she?"

"Don't you recognize her?" Rafferty quizzed back with a quick smile. He moved ahead to reclaim Gillian's hand and returned her to the spot where they had left her aunt.

Gilbey was there with the countess, and he greeted Brinton warmly. The earl seized the opportunity while both twins were together with their aunt to broach the subject of introducing his family. Gilbey had already met some of them the previous night at the theater.

"Oh, dear," responded Gillian with a surprising show of nervousness. "Could I not do something first about my hair?"

With good-natured chuckles, the gentlemen agreed to allow her this indulgence, and she headed off with Lady Culcarron toward the small salon that had been designated as a ladies' retiring room. Gilbey excused himself to seek out the young lady who had promised him the next dance, and moments later Spelling reappeared beside the earl.

"The same two, ain't they?" he asked in astonishment. "The two from Taunton? They looked demmed fine, dressed to the gills. Said all along the chit was a prime article. What on earth have you been up to, you old fox?"

Rafferty took Archie by the arm and followed in the wake of Gillian and her aunt, heading for the outer hall. "Let us find a more private spot and I shall reveal all," he promised.

The monstrous pier glass in the ladies' salon more than served the purpose to assist Lady Culcarron in repairing Gillian's coiffure. With the rebellious curls once more anchored by the pearl-trimmed comb, the countess replaced the satin rose and ribbons that had nestled before it in her niece's hair.

"There, my dear," she approved with a satisfied smile. "As lovely as ever."

Gillian adjusted the position of one sleeve at her shoulder and tested a smile in the glass.

"I suppose it would be unspeakably rude not to indulge Lord Brinton by meeting his mother and sisters tonight?"

Her aunt eyed her searchingly. "Do you not wish to meet them? You know, when a gentleman sends such a gift as a fan, it usually indicates he is courting."

Gillian's eyebrows went up in what was almost an unconscious imitation of the gentleman under discussion. She had not previously considered his gift in that light, but after his behavior on the terrace, she could accept that her aunt might be right. Could he really want to marry her? He had sought her out. He had said that he missed her. Her heart began to beat faster. "Perhaps I am just a coward, Aunt Elizabeth. Five sisters! I am so used to having only Gilbey!"

"Tush, child. You are the farthest thing from a coward that I have ever run into. I haven't the slightest doubt that you will charm them all. Let us not keep them waiting!"

In the ballroom, however, there was no sign of Brinton. Gillian expressed her concern as she stood in the doorway, scanning the room.

"Sometimes he has trouble, Aunt Elizabeth, especially in crowds and in overheated rooms. He was wounded at Waterloo, and it left him with a bad lung. I have seen him overcome in just this kind of setting." She did not elaborate, although Lady Culcarron fixed a curious eye upon her. She had omitted certain details from her account of her travels, including the incident in the anteroom at the Assembly Rooms in Bath. "Perhaps I can find his friend, Mr. Spelling. Although I do not see him, either."

She gave her aunt's hand a quick squeeze of reassurance. "I see Gilbey, dancing there in the middle. When the dance ends, could you send him to help me? I am going to see if I can discover what has happened." Before her aunt could protest, Gillian turned and made her way back out into the hall.

The room had marble columns and arched niches with statuary around the walls, but some archways opened onto passages that led to other rooms. There had been no gentlemen in the passage she had come through from the salon, so she started down a different one. Just before she came to the intersection of another passageway, she recognized the voices of the two men she sought.

"They are brother and sister—twins, no less," Brinton was saying. He was not coughing, and he did not sound to be in any distress. She knew she should go back to the ballroom and wait for him, but his next words stopped her. "The bet was made on erroneous assumptions, my friend."

"Ah, but they did go to Gretna Green, you've just told me so yourself," replied Spelling.

"Not for marriage!—to escape one," Brinton protested.

"Believe you wagered that they were not going there, and, if I recall, that the whole business had 'nothing to do with marriage'," Spelling said. "I'd say escaping a marriage is still something to do with the matter."

"You just want to get your hands on my Tristan, Archie. Was that what I said?"

Gillian had heard quite enough. "A wager!" she exclaimed, rounding the corner in high dudgeon. "Was that what it was all about? I could not help overhearing—I was afraid you were in distress and I came to look for you."

Spelling merely looked startled, but Brinton's face had turned ashen.

"Gillian, no! It's not as you think. There was a wager, it's true—Archie and I made it that night in Taunton, but—"

"I did wonder why you were helping us, all those first days! I suspected all sorts of reasons, but I never dreamed of this! After a while I began to believe it was because you cared about us, foolish me."

"I did care. I still care. Gillie, let me explain!"

But Gillian had put her hands over her ears. Their raised voices had attracted some attention, and it was fortunate that Gilbey and Lady Culcarron arrived at that moment.

"Gentlemen! This is most unseemly," admonished the countess.

"Please, Lady Culcarron. I must talk with Gillian, uh, Miss Kentwell," said Brinton, desperation making his voice break. "She has the wrong idea."

The twins' aunt looked at Gillian and shook her head. Gilbey was attempting to talk to his sister, who still had her hands over her ears.

"You must call on us tomorrow," the countess said to Brinton. "She is too upset now to pay attention to what you say. I think we had best just take her home." She sighed, looking at the curious faces around them. "I will have to make my apologies to Lady Darley and her daughter in the morning."

Chapter Twenty

Gillian awoke in the morning, full of remorse. How could she face anyone today after behaving so abominably last night? With a groan she pulled the coverlet up over her head.

She had done the unthinkable—created a scene! She had repaid all of her aunt's kindness by committing one of the worst social sins, and at the very event which had brought her aunt to London. She had also deprived her aunt and her brother of an evening they had been enjoying, but perhaps worst of all, she had been horridly unfair to Brinton.

Why hadn't she let him explain? Why had she let anger overwhelm her common sense? She had so looked forward to being with him. Memories filled her mind: the touch of his hand as they danced in Bath, his smiling eyes as they shared a meal on their journey. The images were so real, she could almost smell his scent and feel the strength in his body. Did it matter if a wager had motivated him in the beginning? Wasn't the important question whether he loved her now?

Gillian threw back the covers and sat up. She would start with apologies to everyone, of course. She would try to atone for her misconduct, if that was possible. When Brinton came, she would listen to anything he wanted to say, and she would tell him that she did not care about the wager. She loved him. Perhaps she would even tell him that!

Her first disappointment of the morning was the discovery that both her aunt and her twin had already gone out by the time she had dressed and descended. She ate a solitary breakfast and pondered what it meant that they had "gone to see the family solicitor," according to the butler. Would her aunt do business with a London firm?

She learned that her aunt had left orders for a nuncheon to be served at noon, so they clearly expected to be back by then. She would find something to occupy her in the meantime. She suspected Brinton was far too proper to call before the afternoon.

During the next hour she frequently consulted the ormolu clock on the library mantel, but it seemed to mark the time very poorly. Its hollow ticking filled the quiet room as she perused the titles upon the shelves. She jumped when the butler, doubling as hall porter, came to announce a visitor.

For a moment she was excited to think that Brinton might have come early. Her second disappointment of the day came when she learned that her caller was Lord Pembermore.

She sighed. "I'll see him in the drawing room, thank you, Thornton." She could think of no excuse not to receive her own guardian, much as she would have preferred to ignore him. If only she could convince him to give up his scheme!

Gillian entered the drawing room with a confident air that belied the mixture of dread and curiosity in her heart. The baron had kept himself very much in the background since their arrival in London, but she was not fooled into believing that he had abandoned his plans.

"Good morning, uncle," she managed to say civilly. "Shall we sit down? Or is it really my Aunt Elizabeth that you would like to speak with?"

"I am aware that your aunt and your brother left the house some time ago and have not yet returned," Pembermore said dampeningly, selecting a chair quite close to her. "My business does not require them."

She had no choice but to sit as well. She held herself stiffly, feeling a shiver of dismay crawl up her spine. How did he know who had already come or gone this morning? Did he have someone watching the house?

Her uncle raised his quizzing glass and surveyed her through it with a grimace of what was apparently approval. "You are looking very well this morning, niece."

His quizzing glass always had the bizarre effect of magnifying one watery blue eye all out of proportion to his other one. Gillian usually found the effect comical, but not this morning. She was at a loss, not knowing why he was there or how she was to convince him that she would never concede to his scheme. "Thank you. Can I offer you tea?" she said finally.

"Not necessary," said the baron. "I have come to tell you that, thanks to your ill-considered attempt to avoid the inevitable, poor Grassington has had to come to London. I have seen him, and I must say that for a man of his advanced years, he weathered the journey surprisingly well."

Gillian said nothing as she registered this unexpected news. Was she supposed to feel guilty that the old man was forced to travel? Most likely it had been at her uncle's request.

"One might begin to think that the man has more years left than we supposed." A wickedly cold smile suddenly creased Pembermore's face.

Now was she supposed to feel threatened? Her patience snapped. "Why are you doing this?" she burst out. "Why do you wish to punish me so? What have I ever done to you?"

"Gillian, Gillian. Such dramatics. I never arranged the betrothal as a punishment for you. You, personally, had little to do with it. You are the only attractive, marriageable female over whom I have any legal control. Still, I do not take it kindly when someone tries to cross me. And you, my dear, have cost me considerable time, trouble, and sums of money I could ill afford to spend." His voice hardened as he spoke. "If I felt any regrets about this earlier, you may be sure that none remain now."

Gillian stared at her uncle with wide eyes. It was clear she would never persuade him to give up his plan. She still did not understand the reason behind it, but she had one other hope. She would have to convince Grassington.

Almost as if he had read her mind, Pembermore said, "Now that he is in town, Lord Grassington wishes to see you. He indicated that this morning would be quite convenient."

"You mean, right now?" Gillian asked in disbelief. Wouldn't the old earl have at least sent a note first? She did not want to go now, with her aunt and brother out, and Brinton expected.

Yet, she thought, if she could just talk to Lord Grassington herself, perhaps he would see how ridiculous the whole scheme was. Perhaps she could succeed where Gilbey had failed. Perhaps she could get back again before Brinton arrived, and could greet him with the news that the problem with their uncles was solved!

That idea had enormous appeal. After all his help, she wanted to prove that she was capable of dealing with at least some part of her own troubles. "All right," she said, "I'll go. I'll fetch my bonnet and pelisse."

Her uncle was clearly surprised, but he recovered quickly. "Now, that's what I call a good, obliging girl." As Gillian left the room, she thought she heard him add, "So much easier if you come along willingly."

At almost precisely the stroke of noon, Brinton arrived at Lady Culcarron's rented house in Mount Street. He stuck the square package he was carrying under his arm and had already begun to strip off one glove when he was surprised to learn that no one was at home.

"I'm quite sure they were expecting me," he said, handing the butler his card with a sinking heart. Had Gillian decided she did not wish to see him? Could such a foolish thing as a wager ruin his entire future happiness?

Thornton's furrowed brow cleared as he peered at the earl's engraved name. "The young lady, Miss Kentwell, left a message for you, my lord, in case she had not yet returned."

Ah, there was hope.

"Let me see, she went with Lord Pembermore—"

"Pembermore! The devil she did!" Brinton's burgeoning hope turned instantly into an angry, black despair. He advanced on the poor butler. "Where did he take her? When?"

Thornton recoiled from the unexpected onslaught. "If you would allow me, sir. She went with him something less than an hour ago. She said they were going to Lord Grassington's."

"Was that the message?"

"She said to inform you that she hoped to be back shortly."

"How much less than an hour ago?"

"Well, I would say it was most of an hour, my lord—just after eleven."

The front door opened behind the earl and he turned quickly, hoping to see Gillian safely returned. He stared

blankly into the faces of Lady Culcarron and young Cranford, instead.

"Lord Brinton! Whatever is the matter?" exclaimed the
countess, clearly astonished by the scene she had interrupted.

"Pembermore was here. He's taken Gillian to my
uncle's, or at least that is the message she left. I do not
know that my uncle is in town, or that his house is even
open. I don't know what to think, but—begging your par-
don, Lady Culcarron—I'll be damned before I'll stand here
and do nothing about it. I will go first to my uncle's and see
if anyone is there."

"Of course," said the good lady faintly, "and we will go
with you."

Gilbey said nothing at all, but disappeared out the door
in a flash. "I think he will try to catch our carriage before it
turns into the mews," Lady Culcarron said. "Oh, dear. And
to think we thought we were bearing such helpful news.
Perhaps it will still be of some use, however. We will tell
you on the way. Where is your uncle's London house?"

Gillian had not counted on Lord Grassington's residence
being quite so far from the fashionable West End. As Lord
Pembermore's carriage drove westward beyond the familiar
parks and Kensington Palace, she realized she would be completely dependent upon her uncle or Lord Grassington to
transport her back to Mount Street, and she would not be able
to accomplish her mission as quickly as she had hoped. She
had begun to wonder, too, how Brinton would react to the
message she had left for him if he called before her return.

Her uncle had sat opposite her in the closed carriage, saying little. Her growing concerns must have been apparent,
however, for at length he had said, "Do I see a little frown
of worry on that pale face, Gillian? Having second thoughts
are you?" He had smiled coldly, but added nothing more.

After what seemed to Gillian a painfully long interval,
the carriage entered a lane lined with stately chestnut trees
and stopped before a handsome Georgian house of mellow
brick. Pembermore assisted her out and took her arm, patting her hand in a way that to most observers would have
appeared fatherly and reassuring.

"Did I mention to you that Grassington had succeeded

in obtaining a special license from the Archbishop of Canterbury?" he said with an expression of mock innocence. "It seems that there is nothing left now to hold up your wedding except the arrival of the parson. Congratulations, my dear."

"No!" cried Gillian angrily, struggling to pull her arm away from him. "You cannot do this! You have tricked me! I won't go through with it!"

He tightened his grasp. "I want you to know, Gillian, that there will be no going back from this point on. To do so would mean scandal and ruin for our entire family, including your precious brother. Grassington can sue for breach of promise. If you do not cooperate, I am prepared to sedate you. Anger me enough, and I will keep you drugged right through your wedding night, just to be certain there is no talk of annulment. Do you understand?" He paused at the door, squeezing her arm painfully.

Gillian realized she had better keep her wits about her. Although his words shocked her, she nodded, covering her thoughts with an air of submission. Once they were inside, her uncle instructed the servants to take her to a room where she might refresh herself, and to see that she remained there.

Gillian considered resistance—outright rebellion right there at the bottom of the stairs. She could kick up a great fuss, yelling and screaming and fighting until the old earl himself appeared, assuming that this was indeed his house. But if Lord Grassington was here, a fit of screaming hysteria was not likely to incline him to listen to her. If she demanded to see him immediately, then her uncle would suspect her motives. Meekly she allowed herself to be led upstairs.

When she heard the key turn in the lock, however, icy fingers of panic gripped her heart. Could they really go through with the wedding? What if her uncle tried to drug her? How much time did she have? She had to get out, and she had to find Grassington. But she must act calmly.

She waited a few minutes to be certain that she had been left alone, and then began a thorough exploration of the room. It was an old-fashioned salon, its walls covered from floor to ceiling with painted and gilded paneling. Such rooms often had a connecting door disguised by panels that natched the surrounding walls. If she was lucky, it might not be locked.

She found it in a matter of minutes and cautiously slipped into the next room. From there she made her way down the hall, listening at doors, with stealth perfected in childhood practice. She stopped when she reached a chamber where she could clearly identify her uncle's voice.

"Oh, yes, I believe she is eager now to get back to Devonshire after her little adventure," the baron was saying. "You could even leave this afternoon, after the ceremony. She has acquired a few things since she left home, but you could send for them later. I imagine you will want to dress her to your own taste, my lord."

The other person had to be Grassington. Gillian took a deep breath to calm herself. Now was not the time to be angry, although Pembermore's words made her furious. For the moment she would have to play a role befitting a stage actress. She adjusted the pleated ruff that showed above the collar of her pelisse and stuck out her chin. Brinton had said that confidence was the secret of command. Pasting a determined smile in place, she opened the door and sailed in.

"Gillian!"

"Miss Kentwell!"

"Why, uncle, here you are with the earl. I grew so tired of waiting, I just had to come find you!" She relished the look of astonishment on Pembermore's face as he rose from his chair.

"My dear, we are not ready—the parson is not yet arrived," Grassington began, also struggling to his feet. Although he must have once been tall and imposing, he looked now as if a light wind would quite blow him away. He was every bit as wrinkled and frail as she remembered. Only his thick crop of wavy, snow white hair gave any clue that there was still vitality left in him.

"We won't be needing him," Gillian said, her smile disappearing. She hoped her revelation would not be too great a shock for the elderly earl. "I believe my uncle has misrepresented certain things to you, my lord. I do not wish to marry you. I have been opposed to it from the beginning." She spoke quickly, before her uncle could stop her.

"Stuff and nonsense!" exploded Pembermore. "Pay no

heed, Grassington. She is suffering badly from maidenly nerves."

"Is she?" the old earl said, suddenly choosing to sit down again. He looked thoughtfully from one to the other of them.

"Gillian, I warned you," hissed the baron.

"Yes, you did, Uncle William. You have threatened and cajoled and misled me! You said that Lord Grassington would bring suit and ruin us, but I don't happen to believe you. I believe Lord Grassington is an honorable man. You said you would drug me if necessary, but I'm telling you that I will continue to refuse to cooperate as long as there is still breath in my body."

"That is stating things plainly, Miss Kentwell," said Grassington rather faintly. The expression on his face reminded Gillian of someone who had bitten a lemon by mistake. "What makes you believe I am so honorable, when your own uncle has apparently played you so falsely?"

"By chance I have become acquainted with your nephew. He has staunchly defended your part in this scheme and insists that you believed I was willing to be your wife. As it happens," she added softly, "I believe him."

If what Brinton had told her was not true, she had just gambled her freedom and lost. She had believed him enough to walk into the lion's den. If she had misplaced her trust, then she would no longer care what happened. She loved him that much.

"My nephew, eh?" The look in the old earl's eyes changed to one Gillian could not read.

She decided to sit down. She suddenly felt rather shaky.

"What have you to say, Pembermore?" Grassington looked now at her uncle. "Perhaps I was a fool not to have guessed from the start that you would try to cheat me."

The baron was distractedly swinging his quizzing glass by the cord. Instead of sitting, he began to pace with a stiff, agitated stride. "I had no idea she would be so disobedient and willful. I did not expect her to object to the match."

Gillian interrupted. "I do not understand why either of you wished it in the first place! Why?"

Before either man could answer, they were all startled by a commotion coming from the central stairway down the hall. Angry voices and rapid footsteps approached as their eyes turned uncertainly toward the door. A moment later it flew open and Brinton barged into the room. He was followed by a cowering footman, Lady Culcarron, and Gilbey.

Brinton did not pause until he reached a spot in the middle of the three original occupants of the room.

"Gillian, are you all right?" he asked first, turning a fiercely sharp eye upon her.

She had never seen him like this. He was like an enraged animal, magnificent and dangerous. An aura of violence charged the very air around him. She was too astonished to speak, so she nodded.

She had no sooner done so than Brinton took a step toward her uncle. "You vile pig," he growled and slammed his fist right into the baron's midriff.

"Rafferty!" Gillian jumped to her feet in alarm.

Pembermore folded in half just like a letter opener. He staggered backward and landed fortuitously in a chair that was directly behind him. He stared at Brinton, gasping for breath.

"You are too low to even be challenged to grass," Brinton said. "If we did meet there, you would be cut down like a weed in a farmer's field and mourned as much."

Gillian reached his side and put her small hands over the clenched fist he still held at the ready. Cradling his hand against her cheek, she looked up into his face. "Rafferty, no," she said in a soothing voice she might have used on a child. "I do not think you fully understand the situation."

"I understand it," he said through his teeth, his anger just barely contained. "They are the ones who do not understand." He tore his eyes from Pembermore to frown at his own uncle. "There is to be no wedding. The lady does not wish it, and I am here to enforce her wish."

"Rafferty," Gillian repeated, reaching up to touch his face.

Finally, he looked down at her, his fierceness softening. In that moment she loved him even more than she had thought possible. Her eyes must have betrayed some hint of this, for the earl put his arms around her and hugged her to him, apparently quite oblivious now to the other five people still in the room.

"You called me Rafferty," he said in a voice filled with wonder.

"I do not see Lord Brinton anywhere," she said bravely. "He would never show such passion or lack of control." She stared up into his eyes, knowing she could be lost in them forever. "I love you."

"Gillian." He sighed and hugged her even tighter. "I love you so much it is making me insane."

"If this is insanity, I think I like it," she answered. Then she suddenly pushed back from him. "Oh, dear. I think I have done it again."

"What?"

"Broken the rules. Is not the man supposed to declare himself first?"

"And couples should not be hugging or kissing if they are not at least betrothed," he added. He lowered his head and brazenly claimed a kiss from the lips she had opened to form a reply. "I can remedy that, love. Will you marry me?"

"I had better say yes, hadn't I?"

"You won't have the free life you hoped to have. As Countess of Brinton you will have duties and obligations."

"I'll try my best. Will you mind if your Lady Brinton is not as polished as other ladies?"

He did not need words to reassure her.

Lord Grassington cleared his throat, reclaiming their attention. "So it seems there is to be a wedding, after all."

Gillian and Brinton broke apart then. The young earl turned to the old earl and grinned. "I guess you are right, uncle. She seems to have accepted me in your place. You would never have suited, at any rate. She is a hellion with no sense of propriety, and far too willful for her own good."

"I must bestow my blessing," Grassington observed. "If you would accept it, I would like to offer you the ring that I had hoped to use." As the young couple expressed their gratitude, the old earl smiled at Lady Culcarron and Gilbey. "This is a happy moment to be shared among friends. I recognize young Cranford, but I do not believe this charming lady and I are acquainted."

The introductions were made, and the new arrivals finally seated. As Brinton settled on a sofa beside Gillian, he fixed his grin upon her and said, "Can you ever forgive me for wagering? I have lost my best black stallion now, you know. If there was any doubt over the outcome of my wager with Archie, I have certainly fixed it now! But I can bear losing Tristan," he added softly, "because I have found you."

Gillian tried to look at him severely, but the corners of her mouth would not stay down. "I can forgive you—this time. You must promise not to make such wagers! You must also promise not to strike my uncle anymore," she added sternly. "He has been very bad, but it was my own decision to come here."

"But why did you not wait until all of us could have come with you? You would have been safer."

"I did not think of that," she admitted. "I thought if I could just speak with your uncle, he would see reason. You had told me he was honorable, so I gambled that I could trust him."

Brinton took her hand. "I was upset to discover you were not at home when I arrived there. I went mad when I learned you had gone with Pembermore. I had not dreamed that my uncle was in town, and I was afraid that we would not find you."

"Pembermore sent word to me that you were in London, Miss Kentwell, and suggested that I come," Grassington explained. "He assured me that you had recovered from the nervousness that had sent you off to Scotland."

"It seems Uncle William was not exactly straightforward even with his own solicitor," put in Gilbey. "When you communicated with Mr. Worsley in view of the pending nuptials, he decided to come to town with you, because he was worried about all the complications he saw developing."

The young viscount paused to look around the room, his gaze stopping at his defeated uncle. "Aunt Elizabeth and I met with Mr. Worsley this morning. He had discovered that Uncle William had been cheating us, draining money from our trust funds."

"But why?" Gillian also turned to her uncle. "Why did you have to steal from our trust funds? And why did you want me to marry Lord Grassington? I still do not understand."

"Your uncle, like many, has a weakness for the gaming tables," Grassington said with a note of regret in his voice. "When he is in Devon, he finds a substitute for the more exciting stakes of London's clubs in a small group of players to which I belong. Over time, I have come to hold the majority of his vowels, including some notes he originally owed to others. Whenever I demanded payment in the past, he always came up with the ready. I had no idea he was so strapped. He told me this last time, however, that he could not pay. He offered something worth far more to me than the amount of his debts."

He stopped and looked pointedly at Gillian and Brinton. "Since my designated heir was showing no inclination whatsoever toward matrimony, I had begun to despair that he ever intended to do his duty to continue our lines—his own or mine. I admit to being a foolish, vain old man, but when Pembermore suggested he could provide me with a young, willing bride, I was quite willing to cancel his notes. It seemed the perfect solution. I might get a new heir, or Rafferty might suddenly feel pushed to do something. Either way, I would have pleasant companionship."

Brinton groaned. "What is the total amount of his debt?"

"Thirty thousand pounds." The answer came from Pembermore, who was sitting erect now, his face ashen but his eyes defiant.

"Both Brinton and Gilbey whistled.

Gillian sat in shock. "He sold me for that!"

"Uncle William, why did you not come to us for help?" Gilbey asked. "Surely we could have worked out some reasonable repayment plan. I would have helped you. I am still willing to help you, on one condition. You must give your blessing and permission for Gillian and Brinton to marry."

"You would be wise to do so, Lord Pembermore," Lady Culcarron spoke up. "If you do not, I will see your name dragged through the mud. You have certainly abused your position as the twins' guardian. I would not hesitate to challenge it and publish the reasons."

"What do you intend to do about Pembermore's vowels now?" Brinton asked.

"I would cancel them if he agreed to give up gambling."

It was Pembermore's turn to groan. "What would I do with my time?" he asked helplessly.

"Perhaps you would spend less of it manipulating and

cheating other people," Brinton said acidly. "Travel on the Continent is popular once again."

"Perhaps he could discover that he is part of a family," Gillian suggested. Her happiness seemed too great not to be shared. She had found a tiny scrap of gratitude in her soft heart for her uncle's part in bringing Brinton into her life. "He might learn something about love and trust." She looked shyly at her husband-to-be. "I know I have," she whispered.

"Have you?" came his soft reply. "What did you learn?"

"That sometimes love and trust are found where and when you least expect them."

"I've learned that, too," he said huskily, putting an arm around her and drawing her close. "Our grandchildren will never believe our stories of how we met."

"Speaking of meetings," said Gilbey suddenly, "you were carrying this package, Brinton, and left it behind in the carriage."

Brinton's face lit. "That is for Gillian! I quite forgot. We will have to send you to Oxford, Cranford, since you are so smart. Open it now, love. It is very fitting."

With trembling fingers Gillian pulled at the strings and undid the brown paper. Four small volumes bound in brown leather spilled into her lap. "Oh, Rafferty," she said, barely breathing with delight. "Ramsay's *Tea-Table Miscellany*!"

"You will have to learn some new old songs, I fear. I could not find copies of the ones you had before, at least this time," Brinton told her. "But we can go hunting and can work together to rebuild your collection."

"Perhaps you can find some when you come to see me in Scotland," said Lady Culcarron.

"We will be free to travel, sometimes, with five aunts for our children to visit. Do you think my mother and sisters will overwhelm you, love?"

She shook her head, smiling. The idea of a big, wonderful family greatly appealed to her, with Brinton at its center.

He enfolded one of her small hands inside his large one and answered her warm smile with one of his own. "We are bound to want their help, sometimes. After all, there are still a few roads left in England we have yet to travel down!"